# STEMMA

### BECA LEWIS

PERCEPTION PUBLISHING

# CONTENTS

# ONE

E dward wanted to be more like the rock that jutted out from the ocean. Waves swirled around it smoothing it out, making it change shape over the centuries. But despite the constant pressure of the wind and waves, the rock remained itself, solid and in place. It had nowhere to go. It didn't have to be anything other than a rock. It was a symbol of stability, holding the history of all that moved around it.

But Edward was not like a rock at all. He had spent his whole life on the move, always changing into someone else, depending on where he landed and what was needed to survive. Edward had spent so many years being whatever he needed to be, he was no longer sure that he knew who he was. Except for one thing. Edward knew where he came from, and he knew now he had to go back. Needed to, not wanted to.

Edward didn't want to return to his hometown. It was only his promise to his mother that urged him on. It was the same promise that kept him running. Now he was the perfect symbol of a rolling stone. Not a rock like he wanted to be.

If Edward hadn't promised his mother to bring proof of what his father did—but not until it was safe—he would have settled down and had a normal life.

Perhaps he could have gotten married, had kids. It's not too late, he mused. He was only forty-eight. They didn't even have to be his kids. He could find a good woman with children and settle down with them and be a family.

Sure, there had been women in his life. A few, given different circumstances, could have tempted him to settle down. But knowing his family history, he couldn't burden them with a past that he couldn't share, a family that terrified him, and a promise he knew he would have to keep.

Edward thought it was ironic that he desired a normal life when instead he had lived as far from a normal life as possible. He was a nomad and shapeshifter. Although he longed for home, family, and community, as soon as he got too close to someone, or met too many people who recognized him, he had to move on. Each time, he changed his name. Each time, he became a new person with a different past.

It wasn't hard to do. Edward could always find someone who would provide him with a new identity and history. He had become a master at being someone else. So good at it, in fact, that it scared him. What if he was no longer himself? Sometimes he was even afraid he would forget his real name.

But then he would look at his mother's letter, addressed to him, and he would remember. The front of the envelope said his full name: Edward Hellard. But he had crossed out the hated Hellard name and replaced it with his mother's last name, Miller. He was Edward Miller.

After all this time, Edward wasn't in a hurry to get to his hometown of Doveland. He had already stalled for months, knowing he needed to go, but not wanting to.

What did a few months matter, anyway? After all, he had been gone thirty-three years.

He could take his time and do what he loved to do most. Meet people and see things, both the ordinary and extraordinary, while he traveled.

Edward finished packing his suitcase and took one last walk around the apartment he had been living in the previous few years. Like all the apartments he had rented, it was nondescript. It was just a place to eat and sleep. However, no matter how dull the apartments had been, they were always better than living on the street as he had done when he first ran away at fifteen.

Every time Edward moved on, he missed the friends he had made. He thought that the one silver lining in returning to Doveland and his past was that it meant he would never have to run again. Perhaps once he did everything that he promised his mother he would do, he would find all those friends and tell them his real name. Maybe they would still like him. Perhaps he could be normal. Like other people.

Sure, Edward thought. Like other people who have fathers like mine.

Edward was terrified of his father. After he ran away, he had lived in constant fear his father would find him. But what scared Edward the most was the possibility that he would be like his father, a murdering psychopath. A brilliant, murdering psychopath.

Edward had seen pictures of his father during his weekly internet search to keep up with what his father was doing. That he looked so much like his father intensified Edward's fears that he would be like him, too. A picture of his father when he was forty-eight was almost identical to what Edward now saw when he looked in the mirror.

He had the same brown hair with a slight wave if he let it grow longer. He had a straight nose, eyebrows that tended towards bushy if not trimmed, brown eyes, and a square jaw. The same face.

Edward had tried to look different by growing a beard, but then he saw a picture of his father with the same look and had immediately shaved it off.

Edward had noticed that his father had grown a little pot belly in recent years, and he vowed never to let that happen to him. Not that pot bellies were bad. It was just something he could control that would keep him from being like his father.

Everything he did had to be measured against whether or not his father would approve or disapprove. However, unlike most sons, Edward was not looking for approval. He was actively seeking his father's disapproval.

Not that his father would ever know what he was doing. Because that was the point. Never be found.

Besides, finally his father had left the country. That was why it was time for him to return home. It was time to keep his promise to his mother to get justice for those poor women.

Edward knew it was best not to think about what he wanted, or wished for in his life. There was no telling what the future would be like for him. For now, he was going on a road trip home. See some sights, get it all out of his system. Because once he reached Doveland, if he did what he intended to do, he might never leave home again.

Because in one way Edward was like the rock. He held the history of what had gone on around him when he was just a boy. As a man, he was going to release that history, and he and everyone else involved would have to live with the consequences.

# TWO

When someone brought up the idea of a going-away party for Johnny, Tom Merrifield jumped in and said that he and Mandy would have it at their house.

Everyone looked at him as if he had grown a third head. "Parties are always at Ava and Evan's house," Mira, Tom's twin sister, pointed out.

Tom answered, "That's true. We do hold parties and big meetings to discuss problems at their house. However, I want Johnny's party to be entirely different. Nobody has ever come to our house for a party. Johnny can invite all his friends, you can all come, and it will be just what it is supposed to be—a send-off for Johnny."

Turning to Johnny, Tom added, "And a place you can always come home to."

Mandy was as surprised as everyone at Tom's announcement. But other than thinking she had to have a talk with Tom about consulting her on things that affected her too, she agreed.

Their house was now the perfect place for Johnny's party. A few members of Hank's construction crew had just finished installing a new patio that ran the length of the back of their house.

Tom also had them build in a fire pit and a pergola that shaded the back half of the patio.

At first, Mandy had thought it was excellent timing that the house was ready for a party. Then she realized that Tom had planned to do this all along. Still, she thought, Tom's training as an excellent future husband needed to include talking to her first.

Planning for the party had given Mandy the opportunity and excuse to do even more design work on their home. She knew she was lucky because she never had to worry about spending money on her projects. There was always enough. Tom had taken his inheritance and grown it. Neither of them worried about money anymore, nor did they believe in hoarding it.

They continued what Tom had started years ago, using much of their money to do good. Sometimes it was through Tom's non-profit company, and sometimes they gave money on their own. They considered using money that way a selfish act because it gave them both so much pleasure.

Having the party gave Mandy pleasure, too. Everything about it was lovely. All their friends were together, celebrating one of their own. Mandy thought Johnny was handling the pressure of being the center of attention beautifully.

Everyone they had invited had come, and it was a lovely mix of young and old. Johnny's brother Lex, and Ava and Evan's daughter, Hannah, had asked a few of their friends to come, and those eleven-year-olds kept the party from being too stodgy.

Tom and Mandy had installed a horseshoe throw on one section of their lawn. On the other side of the yard, they set up a badminton net. Games that didn't involve staring at the phone or TV were the only ones allowed that day. That included card games, Trivial Pursuit, and conversation groupings.

Mandy had placed baskets for all phones to be put into while the party was in progress. She decided she liked the idea so much she would keep doing it for all future fun parties. As much as Mandy loved technology, she knew it needed to be in moderation and balanced with physical connections.

Everyone had come, and as always, they brought the food. It was no longer something the group planned. It just happened. Mandy and Grace had brought some of the deserts Mandy had made for the coffee shop that they owned together. Pete and Barbara Mann brought food from their Diner.

Sam Long, ex FBI and current caterer, had brought some of his latest creations. Sam was always testing out food on the group. No one complained about being a test case. His food was consistently delicious, although not everyone appreciated every dish. But Mandy thought that was the point. Variety.

Sometimes while watching Sam run a catering company, she forgot he used to be an FBI agent because food seemed to be so much a part of him. She knew he was glad to be done with being in that world. But Sam had agreed to be a consultant on some cases. Especially on the ones that happened in Doveland.

Like the case of the four women's bodies found on Emily's hill last spring. The investigation into what happened had been going on for months, and it still wasn't solved. That meant Sam continued to be on call to the FBI. Mandy knew Sam wasn't happy about it. Especially since everyone else was trying to forget it.

The person most of them suspected of being the murderer had left town, and that meant, for Mandy anyway, it was time to move on and stop wondering what happened. Maybe they would never know.

One way Mandy was moving on was daydreaming about starting her own design company. She was almost ready to talk to Tom about it. He would approve, of course, even so, what if he didn't?

As more people arrived, the joyful chaos grew. Hugs were exchanged, and gifts for Johnny continued to pile up on the table. Sarah Morgan brought flowers from her garden and arranged a gigantic bouquet of them on the center table. Mandy marveled at how many flowers Sarah could grow in such a tiny space. The arrangement was filled with late summer and early fall flowers, which meant there were lots of oranges and yellows mixed into the bouquet.

Mandy watched everyone work together as if they had been together for centuries. The thought made Mandy chuckle to herself. Sarah said they had been. Together. For many lifetimes. They might look different each time, but their essence remained the same, and they circled around each other no matter what lifetime they were in.

It made sense to her intuitively, but she had given up trying to understand how it worked. The point was, they were together, and gathering more people as time went by, and that fact had changed her life.

Johnny's mother Valerie stood on the far end of the patio and watched the party. Her two sons were enjoying themselves, which made her heart happy. For what felt like the millionth time, Valerie thanked God for all her friends who had stepped up for her and her sons after her husband, Harold, died. They were all here for Johnny.

The one person not at the party was Tina Franks. Tina had moved to Pittsburgh with her two children a few months before. The bond between Valerie and Tina had not dissipated, though. In a world of social media, it was easy to keep connected, and Tina promised to visit after she and her children settled into their new home.

Halfway through the party, Sam, Pete, and Hank grabbed Johnny and brought him to the front of the patio. Valerie, as the principal of the school, was used to bringing crowds to attention, and within seconds of her raising her hand for silence, they all quieted down and turned their attention to the four men standing together.

Hank and Pete had their arms on Johnny's shoulder, and Sam stood slightly in front, holding an envelope. Johnny was doing his best to let himself be the center of attention. Although his face was flushed, he didn't flinch as all eyes turned to see him. Johnny was no longer dressed in all black and his pierced nose and eyebrows had closed up long ago. He looked the part of a young man going off to college.

All four of the men were about the same height, emphasizing that Johnny was now a young man. Valerie found that even before they started speaking, tears had begun to run down her cheeks. Grace came to stand beside her and passed her a tissue, and Valerie smiled at her gratefully.

Sam handed Johnny the envelope, and then said, "All of us couldn't be more proud of you, Johnny. Not only do you have the three of us as stand-in dads, you have our entire community behind you. Don't be worried about making mistakes. We all make them. Just let us know so we can help. In return, we expect we can count on you when we need help."

Johnny nodded, aware that he was crying, and yet he didn't care. "I promise," he said.

"Here, here!" the crowded shouted back at him. As everyone lined up to hug him, Johnny handed the envelope to his mother and whispered thank you.

Standing to the side, Craig Lester watched and wondered if he would ever feel the same about this group of people. Friends, yes, but since he didn't believe what they believed, did he fit in anymore? Answering his unspoken question, Leif Morgan materialized out of nowhere, as he often did, and said, "It's up to you, Craig."

Craig turned to his long-time friend and asked, "Is it? Like it was up to you to choose to take Eric to the Forest Circle, so you had to leave your wife?"

"I didn't leave, Craig. You can still see me, and I am still here for you and Sarah. Let your friends be here for you, too."

Craig shook his head. "I don't know if I can," he said and turned back to watch the party, leaving Leif to shake his head sadly as Craig slipped away.

# THREE

They had agreed not to lie to each other, so when Johnny Price asked his mother if her tears were happy or sad, she truthfully answered, "Both." Being wise beyond his years, Johnny, still only a boy of eighteen, had not demanded to know why she was both. Instead, he said, "Me too."

They had hugged for a moment, there in the doorway to his bedroom, and then he laughed. "But I know someone who is completely happy about me leaving," he said, and lightly punched his brother Lex as he came up the stairs to get another load of stuff to put in the car.

"You're right about that, Johnny," Lex said as he punched his brother back. "No more listening to you sing off key in the shower, or you eating all the ice cream before I get any."

Valerie watched her two sons pretend to fight and felt a bubble of gratitude well up in her heart. They were acting normal again. When their dad, Harold, died a few months before, it had thrown the entire family into a tailspin. No one knew what had killed him. That was still a mystery. But after he died, questions about his past had come to the surface. Questions without answers.

All three of them felt that perhaps they never knew Harold. Maybe he had been lying to them all along. *No "maybe" to it,* Valerie thought. Harold had lied. Sure, they had known his flaws and overlooked them, because most of the time Harold had been a loving father, and in the beginning, he was a good husband.

Then the bodies on Emily's hill were discovered, and everything they knew about him had been thrown up into the air. All of Harold's bad traits got worse, and his good ones faded into the background.

When he died, he took with him the answers to questions they hadn't known to ask. So they had to speculate about how much he was responsible for those women dying. What had he been doing all their lives that they didn't know about? Because they didn't know, many of the pieces of their lives remained suspended in the air. It felt as if everything in Harold's life was an open question, and if probed, an open wound in theirs.

They decided not to probe. Instead, the three of them chose to move on together. They decided to table their questions and wait until someone else found the answers. They would not pursue the answers themselves. Sarah Morgan had assured them they would find out what had happened, and Valerie believed her.

In the meantime, she and her boys had to get on with their lives. Which meant she had to let Johnny go. As painful as it was to watch him pack his room, she was proud of him. More proud than she could ever put into words. He had taken the lifeline thrown to him by Hank, Pete, and Sam and pulled away from a life of petty crime. Johnny had learned that he didn't need to act out to be seen. He chose instead to be the best person possible for him to be.

Valerie thought back to their conversation when he told her he wanted to study psychology in college. It had been another proud and heart-wrenching moment when he had torn open the letter and found out they had accepted him at his dream school, Penn State. She was delighted that the school Johnny wanted to go to was only a few hours away. He could come home on the weekends. "No," he had said. "I have to stay and be part of this new life. I can't keep running home."

When he saw the tears in his mother's eyes, he hugged her and said he would be home for holidays. She had pushed the curl on his forehead back and stared up into his brown eyes and realized that somewhere along the way, her little boy had become a young man.

Perhaps it was what he had done for Grant Hinkey a few summers before that had brought about the change. Johnny had set off the fireworks so that Grant could escape, or perhaps it was Harold's death that had prompted the maturity spurt. Whatever it was, here he stood, a young man yearning to know about himself and the world.

Sitting at the breakfast table the day after getting his acceptance letter, Johnny had looked up from his toast and said, "How do I know I won't be like my father?"

She didn't need time to think about it. She knew the answer. "Because you are who you are, Johnny. You can choose your own way."

"That's an easy answer, mom," Johnny said. "But is it true? Will I be like him no matter what I choose? I don't want to believe that to be true, but I need to know. I need to understand. I need to find out how my family heritage impacts me. I need to discover if I can overcome it."

He paused and asked, "Did you know there is a word for that?"

"A word for what?" Valerie asked.

"The family tree, or pedigree. Stemma. That's the word. I need to understand my stemma. Then perhaps I will see what my choices are and what I learned that I could unlearn, or do better. I have to, mom. I can't be my father. I can't even be you. I have to be who I am meant to be."

At first, Valerie was speechless. He didn't even want to be like her? And then she reached across the table and held his hand and answered, "All I want, Johnny, is for you to be happy and fulfilled. Whatever that takes, I am here to help."

There was probably more they both could have said, but they could hear Lex making a racket as he came down the stairs. Instead, they both laughed at the noise.

"What are you two laughing at?" Lex asked.

They just shook their heads, leaving Lex wondering. Both of them knew they would review the subject over and over again. It was not a one-step answer,

Later that day, though, Valerie had grabbed Johnny and pulled him into a hug and whispered, "I'm proud of you, Johnny."

He had answered, "Thank you, mom. You know I love you, right?"

She had nodded and given him one more hug, and then said she needed to make sure all the clothes he wanted to take to school were clean, so he wouldn't see her crying.

As Valerie carried another load of Johnny's stuff to the car, she couldn't help wondering about something Johnny didn't ask her.

Didn't he also need to know about her mother and father, or perhaps even Harold's mother and father? How far back did stemma go?

The problem was, she wasn't sure who her father was. She knew who her mom said he had been, but something had never felt right about that.

Now her mother was dead, so she couldn't ask her. Nor could Johnny. Would it matter?

If Valerie could have seen the future, she would have known that it did matter. It mattered more than anyone could have imagined.

# FOUR

M andy Minks watched the first leaf release from the tree and
twirl slowly to the ground, dancing in the air. Her favorite
time of the year was coming. If only I could design one room as
beautiful as that leaf, she thought. Design and beauty had been
occupying almost all her thoughts the last few days.

Mandy loved the coffee shop and would be forever grateful that
Grace had picked her to be her business partner. But even while
she was baking and working with Grace, a piece of her brain would
mull over a design project. Any design project. Dresses, business
cards, the way the silverware sat on the table, plants in a garden.
Designing anything made her almost dizzy with happiness.

But it was the homes and business that she had been designing
lately that made her the happiest. Craig's doctor's office, and then
his apartment over the office, had become the talk of the town. She
knew she had done an excellent job when she began to overhear
people talk about how much they loved the new look of Craig's
office.

Because he was the town's doctor, almost everyone had seen it,
and their approval of the work she had done propelled many other
design projects. More often than not these days, she couldn't be

working at the coffee shop waiting tables because she was designing someone's home.

She and Grace had finally given in and hired a friend of Alex's to help, and when the Diner wasn't too busy, Alex would walk across the street to help out at Your Second Home.

At first Mandy had been worried that Grace would be upset at her not being there, but instead, she had hugged her and told her to follow her dream. After all, the coffee shop had been Grace's dream, and it was Mandy's design that made it as beautiful as it was. Grace said she couldn't be prouder.

At the time, Mandy had no words to tell her how much that meant to her, so she just hugged her back and said a simple "thank you."

Mandy knew that she was at a turning point. She had to decide if she was going to go forward with her own business or scale it back to a hobby. But the more projects Mandy completed for homes and businesses, the more it felt as if she belonged in the design world. Even though she was entirely self-taught, it felt as if she had been born with the ability to design tucked up inside herself. It was a part of her being that could never be separated from her.

Finding beauty in design was the way she had survived the ugliness of growing up in foster homes. To keep herself from losing her mind because of the messiness of the life she was forced to live, Mandy had looked for how things went together in harmonious and beautiful ways. At the library, she read the magazine *Architectural Digest* to teach herself about styles that existed far beyond what she was experiencing in everyday life.

She had survived her life by harboring a hidden love for all things beautiful. But she had still felt abandoned and alone. That was until she and Ava met at a laundromat. Ava was a sixteen-year-old runaway. Mandy was a twenty-four-year-old escort. That meeting ten years ago had changed everything.

Now she and Ava were part of a growing Karass. Their circle was filled with friends and family who had found each other in this lifetime and had a purpose together. Now her love of design was out in the open. For Mandy, it felt as if a door had opened into a vista broader and more beautiful than she had ever dreamed possible.

Sometimes Mandy wondered where her love of design came from. Was it her parents? Or maybe her grandparents? Until Mandy started wondering where she had gotten her innate love of design from, she had never thought about the parents that she had never known. Mandy learned early on that it didn't do any good to wish she knew who they were and why they had left her. She had enough heartbreak.

But when Valerie had shared with the women's circle what Johnny had said about his father and his worry that he would become like him, it revealed a fear Mandy had long ago tucked away. It was something she had never allowed herself to think about. Because what kind of parents would abandon their child?

But now that Johnny had brought it up, she wondered not only where she had gotten her love of design but also if her fear of terrible parents was why she kept making decisions that didn't involve having children. Was she worried that she'd be a terrible mother? Would she abandon her child, too?

Until she met Tom, having children wasn't something she had to face. She was never going to have children with the men she met before Tom. Now things had changed, and although they had not discussed children, Mandy knew that Tom was just absent-minded about it. She was the one avoiding it, and time was flying by. Did she want them? Did Tom?

Perhaps Johnny's question about stemma would push them all into finding out answers that they had never intended to ask. She knew that for her, not asking about her parents was because she didn't want to know the answer.

However, if there was one thing Mandy had learned from hanging around the Doveland Karass for the past few years, it was that hidden information was always more dangerous than knowing. Perhaps it was time to look for answers and deal with the outcome rather than having it sneak up on her without warning.

Yes, Mandy thought, I'm always looking for beauty. But sometimes, beauty comes in letting go.

Another leaf dropped from the maple as if confirming the accuracy of her thoughts and reminded her of a Chinese saying that falling leaves return to their roots.

Perhaps it was time for her to discover her roots. But first, there was something she needed to do. She needed to talk to Tom and tell him both her fears and her dream. Mandy thought she knew what he would say about her dream of building a design business. She wasn't so sure what he would say about children. Or her fear of being like her unknown parents.

No time like the present, Mandy thought as she pulled her sweater around her and turned back to the house to find Tom. Ready or not. Here comes my future, she said to herself. Turning back one more time to the maple tree, she asked it to give her strength. Another leaf fell in response.

# FIVE

Craig Lester still went to the Diner and had the same breakfast that he and his friend Dr. Joe had both enjoyed when they met every week for all those months before it all fell apart. Craig knew it was a useless thing to do.

He knew that no amount of pretending or wishing would have Joe waiting for him at the Diner. It was a wish that would never come true. But he did it anyway. Craig couldn't really say why he kept the fabrication alive other than the fact that he missed Joe more than he thought possible. For some reason, Joe's leaving had opened a hole in Craig's life bigger than the one made by his divorce from his wife, Jo Anne.

For the first time in his life, Craig had felt as if he had someone to talk to about healing in the same way that he understood it, or at least tried to understand it. They spoke the same language. They were both driven by a sincere and deep desire to know everything there was to know about the human mind and body connection.

Craig knew the fact that he had bought Dr. Joe's practice had added to that feeling of connection and collaboration. It only took a few meetings before they both were completely comfortable with each other and, as far as Craig was concerned, were honest with each other, too. Joe had never hidden the fact that he would leave as soon as Craig got the practice established in his name. But originally, Joe had planned to stay a whole year to help. But he hadn't. He left early.

Dr. Joe's premature departure had blindsided Craig. Craig told himself it was because he wasn't prepared for Joe to go. However, Craig knew it was more than that. He was stunned that his friends, especially Leif and Sarah, who he had known and loved for years, believed that Joe was a murderer. That Joe was the one who had killed not only the women buried on Emily's hill, but also Valerie's husband, Harold, and Lenny and Frank. If they were to be believed, Joe had probably killed countless others too, using a form of mental suggestion that he had practiced throughout the years.

They believed Joe had not been studying healing because he wanted to heal, but because he wanted to control. That he had been practicing the dark arts of mental malpractice while pretending to care. Craig didn't believe them. If they only knew Joe the way that he knew him, they would understand that they were wrong. There was another explanation. That's what Craig felt, and the pain of not being able to explain it to anyone was eating him up inside.

Even though the subject of Dr. Joe had not come up for months and none of his friends had ever held it against him that he believed in Joe's innocence, Craig felt isolated. And he was not happy about it. He wasn't happy about his anger, and he was not happy that he had pulled back from the warmth and companionship of the group.

As a physician, he knew that keeping his anger, grief, fear, and sorrow inside was not healthy. Craig knew he had to let go and talk to someone, but he couldn't bring himself to do it. Something inside him would not yield. He couldn't bring himself to forgive them, and he didn't understand why. He reasoned with himself all the time that they could be friends and not agree. But his reasoning didn't match what he felt in his heart.

The bell over the door of the Diner dinged, and he looked up to see Valerie walk in. When she saw Craig sitting alone at a table, she waved at him. He waved back and pointed to the open chair across from him. It was only the habit of being gracious that enabled him to smile back at her when she accepted. She paused on her way over to the table to say 'hello' to Pete cooking in the kitchen, and tell Alex that she wanted sourdough toast and a tea, please.

Craig tried not to stare, just as he had been trying not to care about her. So far, it hadn't worked. But he knew Valerie believed that Joe had killed her husband. She didn't know how he had done it. But she thought it, and that meant that there was a yawning crevice between them that hadn't existed before Joe had been accused.

Plus, it had only been a few months since Harold had died, and even though Craig had been aware of Valerie's leaning towards him during that time, he never acted on it, thinking that he had no right. Now, he had no way to cross that gap. So Craig tried to bury his feelings and keep his contact with her as casual as possible.

He was so intent on squashing his feelings, he barely heard Valerie asking him something.

"Oh, sorry," he stuttered. "I was thinking about something. A patient. What was it you asked?"

"It was nothing," Valerie said as she glanced up at Alex, bringing her toast and coffee, nodding her thanks. "I was just wondering how you and your practice are doing."

"Of course! The practice! Yes, mostly just taking care of patients. Haven't been doing anything fun like heading off to New York the way that Pete, Barbara, and I did last spring. Too busy to take time off."

"That's too bad. I know you three had a great time. You mentioned a few months ago that you wanted to hire an assistant and a full-time nurse. Did you find anyone?"

"Not yet. I have a few resumes to look over, but not that many qualified people want to live in a small town. Besides, I'm doing okay by myself."

"Are you?" Valerie asked, and Craig knew that she was asking more than just about the practice.

"Okay, enough," he answered after a long pause. They both knew it was a lie.

Valerie took a long look at Craig, sighed, and picked up her tea. *Men,* she thought. To her, that said it all.

# Six

Keeping a coffee shop running while a new entrance was being put in was nerve-wracking, Grace decided as she watched members of Hank's construction crew muscle one of the two enormous glass doors that were being installed.

During the day, the noise of construction ran through the space like fingernails on a chalkboard. A few minutes of that noise and no one wanted to stay inside to drink their coffee.

Anticipating the noise level to some degree, although she did not know it would be so bad, Grace had received permission from the town council to put extra tables and umbrellas in the town square during the construction.

Even though it was autumn and it required layers of clothing to be comfortable outside, most of her customers took advantage of the outside tables. Instead of staying in the coffee shop to chat as they usually would, they crossed the street to sit in the square. There was still the noise of a few cars making their way around the green, but it was much more pleasant than the hammering and sawing that Hank's crew was doing.

Some of her customers didn't even bother going to the square. They just took their coffee home. Grace was counting on the fact that once the new entrance was complete, everyone would be glad that it happened and would return to the shop to drink, eat, and be social.

After the first day of construction dust, the amount of which Grace had never imagined possible, Mandy suggested that they cover the bookshelves with plastic sheeting so that they didn't have to dust them every night. Book reading and sales were down, but it was temporary. No one wanted to browse books while covering their ears. Even the few patrons who used noise-canceling headphones couldn't stand the noise or the dust for more than a few minutes.

Mandy said that one of the hardest parts of dealing with the construction was making the pastries that customers loved to have with their coffee. Hank had installed plastic sheeting around the small kitchen, but that was so difficult to deal with they ended up moving the baking up into Grace's apartment. Although Mandy and Grace had scaled down to just a few items until construction was over, Grace's apartment was in complete chaos. No longer a quiet sanctuary, it was filled with pots, pans, and cooking utensils. There was no room for her to cook her own meals. On the other hand, Grace decided, it smelled fantastic, and the lack of a kitchen meant she got to eat out every night.

The construction was lasting longer and was much more disruptive than Grace thought it was going to be. She had envisioned a few days of disarray. It wasn't disarray, it was disaster, and it had been going on for almost a week. The good news was that it was nearly done.

Grace knew that everyone understood that what they were doing would make Your Second Home much cozier in the winter. But it would be useful all year long, too. Last spring, Sam had suggested the change and Grace and Mandy decided he was right. So, they hired Hank to build a second door into the shop. Now there would be one door which opened into a pass-through that would double as a place to hang wet coats and leave wet boots before opening the second door into the shop. No more cold wind rushing through when the door was opened. Or even hot air during the summer.

The new construction took out the side window on the right side of the shop, but it was worth it. Grace was thinking about having a local artist do a mural on the new wall it created inside. Mandy was already in the process of talking to local artists. Grace knew that if she gave Mandy a design task, she would be in seventh heaven.

When Hank had said that construction always made a mess in order to make things better, Grace thought that it was the perfect symbol for the past year in Doveland. The discovery of four women, buried for over forty-five years on Emily's hill had thrown everyone in town into a turmoil. Although it had died down, it wasn't over. The primary suspect in many people's eyes, Dr. Joe, had retired and left town, and that had to be good enough for now.

But it was like leaving a construction process half finished, and not knowing when it will start up again. There was a continuing sense of foreboding.

But not today, Grace thought. Today was to be the last day of construction on the project, and her home life and business would return to normal.

"Did you say return to normal?" Eric asked as he materialized beside her and whispered in her ear. Grace had to restrain herself from turning to face him and saying out loud, "Cut that out. You scared me half to death." After all, what would most people think if she yelled at nothing?

Instead, she smiled and said through her teeth, "Nice to see you, Eric. Thanks for doing your trick of scaring me." She meant it literally. Last year, she hadn't been able to see him when he visited. Now, she could. It meant everything to her.

"My pleasure," he said. "Now, what did you say about returning to normal?"

"Well, our version of normal I guess, where my husband lives in another dimension and most of my friends can see dimension travelers, hear other people's thoughts, and teleport themselves. Perfectly normal.

"And, by the way, Eric you read my thoughts, didn't you? How long has that been going on?"

Eric leaned in as close as his non-physical body would let him, which meant that part of him merged with Grace's arm, and said, "It's because I love you, Grace."

By the time Grace turned to tell him that she loved him too, he was gone.

# SEVEN

M elvin's garden was nearing the end of its productive cycle. The corn was long gone, shared with anyone who came to visit. In fact, almost all the vegetables grown over the summer had been picked and eaten. The growing season had ended. All the plants had been pulled up and added to the compost pile, although someone had left the eggplant and the tomatoes. They had probably kept the eggplant because it had a few buds on it and they thought it still had time to grow an eggplant or two. That meant it wasn't Melvin tending the garden because he would have known, as Emily did, that it would never have time to grow before the first frost killed it off.

Even if that didn't happen, the air was too chilly. It was perfect weather for wearing sweaters and breathing in the smell of fallen leaves, but not suitable for growing summer produce. However, the tomato plants were still going strong, but only because there hadn't been a frost. As soon as that happened, they would shrivel up and die along with the eggplant.

Emily pulled her coat tighter around herself as a chilly wind whistled around the corner of Melvin's house, bringing a swirl of autumn leaves with it. She was visiting Melvin as she did at least two times a week. She could see Hank inside the kitchen preparing dinner and watching her stare at the garden. The garden was the picture of the natural order of things. A seed sprouts, blooms, and then recycles its energy into a new season.

In a garden, it was easy to see the process and understand how it worked. There was even a sense of joy in the ending stage. Cleaning a garden at the end of a cycle could be very satisfying, knowing that the way was being prepared for a new season. Seeing the ending stage in a person's life as joyful was not as easy. In fact, Emily found no happiness or joy in the process at all. She was having a hard time watching Melvin wind down to the end of his time on earth.

As another gust of wind rushed around the corner, almost blowing her hat off, Hank opened the back door and yelled, "Hey! Get in here. Dinner's ready and Melvin wants to eat."

Emily smiled a huge smile at Hank and hurried to the house. If Melvin wanted to eat, he must be out of bed and feeling good today. She didn't want to waste one more minute of precious time with him when he was feeling well.

Inside, the kitchen was warm and cozy. Hank had a fire going in the wood stove, and had made a salad and pancakes for dinner. She looked at the weird combination and then at Hank, who winked at her and made a slight gesture towards Melvin.

"Oh, stop pussyfooting around, Hank!" Melvin said. "I wanted pancakes for dinner. Nothing strange about that. Who said that pancakes aren't dinner food? And Hank wanted to make a salad for you with the last of the stuff from the garden."

Hank laughed. "Yep, it was that ole fool who ordered this meal. Perhaps we could put salad dressing on our pancakes and syrup on the salad."

"I know you are testing if I am thinking straight, Hank," Melvin laughed, picking up the maple syrup that he and Hank had harvested in the spring.

It had been a perfect season for gathering syrup, and it had lasted almost until the end of April. No one liked how cold it had stayed all April except for the people who harvested maple syrup. A good season for making maple syrup meant cold nights and warmer days, and they had that in abundance.

Instead of trying to process it themselves Hank and Melvin had taken the raw syrup to the-guy-down-the-road-a-piece—"no I don't know his name," Melvin had said—to prepare it for them and bring it back in the traditional maple syrup jugs. Some to keep and some to give away. Emily knew she would never again be able to eat the fake maple syrup sold in stores. And she was sorely tempted to use the syrup on her salad, despite what Hank said, because it was so good.

In the spring, Melvin had taken the time to carefully explain to Hank how to tap the trees and run the lines. Hank didn't need Melvin to remind him that Melvin was not planning to be around the next spring to help him. Melvin had been preparing everyone for his earthly departure all year.

Last winter, he started telling everyone that he wouldn't be around for another season. As much as Hank hated it, he knew Melvin had made up his mind. And now his body showed that it was true. He wasn't sick. He had just decided it was time. He was tired and ready to see his wife Sally again.

Melvin had finally gone to see Craig because Hank wouldn't stop worrying and he wanted to be sure there wasn't something they could do to prolong Melvin's life. Craig had told Hank that Melvin was right. There was nothing wrong that needed to be fixed, and Hank had finally accepted that Melvin was leaving. He didn't like it at all. But he knew he had to accept it for Melvin's sake so they could enjoy every last day together.

Melvin didn't need Craig to tell him there was nothing wrong. But he also knew it was time to go. Long ago Melvin had learned that many Native Americans knew when it was time to pass through the door into another life, and Melvin had decided that he would know, too. There was no doubt in his mind that he would know when the time had come. And now he did.

Melvin had confided to Hank that when he was younger, sometimes he had been afraid, not of death, but of pain and incapacity. Or an accident. The fact that he could lie down one day and not get up was what he wanted, and that didn't frighten him. It was joyful to him that he could see that was exactly what was going to happen.

He had prepared for this ending the same way he cleaned up gardens at the end of their season. All the legal work was done. He had written to his son and told him that this was his last year. In typical fashion, his son had called him on Father's Day and assured Melvin that it was all in his mind.

"Exactly," was Melvin's reply. His son didn't understand the context, and they hadn't spoken since.

*Tonight is a good night,* Melvin thought. Emily is here. The meal was delicious, and he felt less tired than usual. In fact, he felt fantastic. Melvin wasn't fooled. He knew what that meant. He had been the shepherd and guide for many of his farm animal's passing. He could even see Sally all the time now. Still, she told him to take his time, she would wait.

Once or twice he had even heard Jay's voice, and that increased his joy. He would see him again. Jay's coming into his life had brought all this new family to him, especially Hank, Emily and Hannah, a son and granddaughters. That's how he saw them. So tonight Melvin wanted to hear everything about what Hank and Emily were doing. Tomorrow he would rest.

# EIGHT

E dward didn't go far the first day after he decided to leave. In fact, he had merely checked into a motel on the outskirts of town, and there he stayed for over a month. Every morning, he thought to himself that today would be the day he would start the trip. But instead, he slept, read books, watched TV, and sometimes drank himself into a stupor, something he had never done before.

One day, he woke up, looked at his pathetic self in the mirror and decided he was ready. The time for self-pity was over. Fall had arrived, and he had stalled long enough.

The first thing he did was collect cash. It took a while, although he did most of it online. His economic life had gotten much more efficient since the internet. Before, when he wanted to open different accounts under different names, he had to visit a bank in person, with different identities to set up each account. Now, because the bank accounts were already opened and online, he could move money around quickly without having to change his look every time he visited a bank.

Now that he was ready to begin his trip, he wanted to move enough money to his real identity, which he had kept hidden from the world and his father. Yes, he knew Joe was looking for him.

Edward's mother, May, had told him that he would. Before she died, she and Edward had discussed how he could hide when he was old enough to run. Of course, she didn't know about the internet or being tracked electronically. But the idea of hiding had been instilled early. For a good reason, it turned out.

But for his mother, it had been too late. She was too afraid to leave. And as much as Edward as a young boy had begged her to go, she never would. However, she made him promise that he would leave as soon as he was sure he could take care of himself. In the meantime, she taught him how to block his father from knowing what he was thinking and feeling. "Keep your walls up, and your doors closed," she would say. Edward never understood how she knew all that, and yet somehow hadn't managed to do it for herself. His only explanation was despite all that his father was doing, his mother loved him.

He didn't do his online activity at home. He used the computers in libraries. There used to be many public places to rent a computer by the hour, but with smartphones and PCs, libraries were one of the few places left that he could remain invisible online. He even ran a few online businesses through eBay and Etsy using different identities. It was how he had accumulated so much money over the years. Now he was ready to become just one person–himself.

After he moved a large sum of money into the account with the name he wanted to use, Edward Miller, he went in search of a car. He had decided to drive to Doveland and take his time. On this road trip, he wanted a car that would be comfortable and safe. One that he could sleep in if necessary. After researching his options, he had decided on a Subaru Forester. Not flashy. Safe. Signaled stability. Just what he needed.

It always took longer than it should to buy a car, but once he had worked out a cash deal, he headed out with a new model green Subaru, feeling a little bit freer than he had when the Uber driver dropped him off. Since his old car was in a different name, he had sold it on eBay a few days before.

The Subaru was the car that would introduce him to the current residents of Doveland. It was the part of the picture he wanted to portray. It wasn't a false picture, but it was a new one for him to live. Even though he knew it would take some time for him to stop being more than one person and just be himself, he was willing.

Edward's next stop was at an Apple store where he purchased a new iPhone and a small laptop, again in his own name and also with cash. He was sure the clerk had no idea why the whole time he was there he had alternated between elation and abject fear. Elation, because finally, he was living as himself. Fear, because it meant his father would now probably find him because, without a doubt, Joe would be searching for him as Edward Miller. He would guess that Edward would use his mother's maiden name instead of the hated Hellard name of his father.

But Edward thought it was a chance he would take. Because if Joe came back into America from Morocco where he couldn't be extradited, there was a strong chance they would arrest him on suspicion of murder. Edward figured his father would weigh the alternatives before deciding to return.

Edward made one stop at the bank where he kept a safe deposit box. It contained cash and a duplicate of his mother's letter. It also included the most important papers of all, his actual birth certificate and the passport that went with it. He didn't close out the account, though. His training made him ask himself, what if I still need it?

During that last day, Edward visited a few of the coffee shops and diners he had spent time in and left extra tips for the waiters and waitresses who had been so kind to him while living in their town. Then he stopped at Gander Outdoors and purchased a tent and sleeping bag. The clerk had been both understanding and knowledgeable, so Edward ended up buying more supplies than he had planned to, but once he heard why he might need them, he had said yes. He also decided to buy two kinds of hiking boots and alternate between them until one pair suited him more. He had also heard that practice helped to keep blisters and sore feet at bay.

At every stop, he felt lighter. His last stop in town was to a different barber shop than he usually used. In this one, Edward turned into himself. He asked for a short haircut and clean shave. He was no longer in hiding. He was on a hunt. He was beginning the mission his mother had set him on thirty-three years before.

Edward had intended to stay at the motel one more night before starting his drive. Instead, after he had accomplished all his tasks, he found himself wide awake and ready to start the adventure. He decided to spend the first night out of town so he could feel as if he was on his way. He was also worried he would revert to his self-pity mode and never leave.

Months before, when he realized he would be making the trip home, he had downloaded some songs onto his phone. Now, as he pulled out of town, he played his favorite song by Lou Christie. As the music filled his car, he sang along, "Beyond the blue horizon lies a beautiful day. Goodbye to things that bore me. Joy is waiting for me. I see a new horizon my life has only begun. Beyond the blue horizon lies the rising sun."

In his case, it was the setting sun, but the meaning was clear. His new life had only begun.

# NINE

Mornings felt completely different than they used to before Johnny went off to school and Harold had died. Valerie had been used to her old routine. First, rouse her sleeping and stubborn son Johnny for school while making a complete breakfast for her husband. Harold believed in a wife making three meals a day. Even though he only got two from her, because she was at school during the day, she always knew he felt he was missing a vital part of husband privileges.

It surprised her, now that she didn't have to do those two things, how much time she had every morning. Now that it was just her and Lex, there was hardly anything to do. Lex was a self-starter and "I can do it myself" kind of boy. Lex no longer wanted her to pack his lunch, nor make his breakfast. And unlike his brother, Johnny, Lex was the kid who popped out of bed as soon as he was awake.

Lex had always been easy. Even when he was a toddler, Valerie never had to tell Lex it was bedtime. He already knew it. Lex would grab his blankie, say he was tired, and as soon as she put him into bed and gave him a goodnight kiss, he was asleep.

Now eleven, he had become even more self-sufficient and sure of what he wanted to do with himself. After Johnny left, Lex told his mother that he wasn't going to college. He had other plans. Valerie believed him. Lex was already working on them.

When Johnny was working at the Diner, Lex would often visit and watch Pete and Alex cook. Sometimes, when it wasn't busy, Pete would let Lex come back behind the counter and try his hand at simple things like scrambled eggs. Once Sam noticed Lex's interest in cooking, Sam had invited him to help when he had a banquet coming up. Not only had Lex taken Sam up on the offer, but he was also learning from it. Between Pete, Sam, and Alex, Lex was becoming an excellent cook.

Now Lex made breakfast for both himself and his mother every morning and was moving into making dinner, too. The night before, Lex had made fresh pasta with Sam and brought some home for dinner. It was delicious, and Valerie told him it was the best she ever ate. And it was true.

Lex watched Master Chef Junior reruns and memorized every kid's name on every season. On his wish list for his birthday were cookbooks and cooking supplies. Valerie wasn't surprised when Lex said he wanted to be a chef. Valerie told him she was delighted. She didn't have his gift for cooking and was happy to turn cooking duties over to him as he learned more about what he was doing.

Valerie had even researched a camp for budding chefs for the next summer. But she was waiting to surprise him with it for his next birthday in the spring. Assuming being a chef was still what he wanted.

As for her, she didn't know what she wanted. All the hours spent taking care of Harold and Johnny and the guests at their Bed and Breakfast, were now empty and open. She wanted to fill them with something productive and useful. Something that brought her as much joy as Lex found in cooking.

Being the principal of Doveland's combined elementary and middle schools took up every day of the week, but nights, weekends, and summers were empty. Like her house. She and

Harold had purchased it to run as a bed and breakfast to supplement their income, and Harold liked the company and running the business.

Now she and Lex rambled around the house, and she struggled to keep it clean. She used to have a cleaning service when the Bed and Breakfast was running, but was having trouble justifying the expense now that she had closed it, at least for now. When Harold died, Valerie shut down the website and left a message for anyone that called or emailed, that they were currently closed due to owner's death.

Owner's death. What a ridiculous thing to have happened, Valerie thought. But it was true. What to do next was the question. She had a big house with only two people living in it. Her first thought was to sell the house the way Tina had sold the gas station. But then what would happen? Would they move to another part of town in a smaller house? Would it be easy to sell? Would they find a house they liked as much? Valerie was full of questions.

If she told the truth to herself, she didn't really want to sell. She loved the house. Even empty.

There was a women's council meeting in a few days, so Valerie decided to take the question to them and see if anyone had any ideas as to what to do with the house, and the bigger question, what to do with her life.

Checking her Fitbit she wore because she was trying to walk more and sleep better, she realized it was time to leave for school. Lex, the independent child that he was, had already taken the school bus. Of course, he could have ridden with his mother, but he didn't want to remind everyone in school that his mother was the principal. She didn't blame him. Besides, Valerie was reasonably sure that the other reason he rode the bus was because a pretty little girl named Hannah saved him a seat.

The two of them had gone through quite a bit together, so they felt comfortable with each other. Valerie thought Lex had a crush on Hannah, which worried her a little.

She knew Hannah had her sights set on Johnny, even though he was entirely unaware of her as anything other than his brother's friend. The fact that she teleported to find and help him in the woods last spring seemed to have been erased from his mind. Or perhaps Johnny had chosen to forget it because the circumstances of Hannah needing to rescue him had been so terrible. Valerie couldn't blame him for that. She wished she could forget, but Sarah reminded them all that it wasn't over. They needed to stay vigilant.

As for Hannah and Johnny, the gap in their ages was much too big for now. It didn't matter that Hannah still remembered her past life, which she claimed made her older, or that she had gifts most people didn't have. She was still young in the world's eyes.

As Valerie grabbed her heavier fall coat out of the hall closet, she glanced across the street to the empty gas station. Tina had sold it to a company who said they were going to put in a new gas station, but so far nothing had been done. Instead, it sat as a reminder of how much had changed during the year. All those deaths and no answers to any of them.

# TEN

Melvin had a request. Could they have a going away party? Hank knew what he meant, but he didn't like it, so he didn't answer. Instead, he picked up Melvin's breakfast plate and turned to the sink to wash it. Melvin hadn't wanted much, just a slice of toast with some honey on it. Melvin had eaten one bite and had a sip of tea. He said coffee didn't appeal to him anymore.

"You can give me the silent treatment and keep your back turned as long as you want to, Hank, but eventually you are going to have to turn around and answer me."

"What if I say no?" Hank said, turning around so quickly the dish towel slipped from his fingers onto the floor.

Melvin waited until Hank had retrieved it and waited some more until Hank looked at him. "You know you won't. It's a simple request. One that you and I know you will do for me."

When Hank sank down in the chair opposite Melvin still not saying anything, Melvin reached across and covered Hank's work-roughened hand with his slender, almost translucent hand and said, "I know you think that this party means you are signaling the end. That somehow having the party will make it go faster. But you know this timing has nothing to do with you. Or me. It just is. And having the party gives me something to look forward to. It gives me a few extra days and a lot of joy."

Hank remained speechless. He was afraid to talk. He knew his voice would tremble, and that would start the tears flowing. Melvin gave Hank time to collect himself and then added, "I would like to give everyone something special at the party, and I'll need your help to get stuff ready. Plus, I want to have it in our new barn that the town built for me. I know it might be chilly in there, but the woodstove will make it cozy. And not only do I want your whole family and all your friends to be there, but I would also like all the boys and girls that have been working with you, Sam, and Pete to come too.

"I've been planning this, Hank. I saved some money for it. But I can't do it without your help, and maybe Hannah could come over and help, too."

Melvin's last comment finally brought a smile to Hank's face. "Oh, now I see what you are doing, old man," Hank said. "You just want an excuse to do something with Hannah. And I suppose you want Emily too?"

Melvin's big grin that took over his whole wrinkled face was the answer. "Do you think they could come over tomorrow and stay the night? And could the party be on Sunday?"

"So soon, Melvin?"

Melvin didn't need to answer him. Hank knew what Melvin was telling him. Hank stood up, slapped his hand on the table, and said, "Better make some phone calls. If you want a party, you'll get a party. Now, let's get you settled before I get to work on this shindig."

Hank steadied Melvin as he got up from the table and led him to the bed that they had installed in the living room. Going up and down the stairs had gotten too hard for Melvin, and this way Melvin could see everything happening out on his farm.

Once Hank had Melvin tucked in, Hank went up to his room, shut the door and sank down on his bed, wondering how he was going to pull the party off. The logistics of making this last-minute party happen was easier than having it knowing what Melvin was telling them.

*But,* Hank said to himself, *now is not the time to wallow in grief, now is the time to give Melvin what he wants.*

Hank's first call was to his niece, Ava. He needed permission to pick up Hannah after school and have her stay until after the party. Ava's silence was not a 'no.' It was an acknowledgment of what was happening. Hank waited.

"Of course. Yes to Hannah. Yes to getting family and friends to the party. Yes to coordinating with Pete and Sam for food," Ava said, paused and added, "Thank you, Hank, for being there."

Hank stared at the phone for a minute after they hung up before making the next call to Emily. He thought it was going to be the hardest call to make, but instead, Emily answered cheerfully that she would come and stay. In fact, she would come and stay for days, or weeks. She was bringing clothes with her. She was adamant that it was going to be that way, and when Hank realized she meant it, he almost wept from relief. They both would be with him. He hadn't known how much he wanted help until it was not only offered, but was done.

His last call was to Pete to have him gather the boys and girls that they were training. Or at least he thought it was his last call. Instead, it was to Valerie. Could Johnny come home for the weekend?

Valerie didn't hesitate, just as she knew that Johnny wouldn't. "Yes, he'll be there," she promised.

Downstairs, before drifting off to sleep, Melvin listened to the murmur of Hank's voice. He couldn't hear what he was saying, but he knew what he was doing. Granting him his last wish.

"Won't be long now, Sally, Melvin whispered. "I just have one last thing to do."

As always, Sally's answer hung in the air long after it was spoken. "There's no rush, Melvin. I am always here for you."

· · · ● ·● ● · · ·

His mom's phone call pushed Johnny into action. He told her he would leave in the morning after his last class. He had some social plans for Friday night and the weekend, but he would cancel them immediately.

"There is no place I would rather be, mom," Johnny said, and he meant it.

Johnny decided not to tell his friends the reason for Melvin's party. He had only known them a few months and wasn't sure if any of them would understand how Melvin could know when he was dying and be okay with it. Not be sick or in pain, just aware that the story of his time on earth in this form was over.

Johnny wasn't even sure he understood it. But since all those terrible things happened in the spring, and when his dad died, he had been thrown into situations he didn't think actually existed. Things like the horror of having a voice in his head trying to make him hurt his mentor and friend, Pete. Hannah appearing like a hologram and leading him to Leif. Leif, who lived in another dimension.

Just saying things like that to himself sometimes made him think he was crazy. But then, that meant that all the people that had watched out for him and his family were crazy too, and they lived with that kind of woo-woo stuff all the time.

In fact, to them, it wasn't woo-woo. It was an evolved way of perceiving the world. "Just training," Sarah would say to him.

"We've been trained not to see. An enlightened and expanded perception will always see and experience more of the infinite possibilities always going on around us."

Sometimes he wanted to be bratty and say, "Whatever." On the other hand, he knew she was right. He had seen Leif that night. He had heard the voice that tried to make him do terrible things. He had felt the powerful presence of love that Hannah had shown him.

But no matter what, there was no way he was going to tell his friends or new acquaintances that his friend Melvin wanted a going away party before he died. He'd be labeled as weird, and he wasn't ready for that.

He told them there was a party he just found out about and would be back on Monday. There was no reason to tell them what kind of party.

# ELEVEN

E dward wasn't sure what he expected his road trip to be like, but he thought he would like it. He thought it would inspire him, relax him, and provide a transition between the life of running to a settled life in Doveland. But it didn't work out that way. Although the first few days weren't bad, it wasn't what he imagined it would be.

His plan was to take a few weeks to drive across the country. He had lived all over the United States under different identities, but finding a new place to live had always been chosen logically and out of necessity. This time he wanted a pleasure trip.

Edward decided to take back roads and see where they led him. He planned to stop and hike in forests, stand on hilltops and look at the view. He wouldn't have a destination in mind each day. He would drive until he was hungry or tired, or saw something that interested him.

The first day was okay. It was something new. The views through the back roads of Oregon were magnificent. He could feel the excitement of a new adventure coursing through his system.

His plan was to check the app on his phone that told him what the local attractions were when he stopped for gas, or food, or a brief nap. If they looked remotely interesting, he would head off to see them.

But the problem was that after the first two side trips he noticed that no matter what he was looking at, his mind wasn't present in his body. Nothing he looked at registered. He might as well have been staring at a blank wall.

Instead, his mind would drift off into the land of "what ifs." What if his father had returned to Doveland and was waiting for him? What if he was hiding in a nearby town just waiting to pounce at the right time? What if no one in town wanted him there because he was his father's son? What if no one believed him in spite of the proof that he was bringing?

If his plan was to relax and tune into his true self as he took a road trip across the county, it wasn't working at all. To try and bring his mind back to the present as he drove, he listened to music, podcasts, and NPR. Sometimes it helped. Most of the time, it didn't.

The first night, Edward camped out in a beautiful state park in Idaho. He lay in his new sleeping bag and tent, waiting for nature to give him peace. It didn't work. He couldn't sleep at all. Everything bothered him. The bugs, the owls hooting in the woods, the zipping and unzipping of tent flaps by the campers near him. As soon as it was light enough to roll up his tent, he left and headed straight to a local Starbucks.

Thinking that perhaps he couldn't sleep because he didn't like camping out, the next night, after driving back roads and seeing local sites all day, he stopped at a nice motel, ready to get a good night's rest. The only good part of that night was the hot shower that he took before he went to bed, and the bath he took in the middle of the night, trying to relax enough to sleep.

Finally, at three in the morning, he realized what was happening. He was stalling. His body was stalling. His emotions were stalling.

Those parts of him wanted to put off his return as long as possible. But his mind was ready. With that realization, Edward fell asleep.

The next morning, he packed the car and headed south to route 180 east. It looked like he was going to get there much sooner than he planned. No more stalling. He was ready.

He hoped Doveland was ready for him, too.

· • • • •• • • • • · ·

Over two thousand miles away, the residents of Doveland were not thinking about anything other than giving their beloved friend Melvin the going away party he had asked for. The weekend weather prediction couldn't have been more perfect. It promised to be bright, crisp, and warm for October, the trees full of blazing color. Melvin couldn't have chosen a better day for his event.

Surprisingly, or not surprisingly, considering what was governing Melvin's decision, almost everyone they invited said they were coming, even though they all accepted with mixed emotions. Everyone understood that it was not just a regular going away party. No one had ever attended one that was essentially a goodbye party before. Should they be happy or sad? Ava had explained to those that asked that they could be both. All that Melvin wanted was to see them.

The only person who had declined the invitation was Melvin's son. No one was surprised, including Melvin. He hadn't expected his son to take time from his busy schedule to travel all that way to see him. The only thing that Melvin wished was that his son had somehow been more like his wife, kind and attentive. But he never had been proving to Melvin that not everyone was like their mother or father.

After a delicious breakfast prepared by Sam, he and Hank went out to the barn to get it ready. Since the barn was used as a workspace for the young men and women that they mentored, it was filled with tools and supplies. However, Hank had built in supply closets where everything could be put away. In the back, Hank had added a bathroom and a small kitchen. Hank and Melvin had planned ahead when they built the place. Or, as Hank had once realized, it was Melvin who planned ahead, as if he had a peek into a future the rest of them didn't see.

Hank and Sam were in charge of cleaning up the barn. Tom would bring food from the Diner and Mandy would be coming with him to add all the special touches that would transform the barn into something magical.

After breakfast, while Hank and Sam worked on the barn, Hannah and Emily helped Melvin into a comfortable chair in his living room and declared themselves to be his hands and feet. Direct them. Tell them what to get and where, and they would. To heighten the image of helper elves, Ava had supplied them both with elf hats and aprons. When they put them on, Melvin clapped his hands in delight.

"Okay, young ladies," Melvin said, "We have some work to do. I also need you to write for me. I have all the supplies you need in Sally's desk in the dining room. Other things I will have to send you around the house to get."

"Oh, fun," Hannah said. "Like a treasure hunt?"

"Exactly like a treasure hunt," Melvin answered, and settled down into his chair, ready to direct his personal elves, the young woman and the little girl he thought of as his own. He couldn't have been any happier. It was going to be one of the best weekends of his life.

Standing beside him, Sally put her hand on his shoulder and whispered, "This is wonderful, my love."

Melvin looked up at her and smiled. He could not only see her now, but he could also feel her hand on his shoulder. They were doing this together, as they always had.

# TWELVE

Although they lived together, Tom was always excited to see Mandy walk in the door even if it had only been a few hours since they had parted. When he first realized that he was always watching for Mandy and missing her when she was away, Tom was confused. Was this how he was supposed to feel? Did his father feel that way when he waited for his mother? It was not something Tom had ever expected. But here he was, waiting for her as if he had nothing else to do. Which, he had to admit, he didn't.

After his adopted parents died, Tom had decided to travel wherever and whenever he wanted to see the world. He had the money his parents had left him, and a natural gift for investing and attracting money, so he had the funds. While traveling, Tom realized that he received great joy by helping people, doing good with his money, and doing it anonymously.

After a while, he found other men like him doing the same thing, and they had decided to work together to do more good. Over time, that simple good ole boys club had grown into a full-blown non-profit organization. Mira had requested a name change, so now it was called the Good Ole Dudes Club. It still did good anonymously. However, now that it was organized instead of free-flowing and spontaneous, he didn't enjoy it as much. It could run on its own. Besides, traveling meant he was always saying goodbye to Mandy.

Tom didn't think that his current unease was because he had been happier before. It was just that all the things that had happened in the last few years had changed his entire view of the world. Before, he had thought that he understood how the world worked. Then life intervened and took everything he knew and turned it upside down.

First, the twin sister that he didn't know he had remote viewed him, scaring the crap out of him. Mira was unwittingly helped by one of the members of what was the Good Ole Boys Club, Evan Anders. Uncovering that mystery led to meeting Sarah and Leif and then Craig and Ava in Sandpoint, Idaho. It was there that he and Mira learned they had been adopted. Their parents had let them go to protect them. It was in Sandpoint that Tom and Mira briefly met their mother, Suzanne, who had been waiting for them, knowing they would come there together someday. Their father had died a few years before.

If that wasn't enough to turn his world upside down, Tom found out that his father, mother, and grandparents were part of a circle his friends later named the Forest Circle. The members of the Forest Circle were able to shift or travel between dimensions. Tom could never figure out which one to call it because it was crazy to even think about. Although he now saw his friends, Leif and Eric, all the time as they shifted between dimensions, Tom still thought it was crazy.

Suzanne had hugged her children before she left to join the rest of the Forest Circle, even though she stayed present in both dimensions for a while to make sure they were all doing well. As Tom thought back over the past few years, he realized he hadn't stopped to think how life-changing and downright weird it had been. No wonder he was feeling restless and unfocused.

He was learning to accept a new way of viewing reality, even though he didn't understand it. But he knew it was real because he experienced it for himself. Which brought him full circle back to Mandy. He knew his feelings for her were real too. But he didn't fully understand them either.

When Mandy entered his life, Tom's desire for traveling diminished, mainly because he was going without her. He kept it up anyway, unwilling to admit that she was that important in his life. Reluctant to believe that anyone could be that important. Last spring, Mandy had given him an ultimatum of sorts. Be a couple, stop running away, or let her go.

It was impossible to let her go, so he surrendered. Mandy moved in and transformed their house. Mandy created magic in everything she did. And she had created magic for Tom. As far as Tom was concerned, it was Mandy herself that was magical.

Finally, Tom had given up trying to pretend that his heart wasn't completely taken over by her. It was too late. He was hers. And that was why he was worried. Lately, she seemed preoccupied, and his paranoia was kicking in that it had something to do with him. When he had asked her about it, she said it wasn't the time to talk about it. It was time to focus on Melvin. She was right, of course, so he put his fears away, and pretended that they weren't there.

Sitting at his favorite table at Your Second Home, he watched Grace and Mandy prepare some of the food he and Mandy would be taking out to Melvin's house. They would both say it was just a simple selection, but Mandy and Grace would be downplaying their stunningly delicious sandwiches and desserts. Once again designed by his magical Mandy.

The items needed for transforming Melvin's barn were already in the car. Mandy had spent a few hours going through all her supplies at their house to pull together just what she wanted to complete her vision. While she was working, Tom overheard her muttering that she was going to need a place all her own where she could keep her supplies, increasing his paranoia that she was unhappy with him.

But when she turned to him with twinkling eyes and a full smile, he relaxed a bit. Perhaps he was misreading the signs. After all, he had done it before with his sister, Mira. If nothing else, he would be Mandy's handyman as long as she wanted to have one. He wasn't good with design, but he did know how to run a business. He could be handy that way, too.

Grace waved a hand at him, calling him over. "We're ready for you, Tom."

What would they do without Grace? They found her in Sandpoint, too. Or was it that she found them? Either way, even though she called herself an old busy-body, she wasn't. She was the town's angel, and together she and Mandy had brought joy wherever they went.

Tom hugged them both—surprising Mandy but not Grace, who saw in his eyes both his love and his worry—picked up the food supplies with a grunt and headed out the back to the car.

Grace grabbed Mandy's arm and held her back.

"You better tell him soon, Mandy. He doesn't deserve to be left out."

"I promise. After the women's council meeting when I know more."

"Well, in the meantime, give him extra attention, so he stops panicking."

Mandy turned and hugged Grace, and whispered, "I will. Thank you."

Tom watched them both as he held open the door and started worrying again. Why were they whispering? He smiled at Mandy, and she smiled back at him and then kissed him on the cheek.

It was enough for now. But Tom promised himself after Melvin's party that they would definitely have to talk.

Grace watched them both go and hugged herself. She missed Eric. She knew that both Eric and Leif would be at Melvin's party. She'd see him then. No hugging. But at least she would see him. For that she was grateful.

The new front door dinged, but no cold air came in with the group of teenagers ready to have their late morning coffee. She smiled to herself. The new entrance was working well, and her coffee shop was the perfect place to keep tabs on the town, and that was precisely what she was doing.

"And doing it well," Eric whispered in her ear.

*Dang it,* Grace thought. Now he was teasing her by being invisible. She'd have to talk to him about that. Still, he was always watching out for her. For that, she was forever grateful.

# THIRTEEN

Sarah leaned against the back wall of the barn, watching the party. It was the perfect example of a community working together. As always, everyone brought delicious food and Mandy's decorations had transformed the barn into something both magical and comforting.

Hank had brought Melvin's favorite chair over from the house, and he sat in it looking as happy as she had ever seen him as people took turns talking to him. Wisely, Hank had added a second chair facing Melvin where people could sit. It meant that only one person at a time could speak to him, which was precisely what he wanted, personal time with everyone.

Melvin also had his two elves with him standing on each side of his chair. Emily and Hannah had each put their elf hats and aprons back on and were prepared to run errands for him. They stepped away when Melvin was speaking to each person so it could be a private conversation. Before each person left, Melvin would nod, and one of his elves would get the small package with that person's name on it and hand it to Melvin.

Melvin would make the recipient promise to wait until he left the party before opening it, and then place the gift in their hand.

For those paying attention, which was quite a few, they saw that the real gift he was giving was his direct look into their eyes, where he transferred as much love as possible to them.

There were only a few people left that Melvin hadn't talked to yet, and Sarah could see that his energy was flagging. Would he make it to the end? Was there something she could do? She hadn't received her gift yet. She was waiting for a signal from one of the elves that it was time. She hoped it was soon. Not because she wanted anything. She wanted to give him something instead.

"You don't need to touch him to give him that gift, Sarah," Leif said as he appeared by her side. He and Eric had been at the party since it started drifting in and out. Sarah had once asked Leif why he and Eric never stayed long. He had told her they were still learning how to be in both places at the same time.

Then he launched into some explanation that all dimensions were at the same place at the same time, and that meant everyone was in all of them. At the same time. Together. But he and Eric were beginners, so it was hard for them to be in two places at the same time in a way that people could see them in both places.

He had corrected himself and said so that the inhabitants of both dimensions could see them. She had pondered over that change to the word "inhabitants" but hadn't had the opportunity to find out what he meant by that. She suspected that he and Eric were wondering if they should tell her.

She wasn't worried. He would. Soon. Because she realized she needed to know.

In the meantime, here he was reminding her she didn't need to touch Melvin to give him his gift, so she closed her eyes and imagined Melvin knowing himself as the essence of spirit and love with unflagging energy.

Once she felt the truth of the imagining, she opened her eyes and looked at Melvin.

He was looking straight at her. He knew and felt what she had just done, and he had willingly accepted her gift of knowing his true self as present now. He smiled and straightened up in his chair, ready for his next visitor.

Finally, everyone had been handed either an envelope or a package, and Melvin told his two elves that it was time for him to head to bed. But, to his surprise, one of the children walked up to him and started singing the song "I'll Be There."

Melvin clapped his hands together in utter delight as another child joined in, and then another joined one at a time until all the children and adults were singing and dancing together. When it was over, the whole crowd clapped and cheered, and Melvin told them it was the most beautiful, magical thing he had ever seen.

"How did you do this?" Melvin asked. They pointed to Emily and her musician friend Shawn and said, "They helped us." Shawn and Emily gave a little bow and hugged all the participants. They had put it together at the last minute by sending out a call to anyone who wanted to do a flash mob for Melvin's party to meet at the town hall that morning. They weren't surprised that almost everyone showed up. Melvin had spent the last few years doing as much good as he could, thinking people hadn't noticed. They had.

Once everyone had settled down a bit, Melvin sat back in his chair and looked at Hank. Hank knew what he was telling him. It was time. He, Emily, and Hannah helped him stand. As he slowly left the barn, Melvin waved and smiled at everyone as his chosen family led him into the house.

The party was over. By the time Hank, Emily, and Hannah returned to the barn, people were packing up what they had brought and were leaving. Quietly. It was time to go home and open their gifts from Melvin in private.

Hannah and her parents, Ava and Evan, and her little brother Ben were the last to leave. Hannah wanted to stay but gave in when

Hank reminded her that there was school tomorrow and he and Emily would stay with him. "Besides," he whispered to her as he hugged her, "you always know how to be with people even if they aren't here, don't you?"

She hugged him tighter and nodded, yes. "But you promise to stay with him for me?"

"I do. And Emily said she would stay too. One of us will be here with him as long as he needs us to be."

As they watched Evan and his family leave, Emily turned to Hank and said, "You know I will stay for as long as necessary, but you also know he is leaving tonight, don't you?"

"I do," Hank said, pulling Emily close. The two of them returned to the house knowing they would be awake the rest of the night.

# FOURTEEN

M elvin's funeral was held the next Saturday. True to form, Melvin had written instructions down for what he wanted for his funeral. What everyone else wanted was for him to be there still. Everyone whose life he had touched wanted more. More Melvin.

But they honored his wishes. Except for one thing. He didn't want people to stand up in the front of the church and sing his praises. They did anyway. Each one started by saying, "Melvin, sorry, but I have to say this."

For someone who had spent all of his life on his small farm, Melvin had managed to spread a lot of love. When Jay, Hannah's past-dad, had come to stay at his farm, Melvin had pulled out of the slump he had been in since his wife Sally had died and begun to live as fully as possible. It was partly in honor of Jay's sacrifice of his own life to save Hank's and partially when he recognized that Sally had never left him and expected him to get the most out of the time he had left.

He had found a new family in the people of Doveland, and he let them know he loved them. At home, after his going away party, everyone opened the gifts that he had left them and found something personal. Most of the items were small treasures that he had collected over the years. Not value measured in money, but in memories. Each one had a little story attached to it about where it had come from and what it meant to him and Sally and what he hoped it would mean to them.

Some people got envelopes telling them what they would find in his will. Hank doubled over in pain and joy when he read that he would get all of Melvin's property. Pain because Melvin wouldn't be there, and joy because Melvin had given him something he never had before. A safe home.

Sarah got a long letter that Melvin had written himself. It must have taken him days because she could tell when he had to stop and start. She had read it once and put it away for the time being. Not that the contents weren't important, but because they were.

When Emily opened her package, she burst into tears. What she had in her hands meant Melvin had to have help to accomplish it. It was the four-leaf clover that her mother had left her when she died. It had been given to her mother by her sister almost a half-century ago. Emily was supposed to have found her Aunt Jean and returned it to her.

She did find her. Jean was one of the bodies that were found buried on her hill when she started building her art retreat. Instead of putting it in Jean's urn, she kept the four-leaf clover that had been pressed between two pieces of wax paper all that time, in a little box on her desk.

And now here it was. Melvin had it encased into a piece of glass and hung on a chain. As Emily listened to everyone tell what Melvin meant to them, she held it in her hand, sliding it back and forth on the chain, wishing she had more time with the man she thought of as her grandfather.

She looked down the pew and caught Mandy's eye, who winked at her. What did Tom call Mandy? Magical Mandy? Yes, that was what she was, because now she knew who had helped Melvin with the gift.

Emily placed her hands on her heart and nodded at Mandy, who returned the gesture.

After everyone had said what needed to be said, ignoring Melvin's wishes, they ignored them again by having the same children who had sung at his party, stand up and sing, "This Little Light Of Mine." They figured that if he had known they could do it, he would have asked for it.

Cars with balloons on their antennas and honking horns followed his casket out to the cemetery where he was to be buried beside his wife, Sally. His note to Hank told him he knew he wouldn't be at the cemetery. After all, he saw his wife every day now. She wasn't there either. But they had purchased the plots years before they understood the continuation of life. Therefore, he would honor that tradition. Perhaps it would give them a place to come to talk to him. He'd be listening.

Melvin's son had arrived in time to hear the will read, and briefly attended the funeral. He appeared to be so opposite of Melvin that no one realized who he was until the reading of the will. He was furious that he didn't get the farm.

Not that he wanted it. In fact, he would have sold it, anyway. But it proved to him that life wasn't fair. His dad had left him some money, explaining in the will that it was what he gave him because Melvin knew his son wanted that most. If Melvin's son was honest with himself, he knew his father's words were right. Still. He stayed until all the people started talking about the wonderful man that was his father, and couldn't take it anymore.

Deep in his heart, he knew it was true. That it was his focus on his business and money that had driven them apart. But to admit that it was his fault, well he wasn't ready to do that. So he slipped out of the funeral and went home.

Only a few people saw him go. If he felt the rush of light and love sent to him on the way out by those people he didn't show it. It was the best they could give him at the moment. Sarah knew she was not the only one who sent him love. Someday, perhaps, he would find it.

At the cemetery, they released balloons and doves and threw lavender seeds and rose petals in the air yelling, "Bye, Melvin. We love you!"

After it was all over, there was a gathering at Ava and Evan's. Once again, the community brought food and celebrated. It was the end of an era. Nothing would be the same.

Sarah and Grace walked out together, out across the lawn towards the forest. Although Leif and Eric were there at the party, they let them go alone, watching just in case they were needed.

"Now what?" Grace asked.

"Now, we keep on living," Sarah said. "I should add, living here. Because, of course, life goes on. We just don't see where people go when they leave." She paused and added. "For the most part, anyway."

They turned back to see Leif and Eric watching them.

Grace said, "Well, we learned to live with them without their physical bodies. If we can do that, I suppose we can do anything."

"We can," Sarah laughed, "And I think it's time for a women's council meeting."

Grace laughed, "Amen to that, sister. My place? Monday night?"

When Sarah nodded yes, she and Grace headed back to the gathering, arm in arm, to tell the rest of the women. Even though, watching the two of them head back with a twinkle in their eyes, all the women already knew. They just needed the time and place.

# FIFTEEN

Edward wasn't sure what to do. It had been a peaceful trip across the country, and now he was only a few hours from his destination. He stopped driving early the day before, not ready to make the last leg of his journey.

At the last minute, he had stopped at a motel in Ohio and spent a restless night imagining what would happen when he reached Doveland. Now he sat in the coffee shop across from the motel trying to eat something for breakfast and finding it hard to swallow. Despite all the years of planning, or maybe because of it, he was afraid to go on.

The what-ifs wouldn't leave him alone. Living his life, never being himself, had done something to him. It was as if he had hidden all this time behind a mask, and now he was asking himself to take it off and expose who he was to the world. The resistance to doing that was amazing, and not at all what he had expected. Throughout all the years he had imagined that when he became himself, he would feel free. He had imagined it as if he was rising out of the darkness into the light.

None of that had happened. He wanted to go back to the dark. He wanted to take back one of his made-up lives and go live that.

No one was expecting him. No one knew that he could provide the evidence they were looking for to prove that it was his father who had killed those women. More than those women. Many more.

He told himself that his father was old, and the crimes would probably stop now. Besides, even if he brought the proof of what his father had done, what good would it do? His father had escaped. The argument made sense, but Edward knew he was only justifying his fear.

Yes, Edward thought, I am afraid of becoming myself. But there was another fear, too. It was true that no one was expecting him. Except one person was. Edward knew his father. He knew he had been relentlessly searching for him. It was only a little skill and a lot of luck that had kept Joe from finding him.

However, Edward knew that as soon as he returned to Doveland, his father would know he was there. That was what was terrifying him. Edward held no hope that his father loved him and would never hurt him. He knew that his father would act as if he cared as long as it served his need to project to the world that he healed and helped people. However, if Edward threatened Joe's reputation, even his son would become the enemy.

And that is precisely what Edward was going to do. Take away Dr. Joe's reputation as the hero and reveal him as the villain.

Edward didn't really believe in prayer. He had lived by his wits all these years, but having nowhere else to turn he decided to give praying a try. He wasn't going to pray to a human god, which he knew he could never accept. He could never believe in a god that made evil and sometimes saved people and sometimes didn't, depending on whim, or good luck, or prejudice.

If he were going to believe in a god, it would have to be one that somehow was the intelligent guiding force of the multiverse. How that could be, or what it would look like, or how that affected him was something Edward didn't understand. But he could accept that it was possible. He could allow that if he lived as if it was true, then perhaps it would be. That he could do.

So right there in the coffee shop, he bowed his head, closed his eyes, and waited for an answer. Or some courage. Anything that would move him off his seat and propel him back home. Because as much as he didn't want to go there, he knew he had to. He kept his promises. Because he had to trust himself to keep his promises, otherwise he had nothing.

The door to the coffee shop opened, causing Edward to look up. A little girl wearing pink tights and black leotard came in holding her mother's hand. She was walking on her tiptoes. Edward thought she must be heading to, or coming from, a dance class.

As they crossed in front of him on their way to a table, he overheard their conversation.

"I'm excited, mom. But, I am scared too," the little girl said.

"What are you afraid of, honey?" her mom asked.

"Well, I want to be in the recital, but I don't want people to know it's me, and my name will be in the program. That's what Miss Windy said, anyway. I don't want my name in the program," she said, sighing and looking as if she would burst into tears.

Her mom knelt down beside her daughter and said, "Well, you could change your name for the recital. Make up a new one."

"I can?" the little girl squealed as she hugged her mom. "That's it. I'll make up a new name. Fun!"

Edward lost the rest of the conversation as they moved to their table, but he surmised that it was a joyful discussion because they were both smiling and laughing. The little girl was gesturing with her hands as she spoke. Edward thought she was making up names and trying them out.

Then he laughed to himself. Of course, that was the answer. He had planned to tell his real name when he got to Doveland, and that was what was scaring him the most. He had no idea what the people were like that lived there now. Instead, he could use a different name until he discovered if it was safe—or not—to reveal his identity.

As he prepared to pay his bill, he thought that perhaps there was that infinite intelligence kind of God after all.

On the way out the door, Edward passed by the little girl and her mom and said to the little girl, "You look like a dancer."

She puffed up and said proudly, "I am! And my name is Tina!"

Edward answered, "Nice to meet you, Tina. My name is Ted."

He smiled to himself as he walked to his car. He had no idea if her name was actually Tina, nor was his name Ted. But it didn't matter. Besides, when he did tell people his real name, they wouldn't think much of it. Ted was often a nickname for Edward. Ted Miller. It sounded good to him.

It was time to go home, and now he was ready.

# Sixteen

It had been a while since they had all met at Grace's for a
women's council meeting. Last spring, they had held meetings
weekly while they were trying to decide what to do about the
mystery of the women's bodies found buried on Emily's hill.
Then they met together with the Town Council to plan the
summer solstice which was held at Emily's retreat. Hank and his
construction crew had still been working on completing the retreat
center, but had finished the dance barn and deck enough for the
town's annual celebration.

It had gone off without a hitch, unlike the year before. After
it was over, it was as if everyone took a collective sigh and
settled down into enjoying summer. Which they did. Picnics and
barbecues happened regularly and to everyone's relief, no one died
and no new bodies were discovered.

It wasn't that the women hadn't had council meetings during
the summer. They still met informally. Sometimes at the coffee
shop, or even the Diner. However, because they were meeting in
public, they hadn't talked about anything private or complicated.

Now, they all knew it was time for an official meeting. They
were all restless and were not sure why. At least one of them had a

question that needed to be answered, and both Valerie and Mandy needed help with decisions that had to be made.

The women's council had temporarily added three new members in the spring. Two of them had asked to remain and their request was accepted. The two knew that meant there was an obligation to being part of the council. They would be there for each other, no matter what. They didn't have to agree with each other. In fact, it was often valuable to not agree, because solutions found together were sometimes the best ones. But they always had to respect each other, their different opinions, and ways of doing things. That meant that there was no sharing of any information that was talked about in the council unless permission was given.

General rules about that permission had already been decided upon, and anything outside of that needed to be discussed together before acting on it. It was also agreed that all permissions could be withdrawn at any time. They also knew that once in the council, they were expected to stay. The group needed consistency to build trust. If you knew you couldn't be consistent or if you weren't sure that you could stay, don't join.

The only exception they made was in the spring when they invited Emily, Tina, and Valerie because the three of them were dealing with unexplained deaths. Emily with her Aunt Jean's. Valerie and Tina with their husband's deaths.

It was Emily and Valerie who became permanent members. Tina had decided to move to Pittsburgh, Pennsylvania, with her daughter, Lynn, and son, Manny. They all wished Tina well and looked forward to the time she visited Doveland. But she would remain outside the women's council official meetings on her visits.

It had to be that way. Everyone understood why. There could be many gatherings and coffees and parties and talking with her, but not within the formal council meeting.

Tonight it was a formal meeting. But Grace, who always did everything the way her name implied, had told them they were going to eat first. She loved having the council meeting at her house. It gave her an excuse to do something special in her living room, and tonight she had filled it with baskets of autumn leaves, and she had hung twinkle lights inside her front curtain. The lights and the many candles she had placed around the room set the stage.

Then she had ordered dinner from Sam's Catering Company. He had prepared a feast for them and dropped it off before the women arrived. He had made a tomato bisque soup, homemade potato chips, crusted brussel sprouts, and a variety of sandwiches to meet every woman's taste. He knew them all, so it was truly a specialized meal just for them.

Mira looked at the spread and wondered how she ended up with someone as wonderful as Sam. If nothing else, she and her friends would always eat well. She knew that there was more than that, though. It wasn't her relationship she questioned. It was what she wanted to do with herself.

Her brother Tom had been moving away from the Good Ole Dudes Club, which meant it wasn't as fun for Mira to run anymore. She needed something else. Looking around the room, she wondered how many of the women in the room were thinking that too. Perhaps they all needed something else, but what was it?

Watching Mira, Sarah knew what was on her mind. They were all restless. They all wanted something more in their lives. But it was more than that. It was the unsolved mystery. Well, the mystery had been solved, but not proved. There was no closure.

What Sarah knew, and no one else did, was the person who was bringing closure to them, had just arrived. She also knew she would have to let it play out the way it was meant to play out. She couldn't control or change the flow of what was going to happen. If she tried to, it wouldn't change the outcome in the long run, but it would make the process harder. It was going to be hard enough without her messing with it. That was going to be her lesson. To watch and guide, protect when she could. She would have to trust the flow.

What she could do was help everyone bring up their questions and confusions about what was going on in their lives. Together, they could design something that worked for everyone. That was going to be so much fun she couldn't wait to get started.

So once everyone had eaten their fill and packed up what was left to take home for the next day's lunch, she called the meeting to order.

She reminded them of their intent as a council. And then asked them all to share what they had been doing the last few months. Of course, they had been sharing and talking all along, and the scrumptious dinner had been filled with laughing and talking over each other, which women can do so well and still hear the whole conversation.

But they knew what Sarah meant. Now they could share what was going on within their hearts. What was troubling them. What did they need feedback on? What small and big issues were they working on inside themselves?

They were seated in a circle in Grace's living room. Sarah and Ava sat on the floor where they both liked to sit. Mira and Mandy flanked Emily on the couch. They had gotten in the habit of sitting beside her last spring, and it had remained. They were showing Emily that they understood she still needed extra support. Barbara, Valerie, and Grace sat on comfy chairs that Valerie said made her feel like a queen.

Sarah looked at Ava and realized that they needed to sit level with everyone else, so they moved to the couch facing the other three women.

"Okay," Sarah said, reaching into her bag and pulling out the talking stick they had made over the summer. She handed it to Ava and said, "You start."

# SEVENTEEN

Ava looked at the talking stick, thinking about how much she loved it. They had all designed it together. Hank had made the basic form for them based on pictures he had seen of the talking sticks used by Native Americans. Then each of the council had added something that symbolized who they were. Now the stick had an assortment of items hanging off of it, from feathers to glitter baubles.

It rattled a bit as they randomly passed it from woman to woman. Ava thought of it as a sound that called them together. They loved using it to start their meetings. Everyone knew to turn the focus to the person holding the stick and really listen. After everyone had spoken the meeting would get slightly rowdy as they threw ideas and thoughts back and forth to each other.

Ava shared something they already knew because it had been on her mind for a while. She was looking for something to do with her time. Hannah was in school all day, and Ben was an easy child, leaving her a lot of time on her hands. Even Evan was restless. They enjoyed funding things like the bike trail and fixing the stone church, but it wasn't enough. Ava wanted a purpose. Something to do that was hers, and perhaps something she and Evan could do together.

Barbara said she was content. The Diner was doing well. She and Pete were enjoying running it, spending time together, and helping Sam mentor some of the kids in town who wanted to cook. They were toying with the idea of holding cooking classes in the evenings and putting in the pizza oven that Pete wanted. What did the council think? She received a resounding, "yes," and a suggestion to hold one for the kids in town who had dreams of being chefs.

Barbara sighed in happiness, knowing her next step, and handed the baton to Emily, who brought everyone up to date on the building on her hill. She was plenty busy, restless about something, but happy in the direction her art retreat was going. She'd have more to say next time.

Grace too was happy. Her business, Your Second Home, was thriving. It was just busy enough to be profitable, but not so busy she didn't have any spare time. Plus, she was done doing any construction for a while. Putting in the new entrance was worth it but very disruptive. Grace hinted that she was looking for someone to work in the shop with her. Mandy knew it was because she hadn't been there as much. Grace said she would also volunteer their little kitchen if the cooking classes needed a different space from time to time.

Mira told them that Tom was thinking of passing the entire G.O.D. organization to someone else to own and run. They would participate but no longer be in charge of running it. That meant she could spend more time, perhaps, running Sam's catering business. They were now doing some online orders, and she was thinking of writing a cookbook. She was going to want the council's help on that as she went forward.

Mira leaned over to Barbara and said she and Sam were converting their kitchen to a much bigger commercial kitchen and perhaps sometimes the cooking classes could be at their place if they wanted to try out other foods. Barbara gave her a thumbs up, and everyone said they would love to be a taste tester for the cookbook.

They all turned to Mandy and Valerie because they knew that the meeting had been called primarily for them. The two of them stared at Mira who was holding out the baton for one of them to take.

Finally, Valerie sighed and reached out for it. Mandy relaxed and leaned back to listen. She knew she was next, and hoped that she could put into words what she wanted to do.

"Well," Valerie began, "I think it's pretty obvious what my problem is. I can't make up my mind what to do about the house and bed and breakfast. As you know, Johnny is in college, and only comes home during the breaks. And now that Harold is dead, there is no one there to run the bed and breakfast part which is why we bought the house. Lex loves cooking and is going to be head over heels happy that there will be ongoing cooking classes, but he couldn't be responsible for providing breakfast for guests every morning.

"I am busy teaching, but then I'm not. I like the idea of having a side hustle, but having strangers in my home all the time doesn't appeal to me."

Turning to Ava, she said. "I did love hosting you before the wedding. But you were local, and we were all part of the ceremony.

"So I am looking for answers to two things first. Do I sell the house and move to a smaller one in Doveland, or do I keep it and do something else with all those rooms?"

Sarah, who knew what Mandy was going to say, asked the council if she could ask Valerie a question before they moved on. Everyone nodded assent.

"Valerie, would you mind if your house hosted people you knew? Do you like people in your house, or do you want to have a private home?"

"I know the answer to that," she said. "I love the hustle and bustle of people around me. I do like some private time, so I need my room and some of my own space, but yes, I would be fine with people around me. Probably why I enjoy being a principal. Always something to do, people to care for, and energy that feeds me."

"Thank you," Sarah said.

Mandy looked at Sarah. "You have an idea, don't you?"

"Could be," Sarah answered. "But first, you share."

Mandy paused. "It's not something you all don't already know. I love designing, and I think I am good at it."

A round of "oh, yeses" came from the room and Mandy smiled at them all.

"You are all so wonderful and have been amazingly helpful in giving me a chance to try out my skills. And especially Grace. She has given me such a slide on not helping as much at the coffee shop. First bringing me in as a partner, and then letting me build another business on the side."

Mandy's voice caught as she added, "I can never thank you enough, Grace." Grace smiled back at her with her hand on her heart.

"And now I am stuck. I know that Tom thinks it's because of him. But, it's not. I love him with all my being. I just want my own design business." She paused, amazed that she had said what she wanted out loud.

"Yes, there. I said it. I want my own design business. Now. So how do I do that, and keep my friends, my relationship, and my business with Grace?"

Sarah turned to Mandy, trying not to giggle she was so excited, and asked, "So, are you saying you would like the business to remain based in Doveland, and you need a space to run it out of?"

The room was quiet for only a few seconds, and then everyone got it at once, and the talking over each other began.

In the end, it was agreed. Mandy would open her design studio in part of Valerie's home after Hank had updated it to make it work. Valerie would help with the administration of the business. When Mandy asked Grace if she could call the business Your Second Home Design and would Grace be her partner in that business, Grace burst into tears.

Ava watched the joy and planning, not with disappointment because she still didn't have her answer, but with expectation. They all knew that although they hadn't discovered the solution to Ava's question, its resolution had begun. They just had to wait and see what the future would bring.

All the women were so involved in the planning of the new venture that it was only Sarah who noticed that Suzanne Lawdry was standing in the corner. She waved at Sarah and then vanished.

The Forest Circle had returned. Sarah wondered what that meant. She thought it was probably because of the man who had just arrived in town, but maybe it was more than that. She knew that they would find out soon enough.

# EIGHTEEN

Edward thought that he would recognize more of the area once he turned off the main roads heading to Doveland. Of course, he hadn't been back since he was fifteen, so what did he expect? Places change, just like people. He was no longer the gangly, fresh-faced teenager who hitchhiked out of town one day while his father was working.

His mother had not only left Edward the evidence of his father's crime, but she also left him enough money to run away. A short time before she died, Edward and May had gone to the lake outside Doveland. They told Joe that it was a beautiful day, so they were going on a picnic. They asked if he wanted to come, knowing full well that he had patients all day and would have to turn them down.

Even though he was only ten, Edward knew his father was not happy that they were going somewhere without him, but there was nothing Joe could do. His patients were watching. So he pretended to be thrilled for them, kissed them both, and told them to have a good time.

It was a brilliant move on the part of his mom to wait and ask his father while he had a room full of patients. At the time, they still lived above the clinic, so it made sense for them to come down with a picnic basket and into the waiting room to invite him. Everyone watching thought it was sweet. And even though his father suspected deception, there was nothing he could do about it.

He had looked through the picnic basket and declared everything looked delicious. It wasn't that he wanted to make sure the food was good enough for them, he was checking to make sure his mother wasn't taking something she shouldn't out of the house.

She knew he would do that. They had planned the picnic for weeks. Everything she wanted to take without Joe's knowledge, she had sewed piece by piece into the clothes they were wearing.

On the way out of town, they stopped at the hardware store and purchased a small watertight safe. His mom knew that it was the one thing that might go wrong. The man who ran the hardware store might ask Joe how he liked the safe that his wife bought him.

However, he was also sweet on Edward's mother. So when May asked him to please not spoil the surprise and talk to Joe about it he said he understood. She said she was going to put something very special in it as a surprise for her husband and she didn't want it to be spoiled. He nodded and ran his fingers across his lips like closing a zipper, laid his hand on his heart, and promised to keep it a secret.

The fact that his mom died just a few weeks later ensured that he never told Joe about the safe. He had promised. Even if he had, it was too late. That day at the lake, his mother removed the letter, a few cassette tapes, and bundles of cash from their clothes, and put them in the safe. It had taken her years to accumulate all of the money. She had hidden it in places Joe would never look. Still, Edward realized she must have always been frightened that her husband would find it.

They buried the safe together in the forest around the lake, near a huge oak tree that would be easy to spot years later. Together they rolled a large stone over where they had buried it. One key to the safe May then sewed into his jacket, and the other they buried under another rock on the other side of the tree. Just in case.

She wasn't worried that Edward wouldn't be able to find the tree. They sat and talked about all the ways that he could find his way back there, no matter how long it took. She made Edward promise to leave as soon as he could make it on his own. Edward begged her to go with him that day. Why couldn't the two of them run away together?

But she said Edward would never be safe if they went together. She would stay and keep Joe happy. Of course, his mother didn't stay. She died. And five years later, Edward walked out of the house and straight to the lake. He quickly found the safe and the hidden key. It was good they buried an extra one. Joe had thrown out the jacket because he had decided that it was too small for Edward. He had done it when Edward wasn't home. It was part of his plan to update Edward's bedroom to look like that of a young man instead of a little boy's room. It was just like his father to plan and do the project while Edward was not home to take part in it.

Edward had come home, and his father had thrown all of his childhood toys away. His room had been cleared of memories. A new bed sat in the middle of the freshly painted room. New clothes were in the closet.

When Edward burst into tears, his father had slapped him and told him to grow up. It was the first time he had physically slapped him. All the other slaps had been psychological.

For the first time in a long time, Edward obeyed his father. He grew up. Edward left the next day. He talked to his dead mother the whole way to the lake and stayed off the roads as she had told him to. "Thank you, mom," he said as he found the key to the safe exactly where they had buried it, just in case.

Now, thirty-three years later, Edward was returning to Doveland, not as a young man running away, but as a grown-up ready to do what needed to be done.

Once Edward found Doveland, he drove around the town square and headed out to the lake and the old oak tree. Pulling into the small parking lot, he had to orient himself. The lake was the same, but the forest had changed. He did as his mom had taught him. He walked to the place the lake jutted out just a bit and stood with his back to it. Then he raised his right hand and pointed straight out in front of him. There it was, rising just over the tree line. Many of the maple tree's brilliant red leaves that surrounded the oak had fallen and the oak's leaves had turned brown. Most of its leaves would drop in the spring. The contrast made it easy to recognize.

He made his way to the tree and sat with his back against it and closed his eyes. He could see his beautiful mom digging in the dirt with the branch they had found, making him promise to be safe and someday to come back and show the world what his father had done. They had pinkie swore, and then she hugged him, dried her tears, and they went back to the lake and had their picnic.

"I kept the first part of the promise to you, mom," Edward said. "And now I am here to keep the second part."

Edward knew that some people could hear their loved ones long after they had died, but he had never heard his mother's voice again. He pretended she had answered, and he envisioned her smiling at him with the same love on her face she always had for him.

He stayed until the sky darkened and a rain cloud formed overhead. Before going, he bowed to the tree, thanking it for staying safe too, and went to find a place to stay for the night.

Tomorrow, he would go into town and start meeting people.

# Nineteen

Hank still couldn't bring himself to eat breakfast at the house by himself, so he had gotten in the habit of eating at the Diner every morning instead. He knew that sooner or later he would have to become comfortable on his own at Melvin's, but he wasn't ready. After all, Melvin had only passed away a week before. Just as he had planned. In his sleep. All his affairs in order.

Ava had arranged to have Melvin's bed moved so that Hank wouldn't see it every morning, but he knew he would have to do something about the rest of the house. Not just because it would help him with missing Melvin, but because Melvin had said in his letter that he had to. He had to substantially change the house within a year, or it reverted to the town.

That was so Melvin. Thinking ahead and knowing Hank so well. Melvin knew Hank would feel guilty about changing the house so this was the way he was helping him do it. Mandy had already told him she would help, and together they had ideas how to open it up. But first, he had to bring his crew in to update the wiring and everything else that hadn't been touched for longer than Hank had been alive.

Hank knew Melvin understood that the whole idea of revitalizing the house would excite Hank once he got over the fact that Melvin was gone. "You ole coot," Hank said to no one. He knew Melvin and Sally had moved on together, but still, he could talk to the house because Melvin's essence would always be there.

On the way out the door to his truck, a cold breeze almost blew his hat off, which made him think that perhaps he would add a big garage to the house. Even if he only got the frame up before winter, he would be able to walk out of the house and into a garage instead of the snow. Zipping his coat against the fall chill, he decided. Yes, he would start there.

The Diner was full, so he slipped onto an empty stool at the counter and signaled to Pete that he wanted his standard breakfast. He was going to stop out at Emily's after he ate to check on the finishing touches for her house, and prepare his crew to come to his. Melvin had left money in his will specifically targeted to fixing the house, so he might as well get started. It would keep both him and the crew busy over the winter, which was always a good thing.

Sam slipped onto the empty stool beside him and, turning his coffee cup upright, nodded to Alex that he was ready to order.

"Figured you'd be here," Sam said.

"Yep, can't get used to being in that house by myself," Hank answered. "What are you doing here? Haven't seen you in the Diner for a while."

"Restless. Everyone is restless. Did you notice? I could put it down to Melvin's passing, but I think it's more than that," Sam answered.

Hank turned to Sam and said, "Every time you say something like that I am afraid you are going to say that Grant is somehow not dead, or something he did is going to show up to bite me in the ass again. Tell me it's not that."

When Sam didn't answer, Hank said, "No really. Not that, please!"

"I don't know," Sam responded. "No, I don't have news like I figured out who murdered those women or know more about how Lenny and Frank died. I don't have any more news at all, really. I just feel it. Mira keeps telling me that information truly comes from within, and I seem to be picking up on that."

He stopped as Alex stood behind the counter, ready to take his order. "Couldn't help overhearing. I agree with you. Everyone seems to be restless, or skittery. Something is happening. Look at how many people are here and yet how quiet it is."

Sam and Hank looked at each other. Alex was right. Instead of the usual loud noise that accompanied lots of people eating together, there was only the murmur of a few voices.

The three of them looked at each other, puzzled.

"Keep your eyes open, will you, Alex?" Sam said. "If you notice anything new or out of place in town, would you let us know?"

As the bell over the door rang, Alex looked up. "Well, that guy's new," he said.

Hank and Sam looked at each other first, and then to the door, where a tall guy wearing jeans and a sweater stood looking for a seat.

They watched as Alex went to him, and guided him to a table that had just opened up. He cleared away the dishes and told him he'd be back with coffee and to take his order.

As he passed by Sam and Hank, Alex said, "He looks familiar. Kinda. Do you guys know him?"

They both shook their heads and turned back to their coffee.

"Feel anything, Sam?" Hank asked. When Sam snorted, Hank said, "No, I'm serious. We couldn't be hanging around with all these people who know things, teleport themselves, and shift from one dimension to another without knowing that feelings are first.

Sam paused. "I felt a change. Like the day you notice that summer has become fall. Sometimes it happens in August and sometimes in September. But you know that day that the air feels and smells different. The shadows of the trees are different. You know what I mean?"

Hank nodded. "Yes. I love that day. Okay, I know what you mean. Something like that just happened to me too."

"So who is that guy?"

That "guy" was watching Sam and Hank. He couldn't hear what they said, but he could see and feel the energy shift that had happened. He hadn't stayed safe all these years without paying attention to subtle changes. His father had taught him that. Not by being a good father, but by being a monster inside the shell of a man.

Yes, those two. He would start there. Time to get to know the town. When Alex came to pour his coffee and take his order, he gestured to the two men at the counter. "I'm new in town. Do you think it would be a good plan to ask those guys to have breakfast with me, to help get me started knowing people?"

Alex only paused for a beat before answering. "Absolutely. It's the perfect place to start. I'll ask them. I'm sure they will want to meet you too."

As he leaned over to invite Hank and Sam to the new guy's table, he said, "Something is up. He wants to meet you. Change is here. I can feel it."

Hank looked over his shoulder, and the new guy gestured to the table. He clapped Alex on the back and said, "Let's go, Sam. Time to find out what the wind has brought us."

It felt as if the whole room watched them walk to the table. And it was entirely likely that it did. Everyone knew that something had changed, whether they wanted it to or not.

# TWENTY

The meeting was cordial. Sam introduced himself as a wannabe chef who owned a catering business. Hank said he was a building contractor and did projects around town. In fact, he was heading out to check on one right after breakfast.

Edward introduced himself as Ted Miller. He ran a few online companies and was in town because he was looking for a place to settle where he could run the business and still find a community that he could interact with when he wasn't working. He was tired of sitting in a room all by himself and not knowing anyone other than the people he met online.

They all told each other the truth, just not the whole story. But then, after all, Sam thought as he listened to their conversation, they had only just met. No one was going to blurt out the whole complicated business that had brought them all together in the first place.

Ted, he now had to think of himself as Ted, asked Hank and Sam if they believed Doveland was a good place to settle down. Were the people friendly? Would he fit in?

When Hank answered, he surprised himself that he told Ted that he had once been an outcast, and it was the people he found in Doveland who had turned him around. They were family. As he said the word 'family,' Ava walked into the Diner followed by Mira.

"Speaking of family," Hank said, "Let me introduce my niece, Ava Evans, and her friend, Mira Michaels. Ava and Mira, this is Ted Miller."

As the two women shook Ted's hand, Hank added, "Ted's new in town. Thinking about staying, but wondered if this was a good place to settle."

Ava caught the undercurrent in Hank's words and took a quick look at Hank. She knew Hank well, so without hesitation, she said, "Well, I know a way you could meet a bunch of us all at one time. My husband and I are having an October Fest around the campfire, before it gets too cold, Friday night. Why not come?"

"Wow," Ted said. "That's awfully kind of you. Sure. What can I bring?"

"Why not just come this time? You will get an idea of what to bring the next time after you meet everyone. Hank will give you the details."

Patting Hank on the shoulder and giving him a quick kiss on his cheek, she added, "Gotta go. We're just collecting Barbara for a quick meeting at the coffee shop."

Barbara had already stepped out of the kitchen, and the three of them headed outside. Ted watched them as they headed across the street.

"Is everyone that friendly?" He asked.

"Well, we have our mysteries, but for the most part, the answer is yes."

Ted didn't have to wonder about at least one of those mysteries. He already knew that they had found the bodies on the hill. It was in all the newspapers, both online and off.

He also knew that there were more bodies. Four more. He would tell them where to find them once he knew it was a safe thing to do. Hank and Sam had acted as if they didn't know much, but Ted knew better than that. Just regular guys. A contractor and a chef. Yea, right, he thought. And I'm bobs-your-uncle.

Ted wasn't planning to waste the next few days waiting to meet everyone at the party. He had some reacquainting to do with the town. He had already set the stage and told Hank and Sam that he loved walking and was planning to do a lot of it to explore Doveland.

They told him about the bike trail that Hank and his crew of teenagers were building. It was one of the projects he had for them to learn a trade, share ideas, and do community service at the same time.

Ted thought all of that was interesting. He wondered who Hank had been before. He'd find out, but first, a little walking around town where he would casually wander past his father's old house. And then, perhaps a drive by the hill to see what was going on there.

• • • • • • • • • • •

On Ted's walk, he noticed that most of the town seemed to be well taken care of. There was a new gazebo in the town square, which now looked beautifully maintained.

One discordant element was the deserted gas station beside the grocery store. Ted remembered that station from when he was a kid. Sometimes his father would get him a Popsicle when they stopped for gas. He always had to eat it quickly since he couldn't have it in the car, and his father was impatient.

The only time he could savor it was if someone came up and started a conversation with Joe. That meant he would have plenty of time since his father never wanted to give anyone else the impression that he was an impatient man. Even as a child, Ted knew that his father's reputation as a healer and kind man was the most important thing to him.

As they would drive up to the station, Ted would say over and over again, "Please let there be someone there for father to talk to." When it worked, he would say, "Thank you," to whatever god had graced him. And if it didn't work, Ted would remind himself that the gods were fickle.

He didn't want to walk straight to the old house just in case that would seem suspicious. Instead, he circled through the blocks, trying not to look like he knew where he was going. Even though the trees had grown or been removed, or the houses run down or been rebuilt, he knew the streets.

He strolled through Doveland for thirty minutes before it struck him that he had actually returned home. Up until then, it was an intellectual knowledge, something that his brain knew. Finally, his heart had caught up with him, and it recognized that he was home. Not as the same person that left, but as a grown man. Ted understood what people meant when they said that you can never return home. The person that left home is not the person that returns. The memories remain, but the person that faces them has changed.

Ted stopped at the corner of a street where his best friend had lived. He wondered if he still lived there. He didn't want to take a chance in case he still did. It was possible that he would recognize him as Edward. Unlikely, but possible.

Instead, Ted turned to go towards his old house, walking slower and slower as he did. Not just because he realized that he was afraid of what he would find. But because he thought his father might have installed cameras. Joe would have told people that the cameras were there to help keep them safe, but it wouldn't be for that reason. It would be to watch for Edward. His father would have wired them so he could always be watching no matter where he lived.

Ted pulled his hat down over his eyes, zipped up his coat, changed his gait to a slow shuffle, and turned the corner. His heart thudded in his chest, and he could feel sweat break out on his forehead under his hat.

Yes, there were cameras. And yes, the house was still there. And the lights were on.

# TWENTY ONE

V alerie parked her car in the little lot behind her house and
wondered if clients would come in the front or the back
door. Valerie thought it would probably be both. That meant they
would definitely need to update the rear door entrance and the
parking lot. She would have to have Hank build a shelter of some
kind over at least part of the lot when he started renovating the
house for its new life. She was sure that Mandy didn't want to run
through rain or snow to get into the house while carrying design
materials.

Renovating the house was going to be a big project, but she was
looking forward to it. Valerie needed something new, something
she had chosen for herself.

She hung up her coat in the closet, hung the keys on the key ring,
kicked her shoes off, collected the mail where it had fallen inside
the front door, and stood at the kitchen counter to sort through
the mail.

She was looking for a specific letter. Johnny's question about
parentage had opened up both a fear and a desire. A desire to find
out who her father really was, and a fear that she wouldn't like what
she found.

Johnny and Lex had never met any of their grandparents. Both Valerie's and Harold's parents had died even before the two of them had met. She and Harold had been their own family unit. They had told each other that they liked that they were alone. They figured they could make their own family traditions. There would be no deciding whose house they would go to for holidays. It would always be theirs.

Now that Johnny had brought up the issue of being afraid that he would be like his father, Valerie wondered what Harold's family had been like. He never talked about them, which in hindsight was strange. She had the impression that they were both distant. Perhaps it was because they were older when they had Harold. Maybe he had been a surprise, perhaps an unwanted one. Because he was an only child, Valerie could only surmise that they didn't intend to have children and that's why they didn't lavish attention on the one that they had.

She thought that the fact that he was basically left on his own was probably one of the reasons Harold had been vulnerable to Dr. Joe's charm. Joe had offered Harold a father figure, and on the surface, Joe had been a good one. Having watched the behavior of children in school, Valerie knew the importance of a boy having a man to learn from. It was one reason she would always be grateful to Sam, Pete, Hank, and Evan for taking her boys, and especially Johnny, under their wing. They had good men watching over them.

As for her parents, she had never shared with Harold that she didn't think the man she called dad was actually her father. There was a certain distance between them. Even though he had been kind and attentive, she always worried that she didn't please him somehow. It was as if she had done something wrong that she wasn't aware of doing.

Like Harold, she was also an only child. As a youngster, she would ask her parents for a brother or sister. They would share a secret look and say that all that they needed was her. They didn't understand that she wasn't asking for them. She was asking for herself.

Over the years, Valerie made up stories about being a stolen princess, or the child of fairies in the forest. Eventually, she outgrew those kinds of stories, but she still didn't think she belonged.

Until her parents died in a car accident when Valerie was eighteen, she would periodically ask her mother if she was really her daughter, and was her dad really her dad. Sometimes her mother laughed at her and ruffled her hair, other times she would snap back, telling her to stop asking such a ridiculous question. "Of course he is your father. Hasn't he always been there for you? Didn't he show love and affection?"

"Yes, mom," Valerie would answer and then say, "But ..." At which point her mother would shush her and say, "That's enough. I don't want to hear any more about this."

After her parents died, Valerie dropped the whole idea, since it didn't matter anymore. But now it did. If only because eventually Johnny would ask and she wouldn't have the answer. So, after researching where to find her official birth certificate, she wrote and asked for one. That was the letter that she was looking for.

It wasn't there. However, even when it came, Valerie wasn't sure what it would tell her that would be helpful. After all, there wouldn't be a note on it saying either, "Yes, this is your real father," or, "No, this isn't your real father." Valerie knew she was still going to need to do research. Track down where her parents came from. See if she could discover where they met, and how long they were married before having her.

Thinking about them getting married reminded Valerie that there was another place she could get information. First, she had to discover where her parents were married. The lack of knowledge about her parents struck her. How had she let it go on so long without knowing? Didn't parents usually tell the "how they fell in love" story to their children? How come she knew nothing at all about their past, including her parent's parents.

As Valerie stood at the kitchen island in her stocking feet, the enormity of the black hole of information struck her. She knew nothing at all about who had come before her.

She decided that it was useless to fret over what she hadn't done before, or try and understand why it never occurred to her that she had no other family other than the two people who said they were her parents.

Instead of beating herself up about what she should have done, she was going to do it now. While she was rebuilding her home, she would rebuild her life, one ancestor at a time, starting with her father.

But she would need help. It was not something she could do on her own. Besides her not knowing how to do it, Valerie also wanted someone to discuss ideas with and help see things differently. It would have to be someone she trusted without question.

As she headed to the shredder to shred the mail she didn't need, Valerie had a light bulb moment. Ava! Ava was looking for something to do. Maybe she would be interested in the search. She would ask her at the party on Friday night.

Lex was staying overnight at Hannah's, something that happened regularly since last spring when Harold died, and Ava had taken them in. That meant she had a whole evening to herself. Valerie smiled at the idea. She could decide exactly what she wanted to do without anyone questioning her actions. It was a new feeling.

Valerie decided she wanted to eat the slice of leftover pizza, and eat it in bed while she read the latest Brandon Sanderson book. Laughing like a schoolgirl, she heated the pizza briefly in the microwave and headed up to bed with her Kindle.

She was beginning to understand what happiness felt like. No matter what she found out about her parents, she would not let anyone take away her freedom again.

# TWENTY TWO

T ed backed up and hid behind a lilac bush. Although the flowers were long gone, the dead leaves hadn't yet fallen off, and the memory of the smell of lilacs calmed him down. Lilacs had been his mother's favorite flower. Every year, Ted would cut a few lilacs off the bush in the front yard to take to her on her birthday. When he was really young, he thought the month of May was named after his mother. It was disappointing to realize that it was the other way around. She told him that her mother couldn't come up with a name for her, so she just picked her birthday month. He never knew if she was joking or not about that. Still, the name fit her perfectly, and May remained his favorite month.

As he stared at the house, terrified that his father had come home, he could still see the old lilac in the front yard and Ted realized he was probably overreacting. Still, he paused, wondering if he should walk past and try to see who was in the house, or perhaps turn around and go the other way.

The decision was made for him. He held his breath as the front door opened and two women came out. One was carrying a sweeper and the other a tote of cleaning supplies. They laughed and joked together as one turned and locked the door. He had been so distracted by the lights on in the house, Ted hadn't noticed the old Volkswagen in the driveway. Something his father would never drive.

The two women got in and pulled away as Ted stepped out from behind the bush and continued his walk. He hoped no one had seen him duck behind the lilac, because he was sure it looked suspicious.

Ted realized it was probably a foolish thing to do, walk past his old house. However, it helped ground in him the reality that he had returned home. Ted had imagined his return so many times that being in Doveland in person was disconcerting. Shoving his hands into his pocket and breathing in the cold air, he continued up the block.

He barely glanced at the house as he went by. Just feeling it close by made his skin tingle and bile rise up into his throat. Ted realized that there was no reason to come back and look at the house again. He now felt the reality of his return. How long he stayed would depend on how long it took to trust people enough to tell them what he knew. After that, he was free to go.

Ted didn't have to guess why his father maintained a house in Doveland while exiling himself in Morocco. Joe intended to come home. Sooner or later, he would be back. It was only a matter of time before he realized that his son, Edward, had come back to Doveland.

All the more reason to find who I can trust in town before he comes back, Ted thought to himself. The party was going to be a big help. He was looking forward to it.

\*\*\*\*\*\*\*

Hannah was looking forward to the party, too. Hannah loved it when all the grownups got together. It gave her a chance to practice her skills. Although she knew everyone that was coming, she always pretended for at least a few minutes that she didn't. She thought that way she would notice things about them that she hadn't seen before.

Of course, everyone now knew that she had unique skills. People called them gifts, which Hannah thought perhaps they were and was grateful for them. When necessary, she could send her spirit out to talk to people, like Johnny, in the woods last spring. She could read minds—most of the time. But she had promised her mother not to do that unless it was absolutely necessary.

Hannah understood there was a right way and a wrong way to do things, and she intended to always be on the right side of the equation. She knew exactly what happened to people who choose to use their gifts for evil under the guise of doing good. Dr. Joe was the perfect example.

Although she had never shared how she felt about it, she knew it was Dr. Joe who had been behind the fire that killed both her and her mother in her past life. Her past-dad, Jay, had died with a broken heart over it.

Although Dr. Joe had not set the fire, he had trained the man, Grant, who then controlled her Uncle Hank. Yes, Hank had set the fire, but he didn't know there were people inside, and Grant did. Uncle Hank had made lots of mistakes, but he was not an evil man. He had been confused. Now, he did everything he could to make up for what he had done in the past.

Hannah loved him more than even he knew. It had made her happy that Hank and Melvin had become close. It helped them both, but it helped her most of all. Melvin understood things that even he didn't know how to express. But it came out in a love for everyone, and she had been the lucky girl who got to spend a lot of time with him.

She could never express how much she missed him, but she knew he was happy, and she would see him again someday.

Yes, she was looking forward to the party. After all, everyone would be there, except Johnny, of course. He was still in college. Besides, she was still too young for him to notice in the way she noticed him. But there was another reason she was looking forward to the party.

Dr. Joe's son would be there. Edward, although he called himself Ted. Hannah didn't blame him for that. He didn't know anyone yet, and he was, rightfully so, afraid of his father.

Hannah wanted to see how he acted. She thought she would like him, and if she did, she would help him with what he wanted to do. Of course, he would have to get to know her. That was another thing she wanted to see. Would he look right past her and not see who she was? Would he only see an eleven-year-old girl with braces and pigtails? It was a test of sorts.

She couldn't wait to see if he passed or failed. It was important that he passed. Much more important than he realized. Or would realize if he knew there was a test.

Hannah laughed to herself. No matter what, she was planning on having a good time, and yes, she would keep her promise to her mother, no mind eavesdropping. Unless it was absolutely necessary.

# TWENTY THREE

The object of everyone's fear, Dr. Joe Hellard, sat in his favorite chair in his new home, thinking about what to do next. He was bored out of his mind. *Was there anything worse thing than being bored,* he wondered, and decided that there was not. Except being caught. But that would never happen. Which meant he had some serious planning to do. Maybe not now, but when he became sure.

A few days ago, one of the many people Joe had hired to look for his son had contacted him and said that there was a small chance that he had found Edward. The fact that it happened only a few months after Joe had left the States made it suspicious. Thirty-three years of looking and suddenly Edward might be visible enough to find?

Joe realized it might be a trap, which is why he was going to bide his time. He had his cameras in Doveland and his spies on the internet. Was it really Edward? He would know soon. Then he had to decide what to do.

The fact that he was bored would have to be considered into the equation. He needed to find something to stimulate his mind. A reunion with his son would definitely help the boredom factor. As he drank his coffee, looking out the window at his million dollar view, Joe had another thought.

Perhaps he could resume practicing his skills. He had stopped, not wanting to draw any attention to himself. For sure, Joe didn't want to contaminate his safe home in Morocco with unexplained deaths. But perhaps he could extend his reach beyond the borders and see what happened. A very exciting thought occurred to him. Maybe it could extend all the way to the United States.

There were a few people in Doveland he had not dealt with in a manner they deserved. They had caused him unnecessary hardship, and just a little fear that they would catch him. Maybe he could reach out and touch someone's mind as far away as that. Although he had never tried to manipulate someone from that far a distance, he couldn't see why it couldn't be done. Despite keeping his agreement to himself to not do any serious mind tricks for the past few months, he thought his skill could easily be revived. He had kept somewhat in practice by mentally suggesting to people to give him good deals or say something they never meant to say. Parlor tricks, really.

He would have to raise his game if he was going to deal with the do-gooders in Doveland. They knew what he could do. Most of them were skilled enough to know when he was messing with them, but not all of them. He knew all of them well enough to know what would sound like their own thoughts talking to them inside their head. If he did it right, they would never know it was him invading their minds. The prospect pleased him. He would watch for his son, and maybe have a little fun in the meantime.

• • • ● • ● • • •

*A party. Just what he needed, another gathering of family and friends.* Craig Lester thought back to only six months before, when a party would have been something he joyfully anticipated. Not anymore. Now he dreaded them.

He still went. He still participated. Brought food and laughed at Sam's corny jokes. Sometimes he joined in the discussions as long as they stayed within the bounds of what was going on in town, or the plans of someone in the group.

Craig knew his friends avoided the subject of Dr. Joe when he was around, and he appreciated the effort. Without talking about it, they had agreed to disagree. He couldn't understand why they insisted that Joe was the person who had killed the women. But most of all, he couldn't understand how he and they could be so diametrically opposite in what they believed.

Until last spring, they were on the same page for everything. Now, although they all remained his friends, there was a gaping hole that lay in the heart of their relationships, and Craig was always afraid that one wrong step would throw them into that pit, never to emerge.

The other reason he was not looking forward to the party was that Valerie would be there. Not because he didn't want to see her, but because he did. So much. He dreamed about her. Her soft smile belied her core strength, that had only become more evident since Harold's passing.

For a brief moment, he had fancied that she had feelings for him, but then the specter of Joe rose up and put a wall between them. What made it worse was it was a wall that he had raised. Now that it was there, he had no idea how to take it down.

She had brought Johnny in for a brief checkup before he headed off to school. Valerie had been kind and attentive to everything that Craig had to say. She told him how much she appreciated Craig's point of view that began with the assumption of health, rather than disease.

Valerie acted as if there wasn't a wall between them, but when he remained solidly on the other side, Craig thought he could see the hurt in her eyes. It was a brief moment, but at that moment Craig's heart hurt more than he thought possible. He would never want to disappoint her, but here he was doing it all the time.

Because of Joe. No, he reminded himself, not because of Joe, but because of his loyalty to him. Craig thought he heard Leif's voice say, "I hope that is worth it to you, Craig." But when he looked for Leif, he was not there. Craig had to put it down to the fact that he and Leif had been friends for so many years his voice was stuck in his head.

Whenever Craig thought about Leif, he would shake his head at the wonder of what he had done. Sacrificed his physical life for a friend who wanted to go to the Forest Circle. Craig was not sure that he would be able to do that for anyone. Give up everything for a friend? He didn't think he could ever be that good a friend. And that made him mad. Not at anyone else. Just at himself.

Craig hoped he could contain his self-loathing that seemed to be growing daily, enough to be pleasant at the party. It was a deadly mixture. Wanting to impress Valerie, keeping her at bay, and hating himself for what he was doing.

He had no idea how much longer he could last playing that double-sided game.

# TWENTY FOUR

A va had told Ted that he didn't need to bring anything to the party, but Ted found himself very uncomfortable arriving empty-handed. So he had stopped at the grocery store and purchased a few bottles of wine. He didn't know if anyone drank wine, but it seemed like the kind of gift that meant you were grateful, and that is what he wanted them to know, that he was grateful that they had invited a perfect stranger to their gathering.

It wasn't hard to find the house. Ava had texted him the address, after having him put his information into her phone, and hers into his. From a lifetime of not giving out information to one where it was given so freely, the act gave him a moment of pure panic. What if he was making a mistake?

*It is too late now*, he told himself, as he made the right hand turn into the driveway. He would have missed it if Ava hadn't told him it was exactly eight-point-five miles from the bike path parking lot that was just outside of town.

To Ted's expert eyes, it was easy to spot all the surveillance cameras. He suspected that there was even more security in a place that he couldn't see.

Although he didn't know their story, he decided that perhaps there was much more to the group than he first imagined.

He had heard about Sam, even though he had not told him when they met at the Diner. As Ted had followed the stories about the bodies buried on the hill, Sam's name had been mentioned a few times. Ted hoped Sam was already on the trail of his father, but he would have to be careful about finding out.

Ted hoped someone would bring it up so he could be the curious stranger who wanted to know more. In this way, he hoped to discover how they would feel if—no, not if—when they found out he was Joe's son.

At the top of the winding drive, Ted found the parking lot in front of the house filled with cars already. Perhaps he had misunderstood the time? Another car came up the drive and pulled in beside him. He and the other man both exited at the same time, and Ted gave a slight wave of his hand at the stranger.

"Hey," the stranger said, "You must be the new guy, Ted, right?"

Ted walked out past his car, and the two shook hands.

"Craig," the stranger said, extending his hand.

"Yes, I'm Ted. I feel a little strange now. Is everyone expecting me?"

Craig clapped him on the back as he said, "Might as well get used to it. News travels fast in a small town. You are the subject of much speculation."

Seeing the flash of panic on Ted's face, Craig laughed. "Don't worry. It's all good. We don't bite."

Ted did his best to smile, and act like this was easy for him. Instead, all the alarms inside his body were firing. "Danger, danger," they flashed. All he could think of was that everyone would know him and perhaps see right through him. Plus, he wouldn't understand the language they spoke. It was as if he was entering a foreign land.

The front door opened as they approached and a cute little girl with pigtails, braces, and blue eyes stood in the doorway. "Hi Craig," she said, and then turned to Ted and said, "Hi, you like to be called Ted, right?"

If anyone had been looking, they would have seen Ted's face turn white as a sheet. What was she saying? Did she know that wasn't his real name? But when he looked at her, she was smiling a sweet, calm smile and had her hand extended.

Ted took it and answered, "Yes, Ted."

"I'm Hannah," she said. "Come in. Don't be afraid. We're here to help."

Whatever Hannah meant, both scared and excited Ted. But he had no choice. The door was open. It was time to walk through it.

• • • • ● • ● • • •

Hannah led the two of them into a large open space that still managed to feel cozy. Ted knew open was the new look, and he liked it. The living room merged into the dining room and then into the kitchen. There was a hallway on the left that Ted decided must lead to bedrooms, but Hannah took them straight back towards the kitchen.

Craig noticed Ted's stare and said, "Beautiful, isn't it? You'll meet Mandy, who helped with the design."

Ted nodded and tried to keep his emotions at bay. *What would it be like to live in a home like this?* Open, cozy, and welcoming to everyone. Different from the way he lived, always hiding away in small, cramped spaces.

He was even more impressed as they stepped out of the kitchen into a screened-in porch and then out onto an amazing deck. The deck had a roof over the part closest to the house and then opened out into a huge backyard. A gravel pathway led to what looked like a bunkhouse and behind that a field and then the forest.

"Wow, this is stunning!" Ted said.

"I'm glad you like it," Ava said as she came to greet him.

"Like it? Love it. You must be very happy here."

"We are," Ava answered. "Let me introduce you to everyone. Don't feel bad if you don't remember our names. There are a lot of us, and it just keeps growing. Something that also makes me very happy!"

It was apparent how much Ava cherished her friends. As Ava introduced Ted to one person after another, she told little anecdotes about each one, repeating their names more than once in the telling. Ted discovered it made it much easier to remember who they were and marveled at Ava's ability to put everyone at ease without effort.

By the time they had made their way around the gathering of people, he felt as if he knew at least half their names and would remember them. He definitely would remember the stories Ava told. The story that Ava told about him, knowing that it was only partially true, did not make him happy. He found himself yearning to be part of a group that knew how to be friends while being themselves.

Just as he said hello to Hank, he heard Hannah, who he now knew to be Ava's daughter, yell, "Lex!"

He turned to see Hannah rush to a young boy who was accompanied by a woman Ted took to be his mother. He felt stuck to the ground and unable to move because seeing her both terrified him and filled him with joy.

Hank, noticing his look, said, "Oh. I know that feeling. Do you think you already know her?"

When Ted simply nodded, Hank added, "It happens a lot with these people. Are you familiar with the term Karass? The writer,

Kurt Vonnegut, made it up. He thought that people find each other throughout lifetimes to fulfill purposes appointed by God.

"What you are looking at in this group of people are people who have felt drawn to each other. We have found each other in some mysterious ways. Perhaps it is true we have known each other before. But for sure, we know each other now.

"There are more strange things about this group, but I don't want to scare you off. In fact, since you are here now, it's entirely possible that you too have some special gifts you didn't know about."

Ted looked at Hank and asked, "Special gifts?"

"Probably best you find out as we go along. In the meantime, let me introduce you to Valerie."

Across the room, Craig watched Valerie turn to meet Ted and was amazed at the amount of jealousy that he felt. Craig was sure that Valerie wasn't aware that she pulled back just a bit, as if she was startled. Did she know him? He hoped that was all it was because the look that passed between them worried him.

But his jealousy worried him more. He had thought he was letting his feelings for Valerie dissolve away. Apparently, he was failing at that, just as he was failing at being part of the group he had once treasured. He had no idea what was wrong with him, but he didn't like it one bit.

# TWENTY FIVE

The party went better for him than Ted could have imagined. Everyone had stories to tell, and they were polite enough to ask him a little about his, but not too much to make him uncomfortable.

Although he already knew about Emily's art retreat, when he met her he pretended not to know anything, and of course, she invited him to come out to the hill to see her "little project," as she called it.

They agreed he would drive out to the hill the next morning and have coffee with her. He also agreed to have lunch with Pete and Hank at the Diner, and at the last minute, he had asked Valerie if she was free for dinner. Afterward, he couldn't believe he had done that. The whole day was going to be stressful, and then he added dinner with a beautiful woman to the end of it. Every moment of the next day was going to be fraught with danger. Ted wondered if the group had bewitched him somehow.

The party broke up not long after Ava sent Hannah off to bed. Before going, Hannah turned and looked directly at Ted and smiled at him. It was a warm and lovely smile, but it caused a ripple of pure panic to flow through all the nerves in his body. What did she know? What was she trying to tell him?

He thought of following her down the hall to her room, but thought better of it when he realized what that would look like to everyone else. A strange man following a little girl to her room without permission? Ted decided that he would have to trust that she was on his side and would eventually tell him what she knew about him.

By chance, he and Craig headed out to their cars together while hugging their coats closed against a chill wind, and as they both clicked the locks on their car doors, Craig asked Ted if he had enjoyed the party.

"I did," Ted replied. "It seems like a group of very good friends. Have you known them for a long time?"

"Not all of them," Craig replied. "I've known Leif the longest."

"Leif? Did I miss him?" Ted asked.

Craig gave a small laugh. "Oh, I forgot. No, you probably didn't see him," he said, as he got into his car and drove away.

Ted watched him go, thinking that was a very strange response. Was Leif there, or wasn't he? He mentally walked through the room, thinking back to meeting someone named Leif but didn't recall seeing him. Odd, that, Ted thought.

Thinking back, Ted realized that all of the conversations with that group of people had a touch of mystery or strangeness. It was as if they all had a hidden side that they hadn't shown him, or maybe they didn't show that side to anyone, not just him. On the surface, they were an ordinary group of people. However, Ted had an idea that wasn't the case at all.

He wasn't sure if that was good for his mission or not. He had a lot more research to do before he could decide.

• • ● ● • ● ● • • •

The next morning, driving to the hill where his father had done his evil deeds, Ted passed through a variety of emotions, the strongest of which was fear. The closer he got to the hill, the more afraid he became. He thought about turning around and going back to the motel by the lake. He could call Emily and tell her he didn't feel well. That would be true, too. The only thing that kept him driving was the knowledge that eventually he would have to face that hill and his memories.

As a boy, he had loved looking at the hill from his father's office. Every season was beautiful. The many colors of green in the spring, the riot of summer wildflowers, the vibrant, warm colors on the leaves in the fall, and the calm, soothing white blanket of winter.

Although the hill was miles away, sometimes he had felt as if the hill was sending out beauty just for him. He would stand at the window, close his eyes, and breathe it in. But that was before the commune had been built—and before his father took him out to meet the women. After that, the hill scared him.

Joe had told Edward that he wanted him to visit the hill because he wanted Edward to see what the women were doing and learn what he was teaching them. But once they arrived, even though Edward was a child, he knew that what his father wanted to show him was how much the women loved Dr. Joe.

Even though he didn't know then what he knew now, Ted understood that it was a misplaced love that he had seen. His father had fooled the women. He had charmed them into believing he was helping them, that he was a good man, and that everything he said to them was true. They acted like love-sick teenagers around him, and Joe lapped it up. Why not? He manipulated them both openly and subversively into being his adoring subjects.

However, it was not just seeing the hill again and what he remembered that scared Ted. He was also worried he would say something that would give him away. He wasn't ready. Besides, when he was ready, it wouldn't be Emily that he would tell his story to. It would have to be Sam and Hank. It was their reaction that would tell him if he should stay or run.

There was another emotion that Ted was feeling. Much better than fear. It was excitement. Ted was surprised to discover how much he was looking forward to seeing what Emily had done with the hill and hearing more about her story.

However, as he approached the hill, he had a reaction to it he hadn't expected. Perhaps it was the difference from the picture in his head from the last time he saw it. A few poorly built A-frame houses, a scraggly garden, and eight women sitting on a blanket listening to his father tell his stories.

Instead, as he drove towards the hill, he could see a large deck jutting out from the side, a barn nestled within a grove of trees, and a small two-story home in the style of a farmhouse sitting between them. Instead of eight women, it was Emily who was sitting on a swing on her front porch, waiting for him. Emily was quite a contrast from the spell-bound women that had last lived on the hill. She was vibrant, aware, and at one with the hill. Ted could see now why people called it Emily's hill.

The specter of death had been erased, and in its place was the joy of self-discovery through all the arts. It was a space filled with life. During his visit with Emily, as she showed him what she was doing to build her dream. Ted discovered he was no longer afraid. Instead of death, he found life.

He knew there were many more hurdles to go, but he had conquered his fear of what he would find on the hill. And that was a gigantic step in the right direction.

# Twenty Six

Emily's enthusiasm and joy stayed with Ted as he made his way towards the Diner and lunch with Pete and Hank. It was still there when he walked in the door to discover that Evan, Sam, and Tom were also waiting for him. Inwardly, he gulped and told himself that they weren't there because they had discovered who he was, but because they were being friendly. And cautious. As they should be, with a stranger in their midst.

At the party, none of them had probed Ted for information about his past. He knew they were being polite, and he appreciated it. However, it appeared that some of his probationary status was at an end.

Hank waved and beckoned Ted over. "We told these guys we were meeting you for lunch and they invited themselves. Hope you don't mind."

To his surprise, Ted spoke the truth when he said, "I don't mind at all. I appreciate you inviting me to join you!"

They all took turns telling Ted what was the best thing to eat there, pretending that it wasn't Pete's Diner they were talking about, but in the end, he ordered Emily's portobello mushroom burger. He told them he had enjoyed his visit with her so much he wanted to see what else made her happy.

Barbara took their orders. She said she waited tables a few days a week because she enjoyed it. Ted envied the look that passed between Barbara and Pete. He knew it was years of learning about each other and living through both happy and sad events that accompanied that look. He hoped to find that look someday with someone. However, realistically, it probably would never happen. He was already almost fifty and unmarried because of his constant running to escape his father. Even if he settled down now, who would want him?

After Barbara left to put their orders in with Alex, Pete asked the group of men sitting around the table, "So are we a men's council now?" They all laughed while Ted looked at them, wondering what they were talking about.

For the next hour, the men swapped stories, talked some sports, laughed at jokes, and ate lunch. Not once did they pester Ted with questions which both surprised and delighted him. If it was a ploy to make him comfortable, it worked.

It gave him a chance to see each man's individuality and experience the closeness of their bond. He realized they were probably not telling the stories about the dangers they had been through together for a reason. Why would they share that with a perfect stranger? It was private.

If he wanted to know all those stories, he would have to stay in town and become a friend. The question was, would he be able to? Would he be able to be a friend once they knew his real name, and would they want him in town? No matter who he was as his own man, he was still his father's son.

Emily's burger turned out to be the perfect choice for him. After everyone had eaten and chatted for a while, one by one the men left. They each had some place they needed to go. Hank had to check on some construction plans at Valerie's; Evan had babysitting duty because Ava was doing something for Mandy; Pete went back to the kitchen to cook and relieve Alex; and Sam had an event to prepare for, which left Ted alone with Tom.

As Ted started to excuse himself, Tom put out his hand and said, "Hold a minute."

Ted's heart started to pound. Maybe this was all a setup, he thought. He sat back down and waited.

Tom didn't say anything at first, twiddling his knife between his fingers. "Ted, a few years ago, this group that you see me with now was smaller, and I was the one that they were afraid of. It's a long story, but it ended up with Mira and I finding each other. It was a complete surprise to us both because we didn't know we were twins. It was also during that time that I met Sarah and Leif, Ava and Evan, and Craig.

"As you can see, it worked out. Our circle has grown. But I remember that feeling of being the outcast, the one that everyone was just a bit afraid of until they knew who I was."

Ted started to speak, but Tom shook his head. "No, you don't have to say anything. In fact, I don't want you to. I just want you to know that I understand that feeling you are having. I know you are hiding something. In fact, we all know.

"Perhaps you have noticed that there are things about some of us that we don't share with others and do our best to keep between us. However, one thing we all have in common is an acute awareness of when something doesn't ring true. What happened last spring increased our awareness of what dishonesty feels like."

By now, Ted felt as if he was going to either faint or throw up. "But," Tom smiled, and said, "Even though we know you aren't telling us the whole story, you also don't feel dangerous to us. We think you are afraid to tell us something. So, let me advise you the best that I can.

"Be ready soon, Ted. And when you are ready, the person you want to talk to first is Sarah. She's the one who understood and guided me into this group of people. She can help you decide what to do, too."

As Tom stood, he stopped and turned back. "Have a nice dinner with Valerie, Ted. Just remember, she is loved by all of us, so be sure you know what you are doing."

Ted stared down at his plate, not knowing what to say. Tom gave him a gentle slap on his back and headed out the door, leaving Ted alone.

Barbara slid into one of the empty seats beside him and took his hand. She patted it with the other. "Don't you worry, Ted. If you were in trouble, he would have never told you all that.

"My advice? Go take one of those walks you like, then get cleaned up and take Valerie out and have fun. She deserves a nice night out on the town. Where are you taking her?"

Ted grasped at the thread of normal conversation, grateful for Barbara bringing him back to earth.

"It seems crazy, but she just wants to go across the square to the Thai place."

"Not crazy," Barbara answered, as she stood up to go, "It's delicious, and a treat."

Ted stood too, and impulsively reached over and hugged Barbara. It shocked him more than it shocked her. It was new and foreign to him to have a rush of feeling for someone he had just met.

"Thank you," Ted said, hoping she understood how much it meant to him.

"You're welcome, young man," she answered.

Ted laughed at the "young man" and was still smiling as he left the Diner.

Pete came out from behind the counter and hugged Barbara, whispering in her ear, "You are an amazing woman."

Barbara smiled up at him and said, "Thank you, my love."

They both watched Ted as he crossed the street to where he had parked his car.

"He is bringing something both good and bad to us, isn't he?" Pete asked.

"Yes, he is. But it's not his fault. He is going to need all the help you can give him," Leif said, standing beside the two of them.

Grateful that they could now see Leif, Pete and Barbara nodded as Leif smiled at them and then drifted away.

Ted looked back and saw Pete and Barbara looking at something he couldn't see. But instead of worrying about it, he decided to take Barbara's advice. There was nothing more he could do at the moment, and he knew he needed all the fortification he could get.

His time was coming, and it was not going to be easy.

# TWENTY SEVEN

V alerie took one thing after another out of her closet, held it up in front of herself and stared in the mirror. Not liking what she saw, she threw it on the bed. When there was a huge pile of clothing on the bed and hardly anything left in the closet, she huffed and sat down on the floor, and that's where her son, Lex, found her.

He eyed the bed, his mother on the floor, and asked, "Need help, mom?"

Valerie laughed and pulled Lex down beside her and said, "I suppose I do. I have no idea what to wear to dinner. Nothing feels right."

"It's just a casual dinner, isn't it? You don't even know him."

"True, but it made me think about what makes me feel good, and none of these clothes do. Or at least I can't figure out how to make them look good."

Lex stood up and rooted through the pile, pulling out a pair of black leggings and a long dark purple tunic top. "Wear the tunic over this blouse," he said as he pulled out a light blue blouse buried at the bottom of the pile.

"And then pull your hair back and clip it. Kinda messy. "See," he said, pulling his mom's hair back, clipping it, and then holding a mirror in front of her. "Looks good. On the other hand, after today, maybe you want a new haircut. Something short and sassy."

"Wait," Valerie said, "did you just say the word 'sassy'?"

"Yep. And I am right about the clothes, too," he said, on his way out the door. "I'm going to Pete and Barbara's now. See ya."

Valerie remained on the floor, looking after her son. All the young people of the day amazed her. They seemed to know so much more than she did at their age. Looking in the mirror he left with her, she agreed. She looked better with her hair pulled back, and it was time for a haircut and some highlights.

Deciding that if Lex was right about the hair, he was right about the clothes, she set them aside for after she took a shower. She would ask Lex to go through the rest of the clothes with her later, and then go shopping. With Lex.

She glanced at her watch and realized she still had time to make an appointment for her hair. She called Ava and asked her who did her hair and then called the salon and asked for Robyn. Ava didn't ask for any explanations. She just said, "I understand," and gave her Robyn's number.

Valerie was ready for a new beginning. Hair, clothes, and perhaps a new man in her life. Yes, she was ready for all three.

• • • ● • ● • • • •

Ava hung up the phone and turned to Evan and said, "Valerie is ready for a new beginning." Then she took a breath and added, "So am I."

Evan was deep into a book when he answered, "That's good," and went back to his reading.

Ava walked over to Evan and gently lowered the book. "Did you hear what I said?"

Evan was wise enough not to lie, so he laid the book down and answered, "Sorry. What was it you said?"

They were sitting out on the back deck watching Ben and Hannah play in the yard. Evan waited while Ava gathered her thoughts.

"I'm bored," she finally said. "Not with you, love, but with myself. I need something else to do, and honestly, I think we both do."

Evan turned his full attention to her and said, "Do you have an idea?"

"Actually, I do. You know that Valerie has closed her bed and breakfast. Instead, Mandy is going to run her design business out of part of the house."

Ava paused and didn't say anything else. She was waiting to see if Evan would come to the same thought that she had a few days before. She had woken up at two in the morning with a full-blown idea in her head.

For the past few days she had kept it to herself, not sure if it was just a passing fantasy, or if it was something she really thought would work, and would want to do.

Evan looked over at Ava leaning back in her chair staring at the sky and realized that she was waiting for him to catch up with her. In the silence, he could hear the whir of bicycle wheels on the bike path down by the road. It was now completed halfway to Concourse. Hank and his crew of teenagers were doing a great job of creating and maintaining it.

He looked at the kids playing in the yard and the empty bunkhouse in the background. Now with Melvin gone, they had an empty room. Actually, they had more than one empty room. They had extra bedrooms in their house and an empty bunkhouse with four bedrooms. Hank used one some of the time, and once in a while, someone would need to stay over. But they always had empty bedrooms.

Empty bedrooms, Bed and Breakfast, connected to both Doveland and Concourse. Bored. Liked to stay home. Loved company.

He jumped up out of his chair and grabbed Ava. "I see it! I do! What a great idea. Let's get Tom to help us. He and Mira know a lot about putting business ventures together."

"I knew you would get it," Ava said. "Do we use the name Bed and Breakfast Inn? That way Valerie's past customers will think it is just a new location, well—and new owners, but still. Shall we ask Valerie what she thinks?"

"Yes and yes and yes," Evan answered.'

"Yes to what?" Hannah asked, joining them while firmly holding Ben's hand.

"What if we turn this house and bunkhouse into a bed and breakfast?"

Hannah looked at Ava and Evan and answered, "Took you a while," and then headed back into the yard to play with Ben.

Ava looked at them and unknowingly echoed what Valerie had said just moments before, "These new kids, they know so much more than we did at that age."

Evan nodded his agreement. "Best get to work then. I know Valerie is going to dinner tonight, but we could have Tom and Mandy over to talk about it."

"Sure, give them a call and see if Mira and Sam want to come too. More people, more ideas."

The two of them went off to make calls and prepare for the meeting, both of them with a lighter heart and step. Hannah knew which person would be first to take them up on their offer of staying at the Bed and Breakfast Inn and she thought it was a great idea that he would do so.

Ben said, "I think so too." Hannah laughed. No one heard him but her. She answered the same way. Silently. Telepathically. "Are you going to speak soon?"

Ben laughed at her as he chased after the ball she threw. Out loud he said what everyone would expect him to say. "Ball!"

On the way into the house Evan heard the word "ball" and excitedly told Ava, "Hey, Ben is learning to talk. He just said, 'ball.'"

Ben and Hannah looked at each other and just laughed. *Adults,* Hannah thought, *can be so clueless.* Ben giggled in agreement.

# Twenty Eight

V alerie felt good about what Lex had picked out for her to wear. She had walked across the street to the Thai Place and asked for a table. She was early. She could have had Ted pick her up and walk over together, but she liked being independent and able to leave when she wanted to. Even if it was just across the street.

She also liked being early. It was a habit she had learned from her years of teaching. Be in the room when the students arrived, and you were automatically more in control of the situation.

Not that she felt as if she needed to be in control, she thought. But then, on closer examination of her motives, she realized that she did. Even though she was just meeting Ted as a new friend, she wanted to set the parameters right away, for herself. It was not a date. Absolutely not.

Ted arrived precisely when he said he would and seemed pleased that Valerie was already there and had secured a table.

Later, neither could remember exactly what they ate, even though they did remember it was delicious. What Ted and Valerie remembered was that they felt as if they already knew each other. They talked long after the meal was over and found many similar interests and points of view.

As the evening wore on, Ted found it harder and harder not to blurt out who he was, and get it over with. But the more rational part of himself knew it was too soon. Besides, he had told Tom he would talk to Sarah first. Instead, he had to be careful to tell the stories of his travels and adventures from the point of view of it always being Ted who did those things.

It worried him. If for some reason Valerie decided to check on him, she wouldn't find all those stories matching with his name. It also concerned him because Valerie might think he was a liar about everything since he was a liar by default.

Ted asked Valerie about her life, and how did she happen to end up in Doveland. When she told him that Harold grew up in Doveland, Ted realized something that made him want to get up and leave. He knew Harold. He knew Valerie's dead husband.

Valerie saw Ted's face blanch and said, "Did I say something wrong, Ted?"

"No, no," he answered. "It was just for a moment I didn't feel well. I'm fine now though. Tell me more about Harold?"

Valerie paused before continuing. She knew something happened when she said Harold grew up in Doveland, but Ted appeared to be okay, so she continued. She gave him a brief and very general outline of what had happened during the last years of their marriage, and then the month before he died.

Having lots of practice compartmentalizing thoughts and feelings, Ted had put away how he felt about Valerie and Harold and the memories he had and asked, "Are they any closer to discovering how he died?"

Valerie sighed, "No. It probably doesn't matter. Not to me. He died. How he died isn't that important, unless..."

"Unless what?" Ted asked.

"No," she replied, "I don't want to bring all that up right now. There is nothing that can be done. Let's talk about more pleasant things."

Ted nodded and suggested they take a stroll around the square together. It was one of those warm October nights that people look forward to. In the middle of advancing cold, nature gives the gift of a few warm days and nights to remind people that summer will return.

After walking around the square a few times, they settled under the gazebo and talked some more. Ted asked Valerie if she needed to be home for Lex, and she assured him that Lex was fine. He was staying over at Pete and Barbara's who loved having him. He practiced cooking while he was there.

"I don't know what I would have done if my friends hadn't stepped up and helped me with the boys. They go way past just being kind. They have turned Lex and Johnny's lives around. And mine too."

Valerie turned to look at Ted. The street lights gave just enough light so she could see him listening. It felt as if his whole being was leaning in and paying attention only to her. It was an odd feeling. She wanted to be able to trust him. It felt wonderful to be with someone who put her at ease so quickly and easily.

But she remembered Dr. Joe. He did the same thing. And then look at who he was. She never wanted to be taken in by someone again. The difference was, with Joe he meant to be charming. He worked at it. Looking back on how he acted, Valerie could see that he needed to be admired, loved, and respected. It was his reason for everything.

With Ted, it felt different. He didn't seem to know that he was charming. It was subtle and felt honest. So she asked him what she had wanted to ask him since she first saw him walk in the door of the restaurant.

"Are you planning to stay in town?"

Ted didn't answer right away. He knew what she was asking. He felt the same way. Valerie felt like home to him. Would he be able to stay once he told everyone who he was, and what he had brought with him? He didn't know, so he answered as truthfully as he could.

"I want to. Meeting you and your friends has made me believe that this could be the place that I settle down in, and never leave again. But..."

"But what? Valerie asked.

"But there is something I need to do, and once I do that, I don't know what will happen."

"Are you going to tell me what that is?" Valerie asked.

"Yes. I promise I will, but not tonight. There are a few things I need to do first. And honestly, I want to keep tonight as perfect as possible."

Valerie nodded, but inside she worried. What could he be hiding, that would be so terrible he might have to leave town?

Valerie did let Ted walk her to her door, and did agree to meet him for coffee in the morning. It was a gesture of faith, and Ted appreciated it.

Valerie stood in her window and waved at him as he got into his car and drove towards the lake.

Neither of them saw Craig come out of the grocery store and stand stock still, his heart sinking. Valerie and Ted. And there was nothing he could do about it.

# TWENTY NINE

L eif Morgan sat alone on his favorite bench along the bike trail. If someone could have seen him, they would have thought he was sitting, but actually nothing physical was touching the seat. Because Leif wasn't really there. Well, he was. And he wasn't.

It had been over a year since Leif had agreed to take Eric, Grace's husband, to the Forest Circle. Eric had been dying. Taking him to the Forest Circle canceled out his illness. He went from having a material body to not having one, which eliminated a body dying.

Of course, Eric could have chosen to die. He would have simply passed through one door, so to speak, into another version of reality. Eric wouldn't have had a physical body then either. But in that case, he would either have to wait for Grace to join him in what Leif jokingly called the death reality, or choose to come back in a different life, or even a different time or space.

Eric knew that he and Grace would have found each other again, in another lifetime. But having just found Grace at the end of this lifetime, he didn't want to lose her again so soon.

So Eric had asked Leif to help him, and Leif had said yes. Neither Sarah nor Leif had been happy about it. Sarah could still talk to Leif, and see him, but in what some people would think of as a ghost form. But he wasn't a ghost. He was a traveler between dimensions.

Leif had no idea how he knew how to do it. If he did, he might teach someone. In fact, as far as he knew, no one he knew understood how to teach anyone how to leave the human body and become an entity that shifted between dimensions with ease. Leif figured someone knew. In fact, he had heard rumors of a circle that taught others, but he had yet to meet them.

*Perhaps it is best kept a secret,* Leif thought. What if the knowledge was out there for everyone? What a mess. There was enough evil in each dimension that they didn't need evil from different dimensions traveling between them, perhaps doing their evil deeds and then hiding out where no one could find them.

"Hi, Leif," Hannah said, sliding onto the bench to sit beside him. She wasn't actually sitting either, but instead of being in a different dimension, she was projecting herself. "Whacha doing?" Hannah asked.

"I think the better question is what are you doing?" Leif answered. "Where are you right now?"

"In bed reading. Ben is asleep, and mom and dad are in the kitchen talking over the new business idea with Tom, Mandy, Sam, and Mira. They won't be checking on me for a little bit. They are really excited."

"The bed and breakfast idea?" Leif asked.

When Hannah nodded, Leif added, "It's a great idea. You are going to be meeting many new people. It will be good for you."

"So I can learn more about how people behave?" Hannah asked.

"Yes, and so you can learn more about how to be of service, Hannah," Leif answered.

They both sat quietly for a minute as Hannah thought about what he had said. "Is that what you are doing? Being of service?" she asked.

"Actually, it's the same thing I said to you. In some ways, the universe is one big bed and breakfast. The inhabitants of each dimension are each different and have different concepts and cultural patterns. The Forest Circle and I are attempting to adapt and learn and be of service wherever we are needed.

"But of course, I am most comfortable here. Not only are the people I love the most here, but the human race, as messy as it can be, is something I know. I know what the world feels like here. The sun, moon, trees, flowers, birds, they are all familiar. Other places, not so much."

"I've been reading some books where they call other dimensions, realms. Is that the same thing?"

Leif thought for a moment. "Perhaps. I'll think about it, and we can discuss it again. Another thing I want to talk over with you sometime is this ability of yours to just show up, and most people don't know you are there. Have you thought through some of the ramifications of this skill?"

"You mean about is it right to listen in on conversations and stuff?"

"That's a beginning. Think about what you think is the right way to use your gifts, and let's talk about it. You'll be guiding others in this skill, so let's make sure it's in the right direction. Now, best to get back to your bed before someone comes looking for you."

"Well, they will still see me lying there, so it won't be that weird." Hannah paused. "Oh, maybe it would be. I see what you mean, Leif. I have some pondering to do."

"We both do, young lady," Leif said.

They air hugged and said "I love you," at the same time. They both laughed as Hannah disappeared. Leif always felt that disappearing like that was what Lewis Carroll meant when he talked about the Cheshire cat's grin in Alice in Wonderland. Now there was someone who probably understood the proximity of other dimensions. After all, what better example of another dimension than through the looking glass. Or through the closet door in the Narnia books.

Leif shook himself. He didn't want to get himself distracted by going down that rabbit hole, so to speak. Later maybe. Right now, he had much to think about. It wasn't just about other dimensions or realms, either.

This human realm had plenty of things to work out. The biggest one for his friends in Doveland was the new man in town. Leif knew who he was, but he certainly wasn't holding that against him. The sins of the fathers are not meant to be visited on their offspring.

What worried Leif is that Joe knew his son had returned. The fact that Joe might return to Doveland was frightening. Joe was far more dangerous than Grant had ever been. After all, Joe had taught Grant. And it was Joe who understood how to manipulate thinking. In many ways, he created illusions that people believed. It wasn't magic, but it sometimes felt like it.

The problem was not that Joe created illusions; it was the intent behind them. And Joe's intention was never for the good of others. In fact, it was almost always for their harm, especially towards anyone doing good in the world. Joe had to be stopped, but Leif wasn't sure exactly how to do that. He hoped he would figure it out soon, before it was too late.

# THIRTY

Valerie and Ted met for coffee the next morning at Your Second Home. If they thought they were going to be able to meet alone, they were mistaken. It appeared that everyone thought it would be a great idea to go to coffee on the way to church, so Your Second Home was packed with people.

Mandy was at the counter serving coffee and pastries when she saw Valerie and Ted standing inside the door, looking for a seat. Mandy caught their eye and tilted her head to the corner where Sarah was sitting by herself. Sarah smiled and pointed to the two empty seats at her table. Ted had a moment of suspicion. Was it a setup? Did she know?

Glancing around at the full room, he decided he was being paranoid. Mandy and Sarah couldn't have arranged for all those people to be here at the same time to force them to Sarah's table. Could they? It was too late anyway. Valerie was already headed to the table, stopping on her way to say hello to all the people she knew, which turned out to be almost everyone.

He would pause behind her each time, nod hello, and follow her to the next person. Once they reached Sarah, Valerie laughingly turned to him and said, "Sorry about that. I know most of these people from the school."

"Or from organizing the yearly solstice celebration," Sarah said.

"Or from running the Bed and Breakfast," Grace said, coming up behind them.

"Or from just being a good friend to everyone who needs one," Mandy said, as she too arrived at the table, coffeepot in hand.

Ted looked at Valerie, who had turned a bright red and was trying to hide behind a curtain of hair. He hardly knew her, but he realized he was proud to be seen with her, and would be completely run out of town if he did anything to hurt her. By mistake. By telling the truth. He stuffed down his feelings of panic and said, "Well, now I am doubly proud to be seen as your friend too, Valerie."

Valerie pshawed them all, sat beside Sarah, pointed at the coffee Mandy was holding and said, "Yes, please." Ted nodded yes and Mandy left, but not before winking at Valerie, who blushed again.

Sarah saved them both by asking Grace if she would also bring an assortment of pastries to the table. Treats seemed appropriate for such a beautiful Sunday morning. For the next hour, the three of them chatted, sipped coffee, and ate pastries. Sarah led them from one topic to another, until Ted felt utterly at ease.

Eventually, Sarah nodded at Mandy, who brought the bill. Sarah paid, saying it was a pleasure to be the one who got to have coffee with the two of them. She drained her coffee cup, picked the last few crumbs off her plate, and said she had to go. She had some gardening and reading to do which meant she would be home all day. Valerie missed the underlying message, but Ted didn't. He was expected.

• • • ● • ● • • •

It was such a beautiful day that when Sarah got home, she decided she wanted to take a long walk. She dropped off her purse at home, clipped on her fanny pack and her phone, and stepped back out into the day. She knew Ted would stay at the coffee shop and talk to Valerie before he came over, so she had plenty of time.

Sarah did not doubt that Ted got the message. He was obviously attuned to people around him and had more skill than even he knew when it came to knowing what others were thinking.

It was a golden day. Most of the trees had dropped their leaves, which meant the ground was covered with gold, red, and orange leaves. Sarah loved how beautiful the yards and sidewalks looked when people had not yet gathered up the leaves. As she swished through the leaves still on the sidewalk, the aroma of autumn surrounded her, which made the day feel even more magical.

All of her friends knew Sarah loved the month of May, but not everyone knew she loved the month of October just as much. It had occurred to her just a few weeks before that both May and October were transition months. She did not know why she hadn't noticed that before, but now that she had, it was glaringly obvious.

Which meant, she told herself, that she should also love life transitions. Which she couldn't say that she did. So as she walked, Sarah pondered the idea of transitions, starting with May and October. One month was the transition from the quiet and introspection of winter into the riot of color and activity of summer, and the other was the transition from the vibrancy and outward energy of summer into the quiet and subdued colors of winter.

A chill wind blew up the street, swirling the leaves from the sidewalk up around her legs. She zipped her jacket closed and stuffed her hands into her pockets, thinking that mittens and stocking hats were going to be needed soon.

Sarah was looking for inspiration, and nothing was coming to her. She needed to know what to say to Ted. Actually, she wanted him to tell her because he felt safe to do so. After that, perhaps the two of them would know the best way to tell the group. She hoped they would accept that Ted's arriving was a blessing, but they might not. After all, it could mean the return of Dr. Joe, and no one wanted that.

However, what Sarah knew was that it was never a good idea to hide from evil. Sooner or later, it needed to be faced. And that is what she needed to do, go home, and face what Ted would tell her.

Sarah glanced at her watch and realized that she had been gone longer than she thought. Walking back home, she didn't shuffle, or stop to gaze at the sky, or stare at the remaining leaves on the tree wondering what kept some on the tree when all their brothers and sister leaves had let go. Instead, she focused on getting back to the house before Ted got there.

Back home, she slipped off her shoes, hung her coat in the closet, put her fanny pack in the drawer and her phone on the kitchen counter. The house was cold, so she prepared and lit a fire in the wood stove, mentally thanking Leif for showing her how to set one that took off immediately.

She loved the heat from the wood stove. Instead of the hot and then cold feeling of most furnaces, the wood stove's heat was steady and enveloping. Like a blanket, Sarah thought. The wood stove put out enough heat to keep her entire small house warm. Sometimes it was so warm she had to open the window, which only increased the fire's charm. Warmth and a fresh dash of air.

As the fire started to take off, Sarah turned on the coffeemaker and put out a selection of teas. She would have also put out cookies, but knowing that the three of them had just polished off a plate of pastries, she arranged a bowl of fruit instead.

As she worked in her small but very efficient kitchen, Sarah thought about all the places she had lived in her life. While working and living in downtown Los Angeles, she would never have expected to end up in Sandpoint, Idaho with Leif, the love of her life. It was a dramatic change in lifestyle, and they were both happy with how peaceful and fulfilled life became for the two of them.

Then the next transition took place. Mira showed up with a problem. That brought Tom, Craig, and Evan. Looking for Mira and Tom's parents, they met Ava, who led them to their grandfather Earl and his daughter Suzanne, who was their mother. It was in Earl's home that they learned about the Forest Circle and their many lifetimes of connection to each other.

If that wasn't enough, they were told that all of them, including Ava, were part of another circle: the Stone circle. They named themselves that because they were each given a stone, or more accurately a stone had picked them. Although the reason for their stones had yet to be revealed, Sarah knew that every member kept their stone safely tucked away, expecting someday they would know what they meant.

At their first meeting in Earl's house, Ava and Evan had fallen in love. Looking for a place to call home, they left Sandpoint to travel the country. When they found Doveland, Pennsylvania, they knew they had discovered the place they were meant to live. When the Stone Circle came to Doveland to help find Ava and then attend Ava and Evan's wedding, they had all fallen in love with the little village. Within a few years, all of them had moved to Doveland to be together. In the past couple of years, their circle had continued to grow.

No, Sarah thought, I would never have guessed that I would end up in Pennsylvania without Leif, in a little home waiting for Dr. Joe's son to show up and bring the next transition to the growing circle.

Just as Sarah settled into the couch preparing to read a book, the doorbell rang. She sighed. It was time. Ted had arrived.

# THIRTY-ONE

J oe decided not to check any luggage. Even if he stayed a while, he had left clothes and the other things he would need back in his house in Doveland. Just in case he returned. And now he had.

He was nervous, and he was excited. He was also a little amazed to discover that he felt a sliver of fear. What could he possibly be afraid of, he wondered. Was he fearful that Edward wasn't there, or that he was?

Perhaps he was afraid that Edward wouldn't like him. No, that wasn't it. Joe already knew that his son hated him. After all, he had run away thirty-three years before and had stayed away from him all this time. No, Edward did not like his father. That was obvious.

It was also evident that Edward was afraid of him. After all, he had hidden all this time effectively. But why was he afraid of his own father? That was really the question. He believed he had never been mean or unkind to Edward.

Yes, perhaps he had been a distant father. It was true. Fatherhood didn't hold much interest for him. He had other things to do that provided much more mental stimulation and definitely made him more money than raising a kid.

Still, many parents were distant with the children, but that didn't mean that the kids grew up afraid of them. Probably mad at them. But afraid? No. There was something else going on.

Yes, that was what he was afraid of, the idea that Edward had a reason to fear him. And the only way that could be possible was that his mother, May, had told him something. Still, Joe thought, as he folded a change of clothes neatly into his travel bag, it would always be just hearsay.

A grown man's memory of something his mother told him when he was just a boy. After all, May had died when Edward was only ten. Joe sighed. That death was unfortunate. He had enjoyed May quite a bit.

May had been as light-hearted as he was severe. Sometimes her happiness, for no apparent reason, irritated him. It seemed silly and groundless. But most of the time he liked that she could lift him out of any moroseness he might have let himself fall into. He would have loved to keep May around, but it was not to be.

May was curious and interested in what Joe was doing, and that was, in the end, her undoing. When they were first married, May told Joe that she had fallen in love with his kindness and desire to help others. She loved that he was a country doctor and had dedicated his life to healing.

Because she loved his work, May supported him in any way that she could. She kept the records of his patients and watched over the money coming in and going out. She was good at it. Actually, she was good at everything. His patients loved her, and she loved them.

May would sit behind the window in the office and welcome each patient with a warm, bright smile, as if they were the most important person in the world. Little Edward would play quietly in the reception room. It helped everyone feel as if they were going to be as cared for as if they were family. Patients told Joe that May made them feel wanted and his son made them feel peaceful. It was an excellent combination for a country doctor.

But I was more than just a country doctor, wasn't I? Joe told himself as he hefted the bag over his shoulder. He hated that he was now considered old. He felt young, but lifting that bag was a chore, and he walked much slower than he used to.

All of those memories reminded Joe that he had to take care of whatever it was that brought Edward to town. He couldn't afford to leave any loose ends. As much as he regretted it, May had been one of the first loose ends. Then there was Frank and Lenny, which he took care of in the spring. The only loose end left was Edward.

Joe had made the mistake of taking May with him out to the commune. It didn't bother May that the eight young women were young and beautiful and that they adored him. She was used to people flocking to him with admiration. She expected it, and it had never occurred to her that Joe might be unfaithful.

That was because it was something that she would never do. Even if she had been tempted, she wouldn't have done it. May was completely unaffected by the fact that she was beautiful. In fact, Joe was sure that she never thought of herself as beautiful. It wouldn't have mattered to her. But because she was beautiful, along with being kind and intelligent, she could have had her pick of any man.

That she picked him was one of the few things that astonished Joe. Because, for once, he had not made it happen. He had not manipulated her into noticing him, or liking him, or falling in love with him. She had done that all by herself, and for all the years that they were together, she made him happy.

Then she came to the hill and met the women. No, not that they admired him. It wasn't that they were beautiful that caused the problem. No, it was because they each slowly got sick and died.

If May had never met them, if she hadn't gotten to know them personally, she would never have ever figured it out. But she did. Without his knowledge, May had started asking the women questions. She learned there had been other women who had left the commune.

"Where did they go?" She would ask. No one knew. And when each woman got sick, she cared for them without Joe's knowledge. May asked where they were buried when they died. No one knew that either.

Finally, reluctantly, she started going through the old patient records and began to wonder why some of them had died. Why did none of them have an autopsy? Why was it always her husband that signed the death certificate? Had he made up the cause of death? And eventually, she started wondering if Joe had been the cause of the death.

Once it reached that point, even though she thought she had kept what she learned a secret, Joe realized May had to die too. It took longer to make it happen. She was wiser than the women on the hill. She blocked his suggestions. But he was stronger, and she was afraid. Fear is always a weakening agent.

Now Joe was afraid of his son. Edward could destroy everything that Joe had built throughout the years. There was no way he would let him. Edward had to be stopped. But first, Joe had to find out what Edward knew.

Joe stepped into the waiting car after spending a few minutes with the caretaker of his estate in Morocco. He knew he could be making a big mistake by returning to the States, but his pride would not let him walk away and allow his reputation to unravel.

No one had any proof that he had done anything wrong. Besides, he had that fool Craig on his side. Joe was going to take his time getting to Doveland. He had a few things to take care of before arriving in America.

He thought it appropriate that he would arrive during Halloween week. There would be people of all ages wearing masks transforming themselves from an ordinary person into something else. Sometimes they wore monster masks and pretended to be evil.

It made him laugh at the irony of it. He had worn a mask his whole life, the cover of gentleness and love. But there was no way he was going to let people know now that underneath that mask was an actual monster. He never had to pretend to be evil. He just was.

# THIRTY-TWO

S arah closed the door behind Edward, turned to lean on it, and looked back at her living room. The teapot and cups were still on the table between the two chairs where they had sat for the last three hours, and Edward had revealed his secret.

She sighed and waited for an idea of what to do next, now that Edward had told her what she had already known. She didn't tell him that, though. Too much information. Much too soon for the boy. Because, yes, even though he was a grown man, the young boy inside him was still very much in evidence, stuck in fear of the past.

After telling Sarah the story, the first thing he decided to do was to return to his real name of Edward. He was not interested in hiding any longer. He was ready to reveal his secret to her friends in Doveland. But then he wanted Sarah to tell him what to do. Who should he tell, and when?

It wasn't up to her, Sarah had told him. He had to step up fully into this decision, knowing the ramifications of revealing that he was Dr. Joe's son. That in itself was monumental. He had been missing for over thirty years, and now he was back. People were going to want to know why he had come home, and why he had left in the first place. Was he ready to tell them the whole story?

Edward wasn't sure if he could tell that whole story to anyone else yet. Just telling Sarah had taken every bit of courage he had. Sarah asked him if he felt better now that someone besides himself knew the truth. When Edward stopped to think about it, he realized that he did. He decided he might feel even better telling more people right now rather than waiting. Edward also needed to let the right people know that he had proof that Joe had killed the women on the hill, and that there were others. Including his mother.

After much deliberation, Edward decided to do the telling in steps. First, reveal his true identity, and if it went well, or as well as could be expected, then release the rest of the information to Sam and Hank and let them bring in the proper authorities. Telling everyone else was still an option. It was a wait and see proposition.

Sarah reminded him of what he already knew. The person he had to tell first was Valerie. Even though they had only met a few days before, the feeling of knowing each other was so intense, he couldn't deny the connection, and he knew Valerie couldn't either.

From the moment he first saw Valerie at Ava's party, Edward wanted to tell her who he was, but he was afraid she would turn away before she even knew his heart. Now he was even more fearful that she would dismiss him altogether because he had lied to her. A lie of omission, but still a lie.

Sarah thought back to the spring when the women's council had discussed if there were times when it was okay, and sometimes necessary, to lie. One of the criteria was if it was to protect someone and Sarah thought that Edward had met that criteria. He was protecting himself. He was also saving himself so he could save others.

"But will Valerie and then the rest of your friends understand?" Edward asked.

Sarah had answered that the only way to find out was to do it. So while he was sitting in his chair in Sarah's home, he phoned Valerie and asked if he could come over. There was something he needed to tell her.

Valerie had hesitated. Fear gripped her heart. What had she done wrong? He was going to tell her he didn't want to see her anymore; she was sure of it. Yes, she knew she was being totally irrational, but panic set in and her voice shook.

When Ted had told her he was at Sarah's and after talking to Sarah about something important, she had suggested he talk to Valerie about it first, Valerie relaxed a bit. That meant Ted saw her as important enough to be first. Besides, Sarah would not put her in harm's way, even if it was just a breaking heart kind of way.

Just thinking about how much she was worried made Valerie mad. After all, she had only met Ted a few days before. Nothing was going on. He was just a new friend.

All of that talking to herself helped a bit, but it wasn't enough. She asked Ted to put Sarah on the phone.

"Should I be afraid, Sarah?" she had asked.

"No, dear," Sarah had answered, reminding Valerie that she could set fear aside and breathe and that would help the feeling of panic.

"Does he need to tell this only to me?" Valerie had asked next.

When Sarah had said, "No, eventually he will have to tell other people," Valerie requested that Sarah and Ava come over too. And maybe Grace. By the time she had finished asking for people, she had named the entire woman's council.

So plans were made. They would meet at Ava's instead of Valerie's. Lex would come over and spend the night. Ted could tell Valerie and her friends at the same time.

When each of the women had asked if it could wait, Sarah had told them, "No, it can't." In fact, Sarah added, "Although the council will meet at Ava's first, perhaps Sam, Tom, and Hank could be with Evan, just in case they needed to be called into the meeting."

Sarah had a feeling that once they got started, Edward would want to get it all over with. Rip off the band-aid so to speak.

It had been a long day and she was tired, but the sooner this secret came out into the open, the better it would be for everyone, because Leif had told her that Dr. Joe had left his home in Morocco and was on the way.

That was a fact she wasn't sure she would reveal yet. It might be best to wait until everyone absorbed what Edward had to say. They would suspect that Joe would be coming, but did they have to know now?

# THIRTY THREE

I t was a brief phone call, but one that changed everything in Craig's world. Joe called and said that he was coming back to Doveland. Could Craig pick him up at the airport in a few days? *What could he do?* Craig thought. Of course, he had said yes.

At first, the phone call seemed perfectly reasonable. But then Craig started feeling as if there was something wrong. Since he couldn't figure out what was bothering him, he decided to take a walk. That always straightened things out for him. Besides, it was a beautiful fall day at the end of October. As he walked down one tree-lined street to another, shuffling through the leaves, his head cleared, and he figured out what was bothering him. For one thing, when Joe left, he didn't have Craig take him to the airport. He went by himself. He hired a car. He could afford one. Why was he having Craig pick him up? Why was he asking him to drive over an hour each way?

The hopeful part of Craig wanted to believe it was because they were friends and Joe wanted time to talk together. But that made little sense. They always made time to talk together. After all, they had their Tuesday breakfast meetings at the Diner, and Craig often went to Joe's house to talk.

*No,* Craig thought, *this has to do with control.* With perfect clarity, Craig realized that was the game that Joe was playing. That was the game he always played. He did not know why he hadn't noticed Joe's need to control before.

But Craig could see that having him pick up Joe at the airport assured Joe that Craig was still on his side. It would also alienate him even more from his friends when they found out he had picked Joe up. And they would find out. It was a small town. By bringing Joe home, the wall between him and Valerie would grow just a little bit thicker, and Joe knew that. It was why he set it up that way.

Plus, with that new guy in town, Craig's chances with Valerie had pretty much dipped to zero. Oh, yes. He had seen Ted and Valerie together. How could he help it? They seemed to be everywhere that he went. To make matters worse, everyone was talking about how quickly Ted and Valerie hit it off, how cute they looked together, and how Valerie seemed so happy after only a few days of knowing that "perfect" Ted.

What made Craig even angrier was that he knew that the distance between him and Valerie was his fault. He had refused to believe his friends about Dr. Joe. His friends. He had known Leif for much longer than he had known Joe. Why would he choose Joe's version over what Leif had told him?

Thinking he would call Joe back and say he couldn't pick him up because he forgot he had other commitments, Craig realized that the phone that Joe had called him from did not show a phone number.

*Damn it,* Craig thought, slamming his hand onto his desk. Joe did that on purpose. He doesn't want me to call him back. Joe just wants me to be there. He knows that if I can't reach him, I will feel guilty for not going. He thinks I won't just leave him there, waiting. *Well, he's wrong about that. I can. And just maybe, I will.*

• • • ● • ● • • •

Joe hung up the phone and started laughing. He couldn't stop. It was a good thing that he was sitting in a car by himself because it was ridiculous how hard he was laughing. He knew exactly what would happen when Craig hung up. He would start thinking. He would wonder why Joe needed a ride. Then he would decide that Joe was using him.

*Oh, so true,* my friend, Joe thought. *I am using you, but not in the way you think.* Joe put the burner phone he had purchased on the passenger seat and laughed again. Then, rethinking the wisdom of keeping it, he stepped out of the car and smashed the phone under his heel, picked up the pieces and dumped them into the nearest trash container.

Joe had stopped at a roadside rest stop to make the call. He had to stop anyway. The coffee he drank while on the plane had finally caught up with him. Standing by the trash container, he watched the little cloud of breath come out of his mouth as he puffed it out. Playing with his breath. One of the few things he remembered doing as a child. Or at least one of the few slightly pleasant things he did as a child.

Despite being a cheerfully sunny day, the feeling of winter was in the air. Still, it was a beautiful Sunday afternoon. Since his motel reservations weren't until later that day, he thought perhaps a short walk would be a good idea. That is if he could find a place that wasn't polluted with car fumes.

Joe checked his new app on his phone that told him where local parks were and discovered one not far away. As he put the car in gear to reverse out of his parking spot, he started laughing again.

Wouldn't Craig be surprised to discover that instead of being thousands of miles away, he was only a few hours away? Yes, he was back in the States. Early. He had things to prepare before anyone knew that he was there.

Joe had also bought a plane ticket for a few days later, so when Craig picked him up at the airport it really would look as if he had just arrived. It probably wasn't necessary, but he was covering his bases just in case he, or his friend Sam, checked the plane's manifest,

Instead, he had arrived the day before, but not into Pittsburgh. He had flown into Chicago and then rented a car. Under a different name, of course. He decided it would be appropriate to use the name he was born with before he remade himself after his mother's death.

Joe hadn't escaped notice all these years by being predictable, or unprepared. He would be in Doveland later that day, but not as himself. Who did they think taught Grant all about disguises and hiding? Yes, Grant had been a master at it, but he had learned from a master.

Joe wanted to find out what his son was up to, and the best way to do that would be through local gossip. His reservations were for the motel at the lake. It wasn't very upscale, but it would do, especially for the persona that he was invoking.

Joe would be an unknown, down on his luck, writer trying his hand at travel writing. It gave him the perfect motive for asking questions. If his son was going to make problems for him, well, he knew how to eliminate that threat. Blood or no blood, it made no difference to him. After all, who he had become was not because his parents gave it to him. He did it all himself, by himself. And he would take care of the problem of Edward himself, by himself, and then return as Dr. Joe. As a hero, his reputation intact.

That last part? He wasn't sure how he was going to pull that off. He'd have to see what opportunities opened up to him, and then he would exploit them. That was another thing that he was a master of. Exploitation. For a minute he wondered if there was anything he wasn't an expert at, at least at things that mattered, and decided there wasn't.

Still laughing to himself, Joe pulled back onto the highway and headed to Doveland, telling himself he could walk later. He couldn't wait to go home.

# THIRTY FOUR

I t was hard to believe that it was just that morning that they had sipped coffee together. If time were counted by how much had happened, instead of minutes, at least a decade would have passed for Valerie.

On the way over to Ava's, Valerie's heart had thumped so hard she was sure that it sounded like a bass drum coming out of her car as they passed people on the road. Lex had taken one look at his mother's hands trembling on the steering wheel and decided to hold his comments until he knew what was going on.

Over the past year, Lex had become used to being told at the last minute that he was sleeping over at Hannah's house. It had happened so often that he no longer questioned it. Sometimes the summons was for a last-minute party. But more often than not, it was because something serious was going on that needed to be discussed among the grownups.

Whatever it was this time, Lex was sure it wasn't for a party. In fact, if his intuition was working well, it had something to do with that new guy in town, the one his mom had wanted to dress up for. In this case, his intuition didn't have to work overtime. All the signs pointed to it being about Ted.

But it was a test anyway to see how well he was doing as he practiced becoming more intuitive. Lex and Hannah had spent many hours talking about the skill of listening to what was going on around them and then listening to what was going on inside of them.

Hannah said that if he listened well, he would often know things that other people missed. Not because those things were hiding from them, but people were too busy to notice, or pay attention. Lex had decided to be someone that paid attention. Having Hannah as a best friend had changed his life. She knew things, and she wanted to teach someone what she knew. He was a willing pupil. Not only because what Hannah had to teach was awesome, but because he knew that he was different, and that difference would mean he would have to learn to be strong within himself. He would need to be aware of what was going on around him at all times.

At the moment, what was going on was his mom being upset about something, so he decided the best thing that he could do for her was to let her know he loved her no matter what.

When his mom stepped out of the car, he reached up and hugged her and said, "Don't forget that Johnny and I love you."

Valerie looked down into Lex's earnest face and realized that there was nothing that was happening more important than how much she loved her children.

"Just what I needed, Lex. You are so wise and intuitive."

Lex smiled to himself. *It was working!*

During the next few minutes, all the women had arrived, poured coffee, and found their favorite seat in the living room. It was dark and cold outside, not a good place to be discussing important things. Lex went off to play with Hannah. When Sam, Tom, and Hank arrived, they went with Evan into the family room.

The women's council arranged themselves so that they were all facing Ted. Valerie sat directly opposite him, with Mandy and Mira on each side. Valerie had a flash of how Mandy and Mira had become protectors of whoever was in most need at the moment. She remembered them flanking Emily and then Tina, and then herself last spring. Now it was Valerie's turn again.

*Please,* God, she whispered to herself. *Don't let this be about any more dead bodies.* Later, Valerie would think back on that prayer and realize she had been just a bit ahead of herself.

Ted looked across at Valerie and began.

"Although I had wanted to tell this to Valerie first and alone, I see now that it is better that I tell you all at one time. I've already told Sarah the whole story."

Everyone turned to look at Sarah to see if she was going to give anything away. She didn't, so they turned their attention back to Ted.

Ted began by telling them that Ted was a nickname for his real name, Edward.

Then he paused and waited. Sarah had told them that they knew Dr. Joe had a son named Edward, so he understood that it wouldn't take long for them to make the connection.

It didn't. It was Grace who made the connection first.

"Edward? As in Joe's son? That Edward?"

"That Edward," he replied.

A few swear words escaped most of the women's mouths, and then Mandy asked the question that terrified them all.

"Does your father know that you are here?"

"Probably. And, yes, I am sure he will come for me. He's either here already, or on his way."

Valerie was stunned. The man she thought she had a connection to, was the son of the man who she knew killed her husband, Harold, even if she couldn't prove it. The ramifications of that news rolled through her, first making her nauseous and then lighting a fury within her she didn't know existed.

"You lied to me!" she screamed, as she stood and walked towards him. "You are just another liar. Just like your father. Are you a killer, too?"

Edward hung his head and waited until her fury died down enough for Mandy and Mira to pull her back to the couch.

He looked up, his eyes compassionate even though his face was white and his hands were shaking. "No, I am not like my father at all. And I didn't tell you who I was at first because I didn't know any of you. I had no idea if I could trust you or not.

"I have been running from my father my whole life because when he finds me, he will probably try to kill me, just like he killed my mother. We know too much."

Edward realized what he had said as soon as it came out of his mouth. He hadn't intended to tell them that piece of information until he had talked to Sam and Hank.

He turned to Sarah and said, "I might as well tell everyone now."

"I agree," Sarah said. "Ava, would you call in Sam, Tom, Hank, and Evan. We also need Pete and Craig."

As Mandy and Barbara placed calls, Ava asked Sarah, "Don't you think we should move Edward out of the motel at the lake and have him stay here?"

"Good idea, Ava." Turning to Sam who had just come into the room, she said, "Sam, could you go to the motel at the lake and get Edward's things? He's going to be staying here."

"Edward?" Sam asked, and then seeing the women's faces, he added, "That Edward?"

"That Edward," Sarah said. "He has a story to tell, but it's best if everyone is here, and of course you can see the wisdom of his not being on his own."

Sam nodded and went to talk to Edward, who wanted to come too, to which Sam said no. But he did ask Hank to go with him. If they ran into trouble, Hank was the person Sam wanted on his side. He planned to sneak in and get out without being seen. But, just in case, he wanted to be prepared.

Sarah turned back to Edward. "While they are gone, let me tell you about the two men that are here that you can't see."

Edward looked around and said, "What men?"

"It's a long story," Grace and Sarah said together, and began to give Edward the short version of who Leif and Eric were, and how they were present to everyone because they had learned how to see them.

Edward looked at the group and said, "You all see them?"

"And hear them too," laughed Mira.

Edward shook his head and said, "And I thought I had seen everything."

"Nope," Mandy laughed, "You haven't."

# THIRTY FIVE

Edward's revelations left everyone shocked and exhausted. And worried. And frightened. They hadn't realized how much they had hoped Joe would leave Doveland alone forever. After all, he had given all his land away to the town, except his house. He had left bequests everywhere, like the one for Emily to fund students for her classes on the hill.

*Poor Emily,* Valerie thought. *Here it goes again.* It all started when Emily put her dream into action and began building her art retreat. After one day of progress, they discovered the four women buried by the old oak tree. Now it turns out there are more bodies. Edward said there were eight women. They had only found four.

Edward kept it to himself that he had an idea where the other bodies were dumped. He even had an idea who put them there. But he wouldn't say what he thought in front of Valerie. She already had too much to bear thinking about Joe returning, so he kept quiet. But Sam, watching him, knew there was more.

There was quite a bit of discussion about safety. Should they all stay at Ava's? In the end, they decided only Edward would stay, because, as he said, his father would come for him first.

However, after hearing that there might be more bodies to be found, Ava suggested Emily call her friend Stephen and have him come to stay with her. After all, he taught music at her art retreat, and she had extra rooms where he could stay. It would make everyone feel better knowing she wasn't alone out there. What if Joe came to visit?

Edward scoffed at that. He told the group that having Stephen there wouldn't stop his father from doing whatever he wanted to, because he didn't use force. He used something much more dangerous because it was invisible and invasive. Dr. Joe used manipulation, charm, and deceit. He worked within the mind, making you think the thoughts he was sending were yours, or the illusion he placed in front of you was real.

It didn't matter where you were if Joe wanted to hurt you. The only way to stand against him was to continue to declare truth, any truth, and to recognize that any suggestion that was not in the best interest of everyone was not one to be listened to. That went for more than Dr. Joe's manipulations, but at the moment, Joe was the one everyone was worried about.

However, Edward didn't think anyone was truly in danger except for him. Because he had proof. Because he was a traitor. And he was a witness. Yes, he had just been a kid, but he took notes. His mother told him what to do, and how to hide them. And he had recordings his mother made. As soon as Edward told the group that piece of information, Sam asked Edward to be quiet. They needed to find the best way to get the information to the right people who could do something about it. Safely.

Sam's warning to Edward reminded everyone that there was more than one reason Sarah wanted the meeting to be at the Anders. Ava and Evan had years of practice in how to keep the house free of any kind of spy hardware. It was swept daily. The locks were changed every month. The network was as secure as any other network in the world, including governments.

If it were true that wearing tinfoil on your head could keep other people's thoughts out of your head, they would be doing that too.

But all of their precautions would be for naught if someone in their Karass decided to supply Dr. Joe with information, or opened their thoughts to him. That would be their downfall, and what worried all of them was the fact that there could be someone in their midst who might do just that. Unintentionally or not, it was dangerous.

Craig knew they thought it would be him. That he would tell Joe what was happening. And Craig wasn't so sure it wouldn't be. After all, he had betrayed his friends before by not believing them.

He was grateful that they had called him to the meeting. It meant more than he could say that they trusted him enough to want him to be there, even though he had been telling them for months that they were wrong about Joe.

Listening to Edward tell his story, Craig couldn't reconcile the Joe that he knew to the one that Edward was describing. A man who would hunt down and kill his own son? Who could do something like that? Not a man who dedicated his life to healing.

Craig was swaying to the side of his friends and beginning to believe that he had been wrong. Joe's asking Craig to pick him up at the airport was still bothering him, so when everyone started talking about Joe already being in town, Craig finally told them all about Joe's request.

Mandy blurted out what everyone else was thinking, in fact, what Craig had felt too.

"What is that about?" she said. "This is just b.s., Craig. Why would he have you pick him up at the airport?"

Craig shrugged and said he didn't know. It was weird to him too, and he was thinking about not going.

"Seems like a mind game to me," Hank said. "Just to see you get upset, confused, or worried. It's the kind of thing he does."

Seeing Craig tense and pull back, Hank added, "Come on Craig, think about it. And even if you don't agree with us, you are feeling weird about it. Admit it."

Sam added, "Here's a thought. What if he is asking you to pick him up at the airport so that we don't think he is in town yet? When is he supposed to be here?"

"Tomorrow afternoon," Craig said.

"I say you pick him up. Be his friend. Maybe we are wrong, and you are right. This way someone is watching him."

"So you want me to spy on him?" Craig asked.

"I could say no, but I would be lying," Sam said. "If what Edward is telling us is true, and he has proof, then, in the end, it wouldn't be about what we believe anymore. We would have proof. But because Joe might be using you to get to us, I worry if you will be safe."

Craig glanced around the room, his gaze resting on Valerie. Perhaps he had lost her, but he would do everything he knew how to do to keep her safe. And if she loved Edward, he would extend that protection to him, too.

Craig saw all his friends, all standing by him no matter what he decided. There really was no choice. He turned to Sam and said, "Tell me what to do. I'll do it."

# THIRTY SIX

J ohnny needed to know, but Valerie wasn't sure what she was
going to say to him. Maybe she could say, "Hey, hon, guess
who's in town. Edward. Yes. That Edward, Dr. Joe's son. The one
who called himself Ted. Yes, Lex is right. I liked him. A lot."

Just saying all that to herself helped. Perhaps if she practiced it
over and over again, she could say it in a way that wouldn't seem
so traumatic. Besides, it didn't mean that just because Edward was
Joe's son that he would be like his father.

Wasn't that what Johnny had been asking all along? Was he
going to be like his father? If she knew her son was not his father,
couldn't she say the same thing for Edward? It would be a double
standard to say otherwise, wouldn't it?

However, it was easier to believe that about Johnny and Lex,
than to know that about a complete stranger. That stemma,
or family tree, or pedigree wasn't the whole truth of someone.
Otherwise, she would be just like her mother, or her father,
wouldn't she?

Thinking of her father circled Valerie back around to the
question that had been haunting Valerie her whole life. Was the

man she knew as her father, indeed her father? And if he wasn't, who was? She had nowhere to turn to get answers.

Except Johnny may have inadvertently found the solution. Last summer, while registering for his classes, Johnny signed up for a course in his first semester that studied family histories. He had told his mom that he hoped to learn more about his own family in the process.

One of the first things his professor had suggested to the class was to get every willing member of their families to send their DNA sample to one of the many companies offering that service. The professor told the story of sending in his own DNA and discovering a half-sister and a half-brother that he had never known he had. They were his father's children from before his father met his mother. It was a secret his father took to his grave. Without the DNA test, the professor would have never known about his extended family.

Johnny's professor told the class that he loved meeting more members of his family, which also included cousins, nieces, and nephews. He claimed that finding them had been one of the best things to have happened to him. When his students questioned him about how he felt about what his father had done, Johnny's professor said that wasn't the point. There was nothing he could do now about his father's past. But he could open up and embrace the future, which included more family than he had before.

His story inspired Johnny to take on the assignment. Johnny asked Valerie if the three of them could send their DNA to a service to find out their ancestry. He was curious. What if they found another member of their family that they didn't know? "Yes," he told his mom, "I know it's highly unlikely, but think about it. It would be so cool."

At the time, she had agreed because it was so important to him, but she thought it kind of silly, and definitely not cool, if they discovered other members of their family. It would just be one more complication in their lives.

But now she was wondering if it was so silly after all. Perhaps when they got the tests back, she would discover more about her father, and put that old question to rest. Or make new questions, Valerie thought.

No matter what her mindset was at the time, she had agreed, and the three of them had sent off their DNA and were waiting for the results.

Johnny was surprisingly calm about her revelation about Edward when she finally got up the courage to call him. Maybe she had expected a bigger reaction because the night before had been so shocking to her. She hadn't slept much. But now that she had called Johnny and had her first cup of coffee she felt much better.

She didn't have to get Lex up for school. She had left him at Ava's because the meeting lasted much longer than any one of them had thought it would. Lex and Hannah were fast asleep when she went to collect him to go home. Lex had been given a closet at Ava's where he could keep extra clothes and other odds and ends, so she wasn't worried about him not looking good for school.

Last night, while they had waited for Hank and Sam to return with Edward's things, Ava had pulled Valerie aside. She said that she hated bringing one more upsetting piece of news into Valerie's world at that moment, but she didn't want her to hear it from someone else.

When Valerie turned pale and pulled back thinking there was another tragedy, Ava grabbed her hand and said, "I'm so sorry, Valerie. No, this is not a bad thing. At least I don't think so. I was wondering if we could talk about Evan and me making our house into a bed and breakfast."

Valerie was so relieved she had burst out laughing. "That is a fantastic, idea, Ava. This place already is a bed and breakfast!"

It was true. Evan and Ava had been hosting people at their house from the moment they bought it. It was going to be a much better bed and breakfast than the one she and Harold had run. Valerie hugged Ava and said they would talk about it more, but for now, she just wanted her to know she had her blessing.

With a start, Valerie realized she had been thinking over so many things, she was going to be late for school if she didn't get moving. Still, she had time to pop over to Your Second Home and grab a coffee and pastry on her way to school. It was Halloween Week, which meant there was a higher possibility of childish mischief than usual. She would need fortifications. And while she was there, perhaps she and Mandy could set a time to go over the plans for the build out of Mandy's design space in Valerie's house.

Now that Valerie knew that someone else was taking up the mantle of the bed and breakfast, that worry was off her plate, so she could concentrate on the joy of new beginnings.

*And completion of old things, too*, she thought. It would be essential to focus on what was good so that what was wrong would be more visible. Always a good strategy, but even more so now that Joe was coming back to town.

As Valerie waited for her coffee, she glanced around Your Second Home at all her friends and realized that she wasn't afraid anymore. She could hold her own, and she had backup. She wasn't alone. Besides, with Edward back in town, and Joe returning she might get some answers. No, she wasn't afraid. She was determined. Dr. Joe was not going to win this time.

# THIRTY SEVEN

Ava felt around the wristband until she found the hidden ladybug appliqué that Hannah had secretly sewn into her sweater. Ava was finding more and more of them in her clothes these days. Over the past few months, Hannah would take one article of clothing at a time, sew in the ladybug somewhere secret, and then returned it to her mom's closet or drawer. Hannah never said anything. She just waited until Ava discovered it, even if it took weeks.

It was Ava who had the idea first. She had been sewing lady bugs into Hannah's clothes for the past few years. A few months ago, Hannah started doing it for her. Neither of them spoke of it. But once in a while, they would glance at each other, finger their hidden ladybugs, and smile in acknowledgment of what it meant. They were mother and daughter, with a connection that would never go away.

After all, they found each other eight years after they had lost each other. Ava had done what she thought best and given Hannah up for adoption. Eight years later, Ava's past came back to haunt her, but instead of destroying her, she had been gifted with the return of her daughter. It was Mandy who had produced the miracle. She had kept Hannah safe all those years.

And that's why she wasn't at all surprised to see that Mandy also had a hidden ladybug appliqué within her jacket. Ava wondered how many other people had been gifted with Hannah's ladybugs.

Mandy noticed Ava looking at the appliqué and said, "Hannah is already producing a brand. Everyone who sees these will think of her."

"You're right. I wonder where Hannah will go with this idea as she grows up. You probably know where she is getting all of them, don't you?"

"I do! She asked me to help her find different designs and purchase them for her, so I did. In return, she and Lex have agreed to give me feedback on some of my new designs for a line of tee-shirts I am thinking of creating. They both have good eyes for what is fashionable right now, and I am creating them with young people in mind."

Ava and Mandy were sitting at a table in the back of Your Second Home. Monday morning rush hour was over. The kids were off at school, and the grownups had headed to work or back home after a quick coffee, so they were mostly alone. Ava glanced around the shop and thought again about how much she loved this little town of Doveland.

"When we met all those years ago in Los Angeles, Mandy, who would have thought we would end up here together," Ava said.

Mandy laughed and lifted her coffee cup in salute. "Yes, you, the sixteen-year-old runaway, and me, the fancy escort working for that terrible man."

"Yes, that terrible man who ended up being Hannah's father. Do you think any of him is part of Hannah?"

"That question about what we inherit from our parents seems to be floating around a lot right now. Edward doesn't want to be his dad, and neither does Johnny. Now you hope Hannah won't be either. Don't you think we have our own destiny? After all, aren't you part of the Stone Circle and aren't you the people that talk about Karass? That we are here in different lifetimes, but still the same soul, or person, or identity that we have always been?

"Why would any of you think that we will be like our parents? I thought you were into the idea that there is only one creator. Like a God, that designs and runs all of this? And I thought you believed in good as the only power.

"So if that's true, then this crap about inheriting traits from our parents is just that. Crap. A story. We don't have to accept that story, do we? Isn't that what you guys are all about?"

Ava stared at her friend as if she had never seen her before. "Who are you?" she asked.

Mandy laughed, "I'm me, and that's because you and all these wonderful people, have told me that I don't have to be my past or my story. I am designing homes and clothes and loving Tom, all because you all said that I had a choice. I choose this. Now don't go trying to tell me that was all made up because I have seen what happens when we choose the story we want to live. When we work at letting go of the evil things that try to make us something else or destroy us.

"Look at Hank. He did horrible things, for heaven's sake. And no one thinks that is who he really is, and he isn't. He's an amazingly good man. He's your uncle who watches over all of us."

"Did I hear my name?" Hank asked as he walked towards Ava and Mandy. "I see you both hiding back here. What are you talking about?"

"Something you would appreciate, Hank. We aren't our parents."

"Thank God for that," Hank said. "Does this mean you're talking about you-know-who?"

"Who else?" laughed Ava. "How's he doing?"

"Well, he's in Valerie's house right now with Evan. I brought them both along while we talk over the plans of what you want to do, Mandy. Sam doesn't want me to let him out of my sight, so he'll be tagging along everywhere I go for a while. We're going to pass him off as my new assistant. So, Mandy, when you're ready, come on over and let's get started."

"It must be strange for him to be in Valerie's house," Ava said.

"Do you think it's serious between the two of them?" Hank asked.

"Did you see how they looked at each other?" Mandy answered. "I don't know if it's serious, but there is a deep connection there somewhere."

"It's going to be hard for both of them," Hank said, thinking about what Edward had told him and Sam after everyone else had left. He told them the story of how he knew Harold, and how Joe taught Harold. After hearing that, Sam had gone straight to his old boss at the FBI. He wasn't taking any chances this time. They needed to know what was happening, and have a plan in place that would work.

"Is Craig going to pick up Dr. Joe today?" Ava asked, as casually as she could, just in case she was overheard.

"Yes," Hank answered, but didn't add any more information. Both women understood why.

Mandy stood up and leaned over to kiss Ava on the cheek, and started to leave with Hank. Instead, she turned around and came back, pulled out her chair, and set it directly in front of Ava. She was so close their knees were touching.

Reaching out and holding both of Ava's hands, she whispered, "I don't think I have ever told you this, but the day I met you, right there in the Laundromat as we both waited for our clothes to dry, was the best day of my life. And every day since then, I have been grateful for having met you."

Ava felt a tear roll down her cheek as they leaned towards each other and touched foreheads. Ava whispered, "Me too, Mandy."

They stayed like that for a few seconds more, and then Mandy stood up, returned the chair to the table, straightened her jacket, and said to Hank, "Sorry. You probably wouldn't understand."

Hank glanced at Mandy and back to his niece who, in essence, had rescued him from the evil clutches of Grant, and loved him as if he was a good man, and answered, "Oh, yes, I would. And I do."

Mandy hooked her arm through Hank's elbow, and the two of them headed out the door to go build her dream.

*This is what Hank is becoming, a dream builder,* Mandy realized as they walked together. *I wonder if he knows it.* Obviously, he was next on the list to thank for being in her life.

As they crossed the street towards Valerie's, a cold wind whipped up the leaves at their feet and then moved on, but not before Mandy caught a glimpse of someone she didn't know standing in the town square.

"When did you say Joe will be back in town?" she asked.

"Later today," Hank answered. "Why? What did you see?"

Mandy shook her head and mumbled, "Nothing."

Hank looked down at Mandy and knew that she had seen something. He thought he did too, but when he looked again, it had vanished. Some more protection might be in order, he thought, because he wasn't betting that Joe was at the airport.

Time would tell, but in the meantime, they needed to be hyper-vigilant, and they probably needed more manpower. Once they reached Valerie's, Hank took the time to text Sam with the question: "Are you getting us help?"

Sam's answer was pure Sam. Simple and direct. "Yes," he said.

# THIRTY EIGHT

*Did I really think that Joe would be here?* Craig wondered to himself. He was waiting at the new Starbucks installed in the baggage pickup area of the Pittsburgh Airport. He thought if he was going to be driving all this way just to get someone who had the means and money to get his own ride home, he deserved a treat.

He leaned against one of the columns, sipping his Café Americano, watching the escalators. Waiting for Joe to descend. Joe was late. His plane was on time, but no Joe. Craig wondered if Joe would look the same. After all, he had been away for five months in sunny Morocco. He would probably be fit and tan and definitely not stressed out like the rest of them.

Just as Craig decided he was going to leave, he saw him. It was Joe, stepping onto the escalator and waving to him. Craig waved back, thinking that Joe had waited until just the right moment to make his entrance. Was Joe that manipulative? Or was it a coincidence?

As Craig watched Joe descend, he asked himself if he felt anything. Did Joe give off good vibes? Bad vibes? The answer was neither. He gave off nothing. Craig realized that somehow Joe had made himself a void. That thought struck terror in Craig's heart.

*Had Joe been like that the whole time? No,* he thought. *I would have noticed.*

He looked back at Joe as he stepped off the escalator and headed towards Craig. He wasn't a void anymore. He was a warm, caring, human being. A doctor who loved to heal. Had he imagined it? Craig wondered, but he didn't have any time to think it through before Joe was slapping him on the back and shaking his hand, and thanking him for showing up to drive him home.

"No bags?" Craig asked as Joe headed for the sliding door that led to the parking lot.

"No. There wasn't any point in bringing summer type clothes to the cold. I left plenty of clothes back at the house because I didn't want to drag them on and off airplanes.

"Hey," Joe said turning to Craig. "Thanks a bunch for picking me up. I know I could have used a car service, but I was looking forward to seeing you and hearing what you have been up to."

By the time the two men had reached the short-term parking lot where Craig had left his car, Craig was feeling right at home again with Joe. It made sense. Of course, he wanted to catch up with the town news.

All the way home, they chatted. Joe asked probing questions about Craig's practice, and Craig was grateful to have someone to bounce ideas off of again. Craig hadn't realized how much he missed their conversations.

Craig dropped Joe off at his house, but not before the two of them made plans to meet the next day for breakfast at the Diner. Since it would be a Tuesday morning, they would be right back into their routine.

It wasn't until Craig pulled into his parking lot behind his office and home that he began to wonder if all of that was real. *It had to be,* he thought. *No one could pull off that warmness if it weren't real.*

He decided to text Sam that Joe was home, and then turn off his phone, have a nice quiet dinner, and get to bed. He hadn't realized how exhausted he had become worrying about Joe's return. *All for nothing*, he thought. *Which wasn't a bad thing at all.*

• • • ● • ● • • • •

Joe almost didn't make it to the airport on time. He had stayed in town too long, looking for Edward.

After distracting the clerk at the motel the night before, he saw the name Ted Miller in the guest book. He wondered what motel uses guest books anymore. With the advent of computers, the guest book went the way of the dodo. Apparently not in Doveland, though. Lucky for him. Much easier to swing a book around than hack a computer.

Ted was obviously Edward, and Miller was May's last name. Joe figured that Edward had decided not to hide from him anymore. At least he wasn't worrying that Joe would know he was in town, because, of course, Joe would recognize the name.

However, even though Joe waited all night watching the door of Edward's room, Edward never appeared. Two other men did, though. He knew who they were, Sam and Hank. Of course, it was them. That meant Edward had already gone to them and probably told them the story.

After they left, Joe used a trick he had seen on TV to open the motel door and search Edward's room. There was nothing to find, Sam and Hank had taken everything with them.

Joe had been around too long and escaped too many traps to panic. He had no idea what Edward knew so he wasn't going to project possibilities into the situation. For all Joe knew, Edward knew nothing at all. Maybe it was all guessing on his part, which meant Joe could always outsmart him. In fact, even if Edward knew something, it wouldn't be enough, because Joe would always be able to outsmart anyone. Including his son. Especially his son.

But he was overwhelmingly curious about where Edward went. Did Hank take him to the farm? Or Sam to his house? Of course, there was always that bitch Ava who was forever taking people in.

To find out more, and maybe discover where Edward went, Joe decided to go into town. Not as himself, but in his stumbling old man, slightly down on his luck, disguise.

He was rewarded for his initiative and patience when he saw Hank go into Your Second Home and come out a few minutes later with Mandy on his arm. They both went to Valerie's, even though Joe knew that Valerie wasn't home. He had seen her getting coffee and pastry before driving to the school. So now he was curious about what were they doing.

What was going on at Valerie's? It was starting to piss him off that things were going on in town that he didn't know about. Things he hadn't controlled or made happen. Even though he had pretended all last year that it didn't bother him, that was a lie. It ate at him. He was the town's guide, and it was through him that things happened. Only him. No, people weren't aware that it was him. That wasn't the point. He knew it was him. Nothing happened without his knowledge.

Ever since that group that followed Ava and Evan came to town, he had begun to lose control. They started to make things happen without him. Enough was enough. He needed to shut them all down before they took over.

The first step was getting Craig firmly on his side, which meant he needed to be at the airport when he had told him he would be. If Craig didn't show up, well, he had another plan in place. But knowing Craig, he would be there because he said he would.

Joe drove like a crazy man to the airport, stripping off his disguise as he drove. He had a story ready to tell about a patient needing him in case a cop stopped him, but he made the trip without incident. He dropped his rental car off, dropped the disguise in the trash, and ran to baggage claim, almost right into Craig sipping coffee waiting for him.

Taking advantage of the swarm of people coming down the escalator, he walked up the escalator backwards, blending in the people coming down. It was difficult, but he used as many tricks as he knew to focus people's attention away from him. He became invisible.

Once he got to the top, he let go of the mind control of the people around him, including Craig's, and allowed Craig to see him.

*It was easier to pull things like this off years ago,* he thought, *but now too many parts of the airport are restricted without a ticket.* He was lucky. It all worked. Craig believed him, and by the time they were home, Craig was firmly convinced once again that Joe was who he portrayed himself to be.

Now the next part of his plan could take place. Starting with breakfast in the morning.

# Thirty Nine

V alerie came home from school tired and a little cranky. The kids were already wired, and it wasn't even Halloween yet. More than one child had been sent to the office to speak with her for acting out. What would they be like after they collected their candy during Trick Or Treat night?

She wished that there was something other than candy that children could receive on Halloween, and that Halloween had remained something that bound a neighborhood together. Instead, that community aspect of the holiday had turned into carpools of kids driving to wealthier neighborhoods to collect more bounty. What did that teach children about how the world worked? And then there was the aftermath of eating candy as if it was food.

Throwing candy at kids waiting by the side of the road while they were watching parades was another of her pet peeves. She thought whoever started that practice needed to sit in the corner wearing a dunce hat. It was something she was planning to talk to the town council about. Not the dunce hat, the candy throwing. It was a terrible practice. Kids didn't even see the parade. They saw candy. It was dangerous in so many ways. The primary danger was children stepping out into the road to retrieve the goodies between the wheels of the parade floats and vehicles.

She sighed. It was important, but right now she had other things to focus on. Lex wanted to know what was happening, and he certainly had a right to know. However, she wasn't sure what to say. Did she know?

So when she and Lex walked in the door and could hear talking in the kitchen, she wasn't sure if she was happy or sad about it, especially when she recognized Edward's voice.

Mandy, waiting by the back door, grabbed Valerie's purse and helped her off with her coat as she said, "I promise, Valerie, I won't always be in your space like this. But we had so many ideas to run by you I thought we would wait for you. Besides, Sam cooked up his famous spaghetti."

Valerie took one look at her friend's earnest face and almost burst into tears. She had no idea she was that stressed and hungry. She hugged Mandy and whispered, "Thank you," in her ear, and said to everyone else, "I am so hungry I could eat a horse. Well, not a horse, but a plate as big as a horse's head!"

"Me too," Lex said, heading to the table after dropping both his bag and his coat by the door. "Plus, I can't wait to hear about the design project." Mandy smiled at him, a boy after her own heart.

"Okay, let's get everyone fed, then we can talk," Sam said.

No one waited to be asked again. They all lined up with their plates by the big pot on the stove. Sam ladled spaghetti and then sauce, meatless for Mandy, and directed them to the garlic bread waiting on the sideboard.

On the way to the garlic bread, Edward and Valerie brushed shoulders. "Hey," he said. "I'm so sorry, Valerie. I didn't know that I would care about someone the first day I came to town."

Valerie looked up into Edward's eyes and realized she had been holding something against him that wasn't his fault. He didn't ask for all these problems any more than she did.

"It's okay," she answered. "I understand. We can talk more about it later, but for now, just know that I am on your side."

Edward's smile told her all she needed to know.

• • • ● • ● • • •

No one had seen Leif and Eric since Sunday night. It wasn't unusual. They often stayed away, especially when events were happening in the Forest Circle's dimension that had to be dealt with. Grace and Sarah had often tried to pry out of them what they did in that other dimension. But they never found out more than that it was much the same as this one, with a bit more magic, but with the same needs and loves as everyone had in this one.

This time, however, Leif and Eric weren't actually staying away. Instead, they were staying invisible. During the past year, Leif and Eric had learned how to enable people to see them. They had also learned how to stop people from seeing them. They could even stay invisible to those that knew how to see them without their help. Like their beloved wives, Sarah and Grace.

Leif and Eric couldn't take any chances. They were beginning to suspect that Joe had learned how to travel between dimensions, too. They didn't think he was aware of what he was doing, and he wasn't technically going anywhere. It was as if he knew how to stand in the waiting room, but he didn't know how to go through the next door.

Eric had likened it to the new doors installed in Your Second Home. The first door brought you inside. You were no longer standing in the street, but neither were you in the coffee shop. You had to walk through the second door to be in the other "dimension" of the coffee shop.

Opening the first door was how they thought Joe could become what Joe called invisible. Joe thought he was manipulating people's minds not to see him, and perhaps he was doing that too, but Leif and Eric believed that without Joe's awareness, he had tapped into the first skill of dimension traveling.

It worried them. They couldn't have Joe open that second door and escape into another dimension. He could either end up in the Forest Circle dimension or, even worse, in another one that they didn't know how to get to, at least not yet.

So to make sure they were not assisting Joe in any way, the two of them remained invisible—to everyone.

But they were watching. Leif and Eric watched Sam's team, and they watched their friends and family. They had already talked to members of the Forest Circle and asked them if they would be willing to help if Leif and Eric got into trouble with stopping Joe.

There was no hesitation. Tom and Mira's parents and grandparents were part of the Forest Circle, and they would do whatever necessary to protect their children. That's what Suzanne and Jerry had done when they gave Mira and Tom up for adoption. They had protected them. They would do it again.

In the meantime, Leif and Eric waited and watched, ready to step in if necessary. Joe's reign of terror had to come to an end, and as soon as possible, before anyone else died.

# FORTY

U nknown to either Craig or Dr. Joe, they had been followed. Sam was taking no chances. And he wasn't going to tell a single person within his circle what he was doing, except Hank, who knew some, but not all, of it. Sam chose Hank because he knew how to battle evil and was skilled at detecting danger and not being consumed by it.

The only other people who knew were the men on his team, lent to him by his old boss at the FBI. They were handpicked by Sam and vetted so thoroughly Sam knew how many cavities they each had in their mouth.

The first training his team had gone through was how to stop their thoughts from transmitting. It was a skill that had been taught off and on since the Vietnam War, even though no one talked about it. If they did, there would be no record that the training existed. The members of Sam's team were also taught how not to be swayed by illusion. They weren't experts at it, but they were better trained than most of their fellow agents.

Sam's team was a mix of top-notch undercover operatives who were already the best at not being seen, and a few data analysts who could find anything hidden on the web. The latter had been working on Dr. Joe's case since the bodies had been discovered on the hill last May. Some people believed that the case had gone cold, but Sam knew differently.

Last spring, they had accumulated quite of bit of damning circumstantial evidence against Joe, but not enough to convict him. Or even hold him, Sam thought. Then there was the fact that Joe could so easily escape. He had already done it last spring. Although, technically, there was nothing they could have done to stop him then, so Joe didn't need to use any special tricks to disappear.

That wasn't going to be true this time. This time, they would have evidence. Some they had found on their own. But the best evidence they had was what Edward had brought with him. So this time Joe probably already knew that they were coming for him. Therefore, once he had completed his mission in Doveland, he would use whatever tricks he had to vanish and never be found again.

Sam had no illusions about the fact that Joe was probably there to get back at Edward for running out on him, and, of course, to destroy anyone who was trying to ruin his reputation.

Joe could have stayed away, but his monster hubris brought him back, and that was what Sam had been counting on all along. Sam knew that Joe's weakness was his need for validation. His need to have a perfect reputation. Sam knew that someday Joe would return to protect that reputation and gather more appreciation, and Sam wanted to be ready. And he was right. And he was ready.

Sam didn't tell his friends, including Mira. Not because he didn't trust them, but because he knew how Joe worked. Joe read minds. Or at least he read people well enough to know what they were thinking. There was no way Sam was going to put his loved ones in the middle of this mess any more than they already were.

So, although Joe thought he had come back to town without being seen, he was mistaken. Sam and his team knew about Joe's two plane tickets. They knew about the rental car. The minute he left the first plane, Joe had been watched.

They knew Joe was staying at the motel at the lake. That morning, two of Sam's men followed Joe from the motel into town. First, they had watched him break into Edward's room, and then turn into someone no one would recognize. Except if you had already been watching him. Otherwise, he was utterly believable as a down-on-his-luck old man.

They watched Joe as he spied on the people going into Your Second Home. When Joe left for the airport, three more men took up the watch. The three that had been watching Joe split up. The first two stayed in town, watching over Edward and the other people working in Valerie's home. The third man was assigned to watch Ava and Evan's, Tom and Mandy's, and Sam and Mira's homes. They all lived along the same road, so it was easy to keep track of who went up and down that road or traveled the bike path.

Sam even had a drone watching over the town. He wasn't taking any chances. The drone was being paid for by Tom. It was Sam's one concession other than Hank. They couldn't afford all the surveillance without financial help, and Tom was happy to provide it. Sam had told Tom that it was just general protection, and in a way it was.

The three new men trailed Joe to the airport, where another man waited at Starbucks, right beside Craig. That man saw Joe enter the baggage area even though Craig didn't. But then the craziest thing happened. Joe disappeared for about sixty seconds. When the agent saw Joe again, he was descending the escalator as if he had just arrived.

For a moment the agent thought about not reporting what he had just seen, or not seen, but Sam had warned them all that Joe was a master hypnotist, and illusionist, so he knew no one would think it was his fault for losing him. They needed to know.

As soon as Joe and Craig left the airport and the agent knew that the three agents that followed Joe there were back on his trail, he gave Sam a call. Sam wasn't surprised, and thanked him for information. It was more of Joe's tricks they all needed to know about.

Sam asked the agent to check the rental car and trash around the rental car return area and then come back to base. He had some research for him to do. They had set up a command post in the town of Concourse. Actually, it was in Hank's barn. The barn had already been designed to teach students the construction trade, so it was only a matter of moving the equipment off of the tables and setting up computers instead.

Hank had made the barn secure from prying eyes when he first built it. Sam knew that Hank would never stop looking for evil to try and attack him, his family, and his friends. Hank had lived too long under its influence. Hank knew what people like Joe were capable of because Joe's prize master student, Grant, had been Hank's teacher.

The three men trailed Craig from the airport and watched him drop Joe off at his home. Then two of them parked behind the house they had rented directly across from Joe's and set up surveillance for the night. Joe wouldn't suspect any new activity. The team had been taking turns living there since the spring. Sam had not told anyone about this part of the surveillance. None of the agents staying in the house were ever seen by the people in town or the neighborhood. They were, for all accounts, invisible.

The neighbors thought the house was in probate, and waiting for a court's decision. No lights were ever turned on. No noise was ever made. But in that darkness and silence, Sam's team was watching.

They were watching the day Edward walked past his father's house and hid behind the lilacs. They reported the occurrence to Sam, who wasn't surprised at all to discover that the new man in town was Joe's son. Sam had hoped Edward would tell everyone before Sam had to act and was pleased when Edward had come clean on his own.

Another agent watched Craig's house. The men working out of Hank's barn would trade off, so it wasn't always the same person driving by. Sam didn't know for sure if he had Craig watched because he was worried about his safety, or because he was afraid of what Craig would do.

Only time would tell.

# FORTY ONE

C raig and Joe met at the diner the next morning as they had for months before Joe had gone away, as if nothing had happened in between. When they walked in the door together, Pete and Barbara looked at each other and wondered what in the world Craig was thinking. Everybody else was staying as far away from Dr. Joe as possible, and here Craig was bringing Joe into the Diner like Craig was Joe's best friend.

Barbara wasn't sure if Craig was pretending not to be afraid of Dr. Joe, or if he really wasn't. In which case, there was something seriously wrong. But Craig was their friend, and there was no way they were not going to support him, no matter what. So Barbara gave her husband a little hip bump and headed out into the Diner as cheerfully as possible to pour coffee for the two of them, doing her best to pretend that nothing had changed.

As she poured, Dr. Joe smiled up at her and said that he had missed their Diner and was happy to be back in the town where it felt so comfortable to him. At which point, Barbara's hand shook just a little and coffee sloshed out onto the table.

"No problem," Joe said as he sopped up the spill with his napkin. Barbara smiled at him the best that she could and asked if they both wanted their usual. Craig and Joe both said yes, and turned back to their conversation.

As Barbara set the order on the spindle so Alex could start cooking it, the bell on the Diner pinged, and a group of construction workers came in laughing about something. Barbara always loved to see them. They brought cheer and energy into the Diner every morning. But this morning she was even happier than usual to see them. She knew most of them because they worked for Hank. They were what her mother would call "the salt of the earth." Good natured, hardworking, and always grateful for the food that Pete and Alex cooked up for them.

As they slid onto the stools at the counter, one of the men called out, "Hey, Pete, do you have any idea what's going on out at the lake?"

"No, why?" Pete asked, leaning on the counter to talk to them. "What do you mean? What's going on out at the lake?"

"Don't know. Just it looks like there are boats out in the lake, looking for something."

"Yea," another one of the men chimed in, "Dragging it maybe."

"Why would they be doing that?" Barbara asked, coming around to fill their coffee cups.

"Who knows? Things happen all the time that don't make no sense," he answered.

"Huh," Barbara said, and went back to waiting on tables. He was right. Things happen all the time that don't make any sense. But she had an idea what was happening, and so did Pete. He had nudged her, and she knew he meant it was wise to stop the conversation before it went any further.

The problem was, she knew that both Joe and Craig had already overheard what the men had said. Craig just looked curious, because of course, who wouldn't be?

But it was Joe's reaction that scared her. For just a fraction of a second, Joe sat up straighter, his face tightened, and a drop of coffee escaped his cup as he placed it back on the table. He had heard, and for a brief moment in time his calm exterior had cracked. Barbara glanced at Pete and saw that he had also noticed Joe's reaction. The fact that Joe had given himself away for a moment was both affirming that they had been on the right track all along, and terrifying. What would he do now?

Craig and Joe left soon after, Joe remembering that he had an appointment. Clearing their table, Barbara noticed two odd things. Joe hadn't eaten his breakfast, which he always did. In fact, Joe often asked for seconds. This time, he had eaten one bite and put down his fork. And he hadn't left a tip. He always did. A generous one. It was part of his reputation building of being kind and generous. Something had disturbed him so much, he forgot. He had never done that before, either.

It was the lake story. She was sure of it. She texted Sam and told him what happened.

Within seconds, he texted back that he would be right there, and he didn't sound happy at all.

· · ● ●· ● ● · ·

Sam felt like being angry. But who was he going to be angry with? The men who noticed something happening on the lake? He should be grateful that they were always watching out for what was happening in town.

Should he be angry with the team dragging the lake? How could they have hidden that? They had done their best to look like fishermen. But observant people, like Hank's crew, would notice something else. There was nothing anyone could have done differently or better. They had to search the lake.

Sam thought back to just a few days before when he and Edward had gone over all that Edward knew. He had told them that right before the commune had closed for good, there had been eight women. All eight of them had disappeared. Edward had overheard his father and Harold talking about the lake being the perfect burial ground.

Edward was confident that the other four women were in the lake, and Harold had put them there. So the lake had to be dragged. So far they had found nothing, but then it was over forty years ago. Depending on how Harold had dumped them, it could take a while, and they would be lucky if there was anything left.

Still, the fact that Joe heard the conversation meant they were in trouble. They were no longer playing a "let's pretend that it's not Joe" game. The only reason for Joe to become afraid was because he knew what was in the lake. Perhaps, up to now, Joe thought he had eliminated all the people who could point to him and say he was responsible for the deaths of the women they had found last spring.

Sam knew that more people had died by Joe's hand. Sam believed Edward when he told Sam that his father had also killed his mother. She had figured out what he was doing, and Joe had to get rid of his wife. What Joe didn't know was that May was never going to tell. Not because she was afraid for herself, but because she was fearful for her son.

Instead, she protected Edward until he could defend himself. Sam thought about the kind of love Edward's mother, May, must have had for her son. May had taught Edward how to be safe from his father while keeping herself at risk. There might have been another way, but she didn't know what it was.

That long ago, who would have believed her that Dr. Joe was responsible for eight women's death by merely telling them that they were sick and then describing their symptoms to them, over and over again? Testing for the disease that he wanted them to have, and then telling them he found it? He had assured them that he was treating them for it, but eventually, he convinced them it was incurable.

Who would believe that he killed them through suggestion and belief? Even now, people would find it hard to accept. Then, it probably would have meant that May would have been declared insane and her son would have been without protection.

Edward didn't know how his father killed his mother. He didn't think it was the same method his father had used on the women, because May knew how he was killing them, so did her best not to believe anything her husband said. But what about what Joe didn't say? What about what he implied, and whispered, and sent through the airwaves? Was she able to block those too, or did Joe have to employ other methods like poison?

The only way to find out was to dig May up. Edward had given permission. It was the next step. And now, since Joe was aware that they were looking for the women buried in the lake, there was no reason to put it off.

Sam opened his phone and sent off a text, "Ready when you are."

Halfway out the door to go to the Diner, he sent another text to the men watching Craig. It was time to double the watch on him because now Sam knew for a fact that Craig was in trouble.

# FORTY TWO

*Well, this is a fine kettle of fish,* Joe thought, and then wondered where the heck that phrase came from. Still, it was. They were dragging the lake. The only reason they would be doing that was because somehow they knew what had happened. They knew that four other women had never returned home. That meant, of course, that that bitch May had told her son, and Edward had been waiting all these years to betray him.

He should have killed him at the same time he killed his mother. It would have been easy. He could have introduced the same bacteria into Edward's food that he had put in May's. Even though it had taken longer for her to die than he expected, it still worked in the end. He had to admit that May was a strong and intelligent woman. If she had been on his side, they could have conquered the world.

Instead, she felt sorry for those women. Didn't she know they were part of the bigger picture? He had learned how the human mind influences the body. Beliefs made things happen. Change the beliefs and change what happens. He couldn't publish how he knew these things, most people wouldn't understand the necessity of sacrifice for science, but still, his research had made a difference.

The world was beginning to recognize that it was thought that changed the experience. On the other hand, Big Pharma was not happy with his work, either. No money for them if people knew they could eliminate diseases by changing their belief system.

What Big Pharma didn't understand, though, is that most people would never get there, so they had nothing to worry about. It's easier to turn to an outside source for any kind of cure, then to deal with it themselves. The medical community could keep on advertising disease, and most people would still be buying into it. It was just the other side of healing.

So in the end, all his research ended up being for naught. Except for himself, because Joe had learned how to change the world around him through manipulation and suggestion.

Yes, he should have killed Edward then, too. He could have milked the widow and childless status forever, making him even more powerful because people's sympathy opened the door to their minds. But in a moment of weakness, he hadn't. He had hoped that Edward would follow in his footsteps. Even then, Joe knew it was a false hope. Or at least he should have known. Edward was a wimp of a kid. Never tried to control anything, just let the world flow by.

For some reason, Joe thought of the book *The Story Of Ferdinand*, where the bull spent all the time smelling flowers rather than being a bull. May had said it was good to read its message of nonviolence and pacifism. Yes, that reminded him of his pansy son, Edward.

On the other hand, Joe had to admit that he had misjudged Edward's strength and intelligence. Otherwise, how had he managed to stay hidden all these years, and hold that knowledge of what Joe had done until it was the right time to come forward? Edward had waited until people already suspected, and now, obviously, Edward had brought some proof.

The question Joe needed to answer for himself was, did he want to escape or did he want to stay and fight? Could he do either? If they were dragging the lake, they would soon dig up May. And if they were doing that, then they were watching him.

In spite of that, Joe wasn't all that worried. He had alternative ways of getting out of Doveland without being seen. He had hiding places staggered all over the United States waiting for him, each one of them with new identities and money. He could easily be another person for as long as necessary, and when everything died down, he could probably even make his way back to Morocco.

On the other hand, would he be satisfied with that? What about Edward and his betrayal? What about all these people that Grant had tried to eliminate for over two years, and failed? Should they be allowed to survive? They had ruined Grant's life, and now they were going to destroy his. There had to be payback of some kind for their relentlessness.

The question was, could he take revenge and still maintain the reputation he had spent his whole life building? He might have a better chance of retaining what he built by staying than he would by running. If he ran, the word would get out about what he had allegedly done, and then everything would be destroyed.

Glancing out his office window at Emily's hill, Joe thought back to the day he had said yes to Emily's desire to build an art retreat. In that moment of wanting to honor the memory of his wife who loved the arts, he had started this whole mess. If he had said no the bodies wouldn't have been discovered, and nothing in his life would have changed.

It went back further than that. If Harold had only done what he had been told to do, bury all the women in the lake, then his wish to honor May wouldn't have changed anything. Who could he blame for this disaster? Harold! He had already eliminated him. May? He had already taken care of her, too. Emily? She was innocent.

Of course, at the time he said yes to Emily she hadn't told him that she was Jean's niece. So, in a way, Emily wasn't innocent. If she had told him why she had come to town, he wouldn't have said yes. In fact, Emily wouldn't be alive today. Emily had been a loose end that he didn't know about at the time. Yes, she had lied to him. A lie of omission perhaps, but still a lie. She wasn't innocent after all. Maybe she was the one to punish now.

And then there were all those do-gooders with their special talents. They had stopped him already when he had tried to distract them by making their children ill. They knew what to do to overcome that suggestion. They had prevented him from trying to manipulate Johnny into killing Pete. That distraction hadn't worked either. Nothing he or Grant had tried against them had worked.

Joe was sure they had gifts he didn't know about. That worried him more than he was willing to admit. He had one skill. Between them, they appeared to have many. They had forced him into eliminating his top people, like Grant and Lenny. Even that dolt Frank had to go. Sure, there were more people out there he could activate, but Joe wasn't sure he should. Unless it helped get him out of this situation, which maybe it could? Something to think about while planning his next step.

The question was, did he want to punish, or did he want to stop the investigation and turn it around so that he remained the beloved doctor of Doveland? Would it be possible? What could he do to flip the scenario from being the villain to being the hero once again?

Would it be about a person, innocent or guilty didn't matter, or would it be something he did?

There was another problem that Joe hadn't wanted to think about for a long time. Edward was not the only person who had gotten away. One woman had left the hill in the middle of the night. She had snuck out and run away right after he had started his experiments. He never found her. Which meant she knew what he was doing and had hidden on purpose.

Was she still alive? If she was, why hadn't she come forward when the investigation happened last spring? It was in all the papers. She would have seen it and known what it meant. She was either alive and afraid, or dead. If she was dead, he had nothing to worry about.

If she was alive, he needed to find her before she talked. Between Edward and that woman telling what they knew, he might never recover. He would have to run instead.

Joe gave himself the evening to figure it out. By morning, he had to have made a decision and a plan.

Joe turned away from looking out the window at the hill. That was the past. It was the now that he had to plan. And it had to be the best plan he ever made. As complicated and terrible as it was, Joe still wasn't worried. It might have been the worst situation he had faced up to now, but it wasn't the first. He would win. He always did.

# FORTY THREE

Craig didn't go home. Well, he did just in case someone was watching. But he went in the front door, through his office, and out the back door. Over the summer Craig had hired a part-time assistant, so before picking up Joe from the airport, he had her cancel his appointments for the next few days. He wasn't so busy that he couldn't reschedule them for the end of the week, and the doctor in Concourse could handle all emergencies.

Craig had seen the look on Pete and Barbara's face when he walked into the Diner that morning with Joe. They thought he had drunk the Kool-Aid again. He was proud of himself for at least one thing. He had acted as if he believed that Joe was innocent and no one could tell what he was doing, including Joe. They couldn't tell that in the night he had woken up with a clear head. It was as if a fog had been living in his brain and he had no idea that it was there until it was gone.

Now that he was thinking clearly once again, he had to hope that he hadn't given himself away to Joe. It was essential that his thoughts and actions matched someone who believed entirely in Joe and the work that he did. He remembered how that felt when he did believe in Joe and although now it made his skin crawl to pretend he still felt the same way, he did it anyway.

Otherwise, Joe might pick up on something, and his plan would crumble. Craig understood that he was putting himself in great danger by playing this game. But he had to do it. By not accepting what his friends had told him last spring he stepped in the way of the investigation, and perhaps it was his fault that a madman had gone free.

It wasn't going to happen again. This time Craig was going to do everything that needed to be done to bring Joe down. If that meant he went down with him, so be it. Craig had to let Joe believe that he was swayed entirely by Joe's charm. That was the plan. But Craig needed to tell Sam what he was doing.

And that's why he was sneaking out his back door. He planned to either get to the bike path and walk all the way to Evan's where it was safe to talk or wave down one of Sam's agents that were watching him and ask to be taken to Sam's.

Yes, he knew he was being watched. Not because he saw anyone, but because he knew Sam. He would never leave Craig unattended. Sam would have him watched either because he thought he was guilty, or that he was being played and needed protection. Either way, someone was watching.

And because Craig knew that he was being watched, he was confident that Joe knew he was being watched too. Did Sam understand how Joe's mind worked? He would have figured it out a long time ago and would use it against Sam.

Joe would make Sam believe things that weren't there because Sam would be looking for it. He would miss what was really going on because he hadn't opened his thinking to every possibility. Craig had to get to Sam to talk to him about it.

Joe's reaction to whatever was going on at the lake was telling. It meant that Joe realized he didn't have any time left to pull off whatever he was going to do. They had a day or two at the most to figure out Joe's plan and head him off. Otherwise, he would be too far ahead of them, and they would never catch him, and people could die. No, Craig corrected himself, people *would* die.

It turned out that Craig didn't need to worry about finding Sam. Sam found him. As soon as he walked out the back door, he found Sam waiting for him in the garden.

"Figured you would come out this way," Sam said.

Craig stared at his friend whose face was not giving him away, and asked, "Why are you here? Are you here to arrest me or protect me?"

"I heard what happened at the Diner, so I knew I had to find you. Do you want to help or not?"

Craig broke out into a huge smile and bum-rushed his friend with a hug so quickly Sam couldn't stop him.

"Okay," he said, after Craig had released him, "Let's get out of here. We need you to help us figure out what he is going to do next."

Just a few blocks away, Joe laughed to himself. Sometimes he felt just like the wicked witch in Snow White who could look into her mirror and see whatever she wanted to see. In this day and age, it wasn't a mirror. It was a camera. Cameras planted everywhere, including Craig's garden.

So he had lost control of Craig, Joe realized. Well, he thought, two can play this game. When Craig tries to trap me, I will trap him instead. That answered one question for Joe. He was wondering who he could use as bait to catch other people in his web. Craig's friends would do anything for him, including putting themselves at risk. Now all he had to do was set the trap and see how many people fell in.

The only problem was, he wasn't sure that Edward would take the bait. Perhaps he had to use another person to catch Edward, and Joe knew exactly who that person was going to be.

# FORTY FOUR

V alerie woke up with a pounding headache and dreading the day. She wasn't sure which came first, the headache or dreading the day. It was Halloween. Once upon a time, she had looked forward to Halloween and the cute little kids dressed up and pretending to be someone else.

She had a fond memory of being a kid in grade school and wearing the bear costume her mom had made for her. She could still remember what it looked like. Because they had little money, her mother had made the costume out of a few brown terry cloth towels. The inserts of the bear's ear were pink felt.

In school that day she felt so wonderful being a bear and wearing the costume that she wore it to school for the next three days. It didn't stop there. She even wore it every once in a while during the rest of the school year. Thinking back, she wondered how that happened. The teacher had to have been okay with a child showing up dressed as a bear. Her mother must have thought it was okay, and all the kids had gone along with it.

Could that happen today? Probably not.

Instead, there would be rules about when a costume could be worn, and the kids would tease the costumed child so much they would never do it again. Besides, when was the last time she saw a homemade bear costume? she wondered.

The costumes today were slick, shiny, sparkly, store-bought costumes. Not cute animals. Very few bears or bunnies. No ghosts in sheets. Instead, the favorite costumes were superheroes, celebrities, and villains. And they acted that way. It was as if the costumes and masks that made them anonymous permitted them to act out if they wanted to.

Not every child, Valerie thought, as she made her coffee for the day. There were still children who chose to be fairies and princesses, and there were still a few princes and wizards who spread their magic around. Valerie was counting on more of those that day. Maybe even a brown bear would show up in class.

As Valerie popped a few aspirins and packed her lunch, she realized she also had a nagging worry about Hannah and Lex who had decided to go as their favorite fictional detectives. Hannah chose Agatha Christie and Lex decided on Sherlock Holmes. What would the other kids say? If they were laughed at, would they be able to handle it?

Then Valerie laughed at herself. She was worried about Hannah and Lex who had proved over and over again that they were perfectly capable of taking care of themselves. The two people she was really worried about were Dr. Joe and Edward, for two entirely different reasons. She had no idea why she felt so connected to Edward. Perhaps it was just meant to be.

Valerie looked out her front window and laughed again. Speaking of Edward, there he was, ready to drive them off to school. He had already picked up Hannah, and now he was taking her and Lex.

She had no idea why he was doing that. She could have driven, but he offered, and her new response to gifts was to say yes if it felt good. And Edward picking them up felt perfect.

However, she had been a bit worried. Shouldn't he be hiding from Joe? What did Sam say about it?

Edward assured her that all would be fine. He couldn't spend his whole life hiding, and besides Sam and his men were always watching Joe. If he got too close to Edward, they would be there to protect him. Besides, it was just a quick ride to school. What could happen? He was so sure, and she was so delighted to be picked up, she didn't give it any more thought.

After one last look in the mirror, she waved at Hannah from the window as Edward rang the doorbell. Lex clamored down the stairs, dressed as Sherlock Holmes. He looks dashing, Valerie thought. And Hannah looked great with her wig on, and glasses set on her nose. It was going to be a fun ride to school.

• • • • • • • • • •

Sam stared at the results he had in his hand. What he was looking at seemed so impossible that he was sure it was wrong. He wanted it to be wrong. He could ask the lab to rerun the tests, he supposed, but would it make a difference? They would come out the same. He knew the lab hadn't made a mistake.

In fact, he had already asked them to be sure they sent the right results. They were adamant that they were correct, and just a bit insulted that he had doubted them. Of course, they didn't know anything about what the results would mean to his friend, and Sam did. Now he had to make a decision. Should he tell, or should he keep it a secret? Or at least delay telling her.

The problem was, Sam knew that sooner or later he would have to give Valerie the results of what he had found. When he had said yes to doing the test he had no idea what it would lead to. In fact, he assumed it would lead to nothing.

A few weeks before, Valerie had come to him and asked if he would do her a favor. Ava had told her that Sam might be able to run a DNA test for her. Would he? Valerie explained that although Johnny was having their DNA run through one of the commercial programs, all it would tell them was the makeup of their nationality.

Valerie needed more information. She wanted to find out if the man she knew as her father was actually her father. She didn't want everyone to know that she was wondering about that, just Sam and Ava.

Since both of Valerie's parent's had passed away, she had no way to check if the father she knew was her birth father. The only hope she had was that someone in the FBI system was a match to her. It was a long shot, but one Valerie wanted to take. Sam explained that if there was a match it was because somewhere along the way, they had done something to catch their attention. Perhaps she didn't want to know after all?

But she had assured him that she did, so Sam accepted Valerie's request and sent her DNA off to be tested. And now the results were back, and what they showed would be devastating to Valerie.

He didn't want to tell her. If there were a way to hide it from her, he would. But the consequences of not telling were more disastrous than how she would feel when she found out. The timing couldn't be worse. He needed help. Perhaps the women's council could meet, and he could tell all of them at once.

Sarah would know what to do. He'd ask. But it had to be now because he couldn't live with being the only one who knew the results of the test.

And to make matters worse, they had no idea where Dr. Joe was at the moment. Somehow he had slipped away from the people that were watching him. Craig was making a list of all the places that Joe might have gone to, but so far, he was nowhere to be found.

Sam was under no illusions. They were trying to catch up with a madman. This was a nightmare in the making. All of it.

# FORTY FIVE

If Joe were someone with a sense of humor, he would have been laughing. Instead, what passed for a laugh was a smirk. There they were. Together in the same car. And then people wondered if God was on his side. Of course he is, Joe thought. Otherwise, how could this be so easy?

It was perfect. Edward, his useless, good for nothing, traitorous son, was driving Valerie and the two kids to school. It was as if Joe had placed an order with the universe to provide him with the perfect opportunity to take his revenge against Edward and, at the same time, punish the community by taking away that brat, Hannah, too. It couldn't have been more perfect if he had written it out himself.

There was another aspect to the whole scenario that made it even more delicious. It was evident to everyone that Edward had a huge crush on Valerie. So he could hurt Edward even more by hurting Valerie. Before he killed them all, of course. But before that happened, he was going to have some fun.

Add in the bonus that Valerie's death would get back at Craig for betraying him, and it was the best scenario Joe could have devised, and he didn't have to work at it. The thought of Craig's betrayal made Joe furious. He had thought that Craig might turn out to be a friend. Actually, he believed that Craig was his friend. But no, Craig had decided to side with those people instead of sticking with him. Joe knew he didn't have to do anything physical to Craig to make him hurt. Valerie in pain, and then dead, would be enough.

Joe wondered if Valerie, before she died, would regret the day that she married Harold. Would she realize that if she had never met Harold, she might be living happily in some tiny town somewhere? Instead, she had managed to have three men fall in love with her that would make her suffer in the end, because now Joe had her son too. It was going to be so much fun playing with her emotions.

Personally, Joe couldn't see what she had going for her that had caused Harold, Craig, and now Edward to fall for her. But on the other hand, his taste for women had dried up years before. Power was much more seductive.

The trouble was, Joe wasn't quite sure how he was going to make the scenario work so that when it was over, he would be hailed as a savior. Because, after all, his reputation was still his most precious asset. But he trusted that he could come up with something that worked because the opportunity to get them all at one time was just too convenient. It wasn't something he could pass up.

He had to think fast, though. He had to capture them without drawing any attention to what he was doing. Luckily, he had hacked into Emily's phone the year before. Not that at the time he had any plans to do anything with it. At that time, he was the town's beloved doctor, and Emily was merely the woman who had purchased the land on the hill from him.

It was just a habit. If Joe could hack something, he did. In fact, he had hacked Valerie's phone too. It was all about control. He had it when he wanted it. And he wanted it now.

In the middle of the night, Joe had snuck out of his house using the tunnel he had built years before. It ended up outside in the field about one hundred yards from his home. He had a bunker down there too, and that was where he was planning to take the four of them once he got his hands on them. No one knew about either the tunnel or the bunker. The men that had built it for him disappeared right after its completion. Everyone thought they had left town, which they had in a way.

After emerging from the tunnel, its exit hidden within a grove of trees, Joe had taken the back way in the dark into town. He had hidden in the same place that Grant had hidden a few years before, upstairs in the theater where he could watch the village green. Joe figured it was too obvious of a place for them to check, and so far he had been correct. The fact that they hadn't put surveillance in the theater was a sign to Joe that he was right. They were dolts, and he was the genius.

Of course, Sam probably hadn't figured out Joe wasn't home until just recently, so it was a good chance that he would need to move on from this location soon. In the meantime, the theater was the perfect place to scout the town. Lying on his stomach and looking out the small window, he could see the Diner, Your Second Home, and Valerie's house at the same time.

He had been watching Valerie's house when Edward drove up. Joe's original plan was to grab Valerie and use her as bait, but now he had four people. Seriously, he thought, how good can it get?

*Pretty good*, he decided as the four of them piled into the car and headed out of town. Joe waited until Edward had moved away from the traffic circle towards the school before he texted Valerie using Emily's phone number. The text asked Valerie if she would swing by Emily's house to get her. Her car wouldn't start, and she needed to be at the school to help with the Halloween party. Stephen had left much earlier to set up the music, so she was stranded.

Valerie texted back that they would be there in a few minutes, and then Joe counted on what he knew Valerie would do next. She called the school and said they would be a little bit late.

Now Joe had to move fast. He had to stop Edward's car and get to it before anyone else did. So as he texted he ran down the steps to the van he had rented when he first got to town under a different name and had parked behind the theater. He had to time the whole thing perfectly.

He waited until the car was a mile out of town, and then pressed a button that made the car start to stutter and slow down. By that time, Joe was in the van and heading towards Edward's car. Although he had let Valerie's call go through to the school so no one would worry about them, he couldn't allow anyone in the car to make any more calls, so he activated his gadget that stopped signals to their phones.

It wouldn't have mattered whose car Edward would have been driving. His first day in town, Joe had hacked every vehicle in that do-gooder's group that he could find. Edward's car was one of them. Hacking cars was one of those things he learned how to do in the long days by himself in Morocco. He had employed a computer genius who taught him everything and made it so simple to do, a child could do it.

Just a little planning goes a long way, Joe thought as he headed towards Edward's car. Rounding the curve he saw Edward's car parked on the side of the road, hazard lights blinking. They'd be out of it by now, because although the car was not moving, the engine was still running, and his hacking was forcing the carbon monoxide back into the car.

He could have let the gas run long enough to kill them, but what would the fun be in that? He wanted them alive before he killed them himself. He had some experiments to run, and they were the perfect subjects.

# FORTY SIX

Hannah wasn't fooled. But she was the only one in the car who wasn't. Lex was busy playing a game on his phone, Edward was busy driving, and Valerie was busy answering the text that was supposed to be from Emily.

Hannah knew it wasn't. She didn't know what was going on, but she knew it wasn't good. She let Valerie make the phone call to the school, and then she yelled, "Stop the car!"

Edward looked at Hannah in the rearview mirror and said, "What? Why?"

"No, we can't, Hannah," Valerie said. "We have to pick up Emily. We're already going to be late to school."

Lex turned to look at Hannah, who was in the process of removing her wig and glasses, and realized she wasn't kidding. There was something wrong, so he joined her in yelling for them to stop the car.

The two grownups turned around in their seats to say something and then realized that both the children had their costumes off and were deadly serious.

"Look," Hannah said, "Neither of you know me well, but trust me, I know when things are wrong, and something is wrong. I think it's Joe. We have to get out of the car right now. Leif is here too, he says, run. We have to run."

Edward stopped the car in the middle of the road, turned to Valerie and pushed her towards the door. "Go. I'll keep driving and lead him away. Go."

The two children were already out of the car and had opened the passenger door and were pulling Valerie out. Hannah looked at Edward and saw where this would lead. There was nothing she could do to stop it, so instead, she reached across and took his hand and said, "I know you don't see her, but your mother is with you. Don't be afraid."

Edward nodded and, looking at where Valerie and Lex were running, said, "Thank you, Hannah. Take care of them for me."

"I promise," Hannah said, "Now, go, fast!"

Edward gunned the engine and pulled out. He knew it was his father after them. He didn't know what his father planned to do, but there was no way in hell he was going to let him touch Valerie and the children. He needed to get as far away as possible.

He didn't get far before the car started to sputter and then died. He let the car drift off to the side of the road. He would wait for his father and deal with him then. It was his last thought before falling asleep.

The three runners heard the car sputter and stop, and when Edward didn't get out of the car, Valerie fell to her knees and screamed, "No!"

Lex and Hannah pulled her up, pushing her towards the forest. They dragged her until she started running, too. Lex stayed by his mom while Hannah led the way, following Leif, who was showing them the way to safety.

• • • ● • ● • • •

Eric didn't waste any time. While Leif was leading Hannah, Lex, and Valerie to safety, Eric was standing in front of Sam. Sam, who still had trouble seeing the members of the Forest Circle when they came around, had a vague sense that someone was standing in front of him telling him something. But he couldn't make out what it was.

So he yelled at the apparition, whoever it was, to go to Sarah and have her call him. A few seconds later his phone rang. Sarah didn't bother with hello. Instead, she said as calmly as possible, "Edward is in trouble on the road out of town towards Emily's. Valerie, Hannah, and Lex are in the woods but not in danger at the moment.

"I'll call Hank and send him there, too. I'll meet you there."

Before Sam could tell Sarah not to go, she had hung up. Sam realized he would waste precious time trying to stop her when she was going to do exactly what she thought was best. She would find Leif, and he would show her where he was taking the children and Valerie.

Sam needed to get to Edward. He sent an alert out to his men but asked them to stay where they were in case Joe returned. As he was going out the door, he motioned for Craig to join him. Without asking why, Craig ran with Sam to the car. He didn't need to ask. He knew it had to be Joe.

Last spring, Hank had shown Sam the back way to Doveland from the farm. They took the bumpy, unpaved way that dumped them out on the road to Emily's, even so, it was fifteen minutes before they arrived at Edward's car. Hank and Sarah were already there.

Hank had been at breakfast at the Diner when Sarah called. She was on her way there, and she was going to come with him whether he liked it or not. Like Sam, Hank knew not to argue with Sarah when her mind was made up.

Sam squealed to a halt behind Hank's truck, and he and Craig ran to the car. The driver's side door was open, and there was no one inside. They were gone.

"There is no mystery as to what happened here, is there?" Hank asked. "It was Joe. Had to be him.

Barely containing his desire to hit him, Hank turned to Craig. "Why Craig, why didn't you help us before? If you had, we might have been able to catch him last spring. But no," Hank yelled, "you had to stick with Dr. Joe because, hey, he was a doctor and spoke your language. You screwed us, and now your friends and my niece are in danger because of you."

Craig backed up as Hank yelled and headed towards him, but Sam stepped between them. "Stop it, Hank!" Sam said. "This is just what Joe wants. He wants us to fight. He wants to separate us, so we are distracted. He used Craig the same way as he is using your anger now!"

Hank sank to the road and leaned against Edward's car tire with his head in his hands, mumbling, "You're right."

Craig stuck his hand out to help Hank up. "I'm sorry, Hank. I'll do whatever I can to make it up to you. Right now, that's finding Hannah, Lex, Valerie, and then Edward.

"Okay, Craig," Sam said, "You know Joe best. Where is he, then?"

Craig pointed at Sarah, who was staring into the woods. "Maybe Sarah knows?"

Sarah brought herself back from where she had been and said, "No, not yet. I don't know where Edward is, but I do know where Leif took the children and Valerie."

"Great," Hank sighed in relief. "Let's go get them."

"No. I think they are safer where they are right now. First, we need to find Joe. Until then, we don't want to lead him to them."

"He's that aware of what we are doing?" Sam asked.

"Yes," Sarah answered. "He is."

# FORTY SEVEN

J oe was so furious he felt like throwing Edward out onto the
road and running over him, again and again. It was a visual
and kinetic idea that appealed to him. He would be able to feel
the first bump, and then the bump again when he reversed back
over Edward's body. Blood would spurt out. Perhaps he would just
move up Edward's body so that he didn't die right away. Break his
legs, then his hips, then his guts would spill out, and then he would
aim for his head.

He shook himself. As satisfying as killing Edward that way
might be, it would be a short-lived satisfaction, and Joe had long
ago learned how to delay his gratification. That's why he was so
successful. He controlled himself.

Besides, Edward was his son. Even in Joe's demented brain, he
could see that perhaps his reaction to finding only Edward in the
car was a bit over the top for one's son. Even if he was a lazy, no
good betrayer. Even then. Was it his fault that the other three had
deserted him, run away, and left Edward to face his father alone?
Perhaps not.

Joe looked back into the van where Edward lay unconscious on
the floor where Joe had tossed him. It hadn't been easy. He had to

lever Edward out of the car, stick Edward's head into the van, and then flip him the rest of the way into the van by throwing Edward's legs to the side and sliding him in. The slide hadn't done much for Edward's face, or the van, which now had a pool of blood in it.

Thinking about the need to torch the van now that Edward had bled all over it, pissed Joe off even more. It amazed him. All these years of maintaining an even keel temperament, and now he was losing it over a little blood.

No, Joe thought. He was losing it over Edward, and he had to stop it right now. First, he had to decide if he was going to hide Edward before finding the three runaways. He couldn't believe it when he got to the car, and they were gone. How had they known? This was the kind of thing that made them so dangerous.

It was why he had sent Grant after them years before. They knew too much. They saw and understood things they shouldn't be able to. They could even be in two places at once. How could anyone control someone like that? They had to be eliminated. Women, children, all of them.

And that's when Joe got the idea he had been waiting for. Why not go where they least expected him to go? Take Edward there, get them all in one place, and then he could rush in and save one of them from the fire he had set. No one would know it was him, and he would be a hero again, because whoever he rescued would not survive after all. No one would be the wiser. Maybe he would come back to Doveland after all and be a doctor again. Who knew? All possibilities were open.

# FORTY EIGHT

E dward woke up knowing exactly where he was. His was in his father's bunker. He had been there only once before. It was when he was just ten years old, right before his mother's death. At the time, his father still believed that Edward would follow in his footsteps, and showing him the bunker was his way of telling him that he had all their futures well planned out. They would be safe no matter what.

It had been exciting. Edward hadn't yet fully accepted what a monster his father was, so the bunker was an adventure. They had spent the afternoon together. Father and son. Edward explored while his father worked on some papers he pulled out of an old filing cabinet.

His mother hadn't come with them. Now Edward thought it was because it gave her time to hide away some of the proof he would need someday. Or perhaps Joe didn't want her to know about it.

Later, when he had told her about the papers, his father had been working on, she became excited. She asked him question after question about what he had seen, but he was no help at all. He had been too busy looking into all the corners of the bunker to see if he could find hidden treasure.

Maybe I did suspect my father at that time, Edward thought. Why else would I have been looking for secret hiding places? Why else had he hidden his favorite pocket knife behind the filing cabinet? Why else had he done it in a way so that his father couldn't see?

A faint glimmer of hope sparked in Edward. Perhaps that knife was still there. However, even if it was, how could he get to it? At the moment, it seemed impossible. His hands were bound together behind his back with what felt like a zip-tie. When he tried to move, he only got a few feet away from the wall before being jerked back. If he turned, he could barely make out a large hook jutting out from the wall with a chain hooked to whatever was binding his wrists.

The pain on the side of his face told him that the blood he saw on the floor was probably coming from him. Although his feet were free, he was far enough from everything that he couldn't touch anything with them. He tried kneeling, but was so dizzy he toppled over again, back into the pool of blood. Which is where his father found him, his eyes closed, pretending to be still asleep from whatever had been piped into the car.

Joe sat down in his chair and looked at his son lying in the bunker. He didn't think he was still asleep, but he was doing an excellent job of making it look real. This was so different from the last time Edward had been in the bunker. He had been just a kid, enjoying his father's secret hideout. Innocent, still malleable.

Joe had been so close to having the son he really wanted, and then May had come along and spoiled it. He bit his tongue, thinking how much he had grown to hate her over the years. It was especially amazing since he had once worshiped her. May had ruined everything, and now here he was with a son who would kill him if he could. Which wasn't going to happen, because Joe had other plans. Much better ones than dying.

Joe set a bowl of water by Edward and said, "When you stop pretending to be asleep, here's some water for you. I haven't drugged it because I need you wide awake for what is going to happen next. Sorry about your hands. Guess you will have to lap it up just like your favorite cat when you were little. Remember her?

After Joe left, Edward remained where he was, weeping. He had made himself forget about his cat. The end had been so horrible he hadn't wanted to remember even the good parts of having her. But now it came flooding back. His cat, who loved him unconditionally, slept on his bed at night, and snuggled under his arm when he wasn't feeling well. Just a house cat, orange, fluffy, soft, and peaceful. Of course, he named her, Fluffy. He and his mom had laughed at the name because it was so perfect for her.

His father had ignored Fluffy until one day when Edward had done something Joe hadn't liked. Edward couldn't even remember what it had been. He only remembered that it was after his mom had died and his father pretended to like him. Everything Edward did either pissed Joe off, which meant he would react violently, or else he ignored Edward completely. The ignoring part worked well. Edward could keep the secret his mom had passed on to him without worrying about his father noticing.

But when Joe was angry, there was nothing to stop him from doing something that would hurt his son. It was a cold rage. Calculating. Joe enjoyed deciding what was the worst thing he could do to punish Edward. So that day, he locked Fluffy into a closet with one bowl of water and nothing else, and then hid the key. For days Edward could hear her meowing, clawing at the door, until there was nothing but quiet, which was even worse.

It was weeks before the door was opened again, just so that Edward could see his dead friend lying there. Yes, he remembered his cat, and there was no way that he was going to end up like her. He would escape. He was smarter than his father thought he was, and besides, perhaps his knife was still there. His father would never leave him in the bunker to die. He loved his bunker. He wouldn't want a dead body in it. No, he would move him somewhere else to die, and that would be his opportunity, knife or no knife.

He had to be ready. That meant he had to drink the water. As he did, he promised Fluffy he would honor her by living. For a moment, he thought he felt her tongue licking his cheek, but decided it was a result of exhaustion. Time to really sleep.

# FORTY NINE

"Where are they?" Ava screamed at Sam. "I thought you were keeping us safe! How could you let this happen?"

Sam let her scream, and even stood still as she beat her fists into his chest, shaking his head at Evan who tried to stop her. He waited patiently until she collapsed crying into his arms.

Bending down he whispered, "They're safe, and we'll get them back when this is all over."

Ava leaned back and looked up into his honest face and clear dark blue eyes and knew he spoke the truth. She stepped back into Evan's waiting arms while whispering, "I'm sorry, Sam."

"Nothing to be sorry about, Ava." Turning to everyone gathered there he added, "It's me that should be sorry. We had Joe under surveillance, and then he simply disappeared. Leif has assured Sarah that he has Valerie, Hannah, and Lex somewhere safe and he is staying with them until this is resolved. He doesn't want us to know where they are. It's just as a precaution in case Joe has the ability to read minds."

When everyone gasped, he added, "We can't put that past him, can we? After all, how many of you do that already? Perhaps he has learned, or maybe it's just that he has the whole town bugged and wired, so he knows everything that is going on. We can't take the chance.

"In the meantime, we need to find Joe and Edward. We know Joe well enough to know that he has something else planned other than just capturing Edward. He is probably furious that he didn't get all four of them, so perhaps that fury will cloud his thinking."

The group listening to Sam sat quietly, taking in what he was saying, holding hands, intent on being willing and ready to act. Only Craig was moving, energy sparking all over, walking back and forth behind them as they sat in Evan's living room.

"For God's sake, sit down man," Pete said. "Or at least stand still more often. You aren't helping by doing that."

Craig stopped pacing and said through gritted teeth, "Well, nothing I do is helping. I messed up big time, and now I have to do something."

Pete pushed himself out of his seat and crossed the room to where Craig was standing, hands clenched at his side, tears pouring down his face. He put his hands on Craig's shoulders and said, "You can't do this, Craig. You can't indulge this guilt because we need your clear thinking. After this is all over, you can wallow in it for a while if it helps, but right now, you can't afford this kind of emotion. We need your ideas, not your fury."

Pete put his arm around Craig's shoulder and walked him over to sit on the couch beside his wife, Barbara. She helped ease him down and then took Craig's hand in hers and held it. Pete sat on the other side of her and said, "Okay. No one is at fault here. Everyone has done their best. Now, let's step up our game, find them, and stop Joe in the process."

"Amen to that," Tom added. "Any ideas? How did Joe get away? Perhaps it is the same place he is hiding Edward."

"It probably is," Sam answered. "But it won't be where he sets the trap. He is going to let us know where Edward is so that we will think that we can rescue him. But we aren't going to fall for that."

"We're not going to rescue Edward?" Mandy said. "We can't leave him to die at his father's hands! How will we all feel? How will Valerie feel if we don't rescue him? She has obviously fallen for him."

Craig took a huge shuddering breath, and Mandy added, "I'm sorry, Craig, we know how you feel about her."

He shook his head. "Once again, my fault."

"Damn it," Sam muttered.

Everyone turned to look at him as he sat down on the nearest chair. Once again, wishing that he wasn't always the one in charge. Perhaps someone else could do all the dirty work from now on.

"Okay, Sam, out with it," Mira demanded. "We can deal with whatever is going on."

"I'm not all that worried about you all dealing with it. I am more worried about how Valerie and Edward are going to feel."

When no one moved, he sighed and told them about Valerie's request to run her DNA against any matches in the system.

Ava stepped in and said, "Yes, Valerie has always felt that the man she called her father wasn't the man who made her mother pregnant. She was taking a chance, thinking that she would find out something if Sam had the test done for her.

"So, did you find out something, Sam?"

"For better or worse, I found out that Valerie was right. He wasn't her birth father."

"Okay, so what? That's what she thought anyway," Mira said. Then she paused and added, "So what does this have to do with Edward?"

Hank was the one who picked up where Sam was going and asked, "Was Valerie's mother ever in Doveland?"

Sam looked at Hank and nodded. "Apparently. We don't know all the details yet. I had them go back and search through the records of the women who lived in the commune. We know a few were there and left before Joe started killing them off. It's possible that is where he met her."

"What?" Mandy screamed. "What? Joe's Valerie's father?"

When Sam nodded yes, Mandy asked, "Does Valerie know?"

"I just found out this morning, and then all this happened. None of them know, including Joe."

· • • ●·●•· ·

Joe hated it when they all assembled at Evan's house. That place was a fortress. He had tried countless times to bug it, but failed every time. Years before, Hank had bugged it for Grant. That was before Hank had discovered that Ava was his niece, after which he had turned his life away from Grant and evil doings. Since then, there had been no opportunity. They had learned their lesson.

Now, Evan and Ava screened everyone who came in the door. They regularly monitored their electronic equipment and used equipment to sweep the house and everything on the property for any kind of surveillance. They had installed their own security, which Joe was hoping was a weak link, but that hadn't worked either. It was Evan who learned how to keep it all free of hacking. He had become an expert so that he didn't need to hire anyone, so then they wouldn't have to worry about trusting someone else.

That's why they always congregated there. It was safe. Joe would never be able to reach them while they were in the house. He had to draw them out somehow. He had to get them somewhere that he was in charge and where they least expected him to be. Joe had to make them think he had made a mistake. Edward would be the bait. They would be assuming that, but would they be expecting how he would use him?

His original plan was to set fire to the house and burn them all up in it, maybe raising the alarm in time for Joe to pretend to save one of them. But that didn't seem like it was going to be possible. It would take too much advance planning. He probably should have set up this particular scenario a long time ago, but since he didn't, he wasn't going to waste any energy beating himself up over it.

But his lack of planning meant that he was going to have to sacrifice something in order to be safe himself. Perhaps his reputation would suffer, but did he want to be dead with an excellent reputation or be happily alive without it?

It was not going to be an easy decision. And Joe would not be able to kill them all. But if he planned it correctly, some of them would die, and he would be free.

# FIFTY

"Wake up, wake up," Edward opened his eyes out of his dream where someone was saying "wake up" over and over again. The trouble was even when he was sure he was awake, at least his eyes were open, he could still hear the voice.

He would have pinched himself to see if he felt anything, but he already hurt all over, and he didn't think that he would be feeling that much pain if he was dreaming. He was still lying on the cold bunker floor. But somehow in his sleep, he had turned so that he was no longer lying with the hurt side of his face in the blood on the floor.

His logical mind thought that was a good thing because he probably would have been stuck there. He used his legs to push on the floor to help him sit up, and then he scooted around so he could sit up against the wall with his legs straight out in front of him.

"Okay," he said aloud to no one but himself, "I'm awake now."

A voice nearby said, "About time. I was going to have to figure out how to move something to poke you if you didn't wake up soon. And I don't think that's possible, so you saved me the trouble of trying."

At the sound of the voice, Edward was so startled he banged the back of his head on the wall, and said, "Ow!"

"That's it? That's all you have to say? A voice, out of nowhere, speaking to you and all you can say is 'Ow?' Can you see me at all?"

Edward shook his head no, slowly because every movement hurt. "Are you real? Or am I hallucinating? Which means if you tell me that you are real, I could still be hallucinating. Good God, I don't know what to think."

"I'm real, and you know me. Pretend that you can see me. Maybe that will work."

"Hannah?" Edward asked.

"See, told you that you know me. I'm not here. I'm projecting myself to you. I don't know where you are though, so I can't tell anyone so they can rescue you. Do you know?"

"Hannah? Are you doing this? How do I know it's not my father making me believe one of his illusions?"

"Wait," Hannah said. "That's an excellent question. Let me ask Leif. Maybe he can tell you."

'Good God, Leif? Who is Leif? People keep talking about him, but I've never seen him. Hannah, are you there?"

"Yes, she's still here," Leif said. "You know that I'm Sarah's husband. I don't live here, though, which is why you can't see me."

"What do you mean, you don't live here? Of course, you don't live here. This bunker would be a terrible place to live. Wait, are you two on a phone line somewhere, and that's how this is happening. Who answered the phone?"

"Well, that's not a bad analogy, but no. We're not on the phone." Leif answered. "We don't have much time, so you will have to wait for the explanation. As for whether or not it's your father talking to you, did he know where you were until you showed up in Doveland?"

"No. Otherwise, Joe would have come after me."

"I do. You were in Oregon. Do you want me to waste time by telling you everything you did that last day? Or maybe about the little girl in the restaurant that gave you the idea to use a fake name?"

"No, no. I believe you, not that I understand, but I believe that you aren't him. So get me out of here."

"Well, that's the plan, Edward, but first we need to know where you are, and second, you need to get out of the zip-tie and get the knife."

"The knife? How do you know about the knife? Okay, never mind. Don't tell me how you know. But if I could get out, I would have already."

"You can do it. I'm going to ask you to relax and sink into the silence. Once you are there, I will ask you to feel all the energy available to you, and already part of you, storing up inside of your body, and when you are ready and can feel it all stored up, release it outward."

"That's going to work? Are you serious?"

"Come on Edward. You know it will work. Even if you don't know that it will, imagine that it will. Get yourself into that possibility. You are not going to use human willpower, or force. You are going to sink into the Infinite One. This is not manipulation. This is an expression of the Infinite setting you free. That's different. Can you feel the difference?"

Edward nodded. He had lived with his father long enough to know that what you believed to be possible was what you experienced. He had only thought of it as a negative force though. Watching his father kill and manipulate people and situations had skewed the way he saw things.

"Okay, Edward. Hannah and I are with you, and I'll lead you into it. Ready to go there?"

Edward closed his eyes in answer. With all his heart, he wanted to feel the difference between what his father did and what Leif was talking about. If it set him free, that would be a byproduct, because what he wanted most of all was to be free from seeing the world the way his father saw it.

He forgot all about why he was listening. He let himself sink into the wave of Love that Leif was talking about, a light that never faded, that was always with him. He allowed it to fill him up, and when Leif said, "Let it go," he did.

Edward had expected to feel the pop of the zip-tie, to have numb arms, to feel pain from where the zip-tie had rubbed into his wrist. None of that happened. There was no burst of light. There was simply freedom. His hands were free, and his face wasn't burning anymore.

"That was amazing," he whispered.

"It is amazing. Thank you for letting go. Now, could you get your knife? We don't expect you to need it, but if you do, it will be handy. Your father is coming, so be ready."

"Ready? Ready? Ready for what? Wait, you're leaving me here? Don't you need to know where I am?" While Edward was speaking, he crawled over to the file cabinet and reached behind it. His hand was much smaller when he had put it there before, but he kept pushing until the cabinet moved enough to get his fingers on the knife. He pulled it out and put it into his pocket and then scooted back to where Joe had left him.

"It's okay, Edward," he heard Hannah whisper in his ear. "We figured it out, and now we'll tell Sam. Go ahead with Joe's plan. We are binding your wrists again. Well, actually, we are just asking the ties to go back in time, so you will be bound again when Joe comes in.

"So put your hands behind your back for us, please. When it's the right time, do what Leif taught you or use the knife to get yourself free."

"Will you stay with me?" Edward asked, not even bothering to ask how zip-ties could go back in time without everything else doing it too. Then for a moment, he understood. He could go back in time in one computer program without affecting other programs, or the computer. Like rewriting.

"Oh," Hannah said, "That's a good analogy. And yes, I will. Leif is already gone to talk to Sam. Lex, Valerie, and I are safely away from Joe. Oh, and Valerie says she's okay, and can't wait to see you again."

Edward whispered, "Thank you," just as the tie snapped again around his wrist, the door opened, and the monster he had called, "Father," walked in with a grin on his face.

# FIFTY ONE

S am, like everyone else, had spent the night at Evan and Ava's house. No one had really slept, but instead watched and waited for information. No one had any idea where Edward had been taken, so when Eric showed him the location, Sam didn't waste any time. He sent a coded message to his team that was watching the house to wait for movement back in the field about 100 yards.

He told them that once Joe and Edward emerged from the tunnel, he wanted his men to stop them if it was safe for Edward. If not, follow them until it was. He didn't have to tell them to make sure they weren't seen, but he did it anyway.

He hoped he had trained them well enough that they would remember to continually pull their energy back so that they weren't projecting to anyone listening or watching for their energy signals. But the technique was new to them, and they might forget in the heat of the moment.

Detecting projected energy worked much the same way as thermal imaging devices worked. However, someone who knew how to feel for projected energy didn't need a tool. It was a skill that could be learned, and Sam was sure that Joe knew how.

Sam wanted his men to hide in plain sight using the absence of projection of energy in a way that would create an illusion that they weren't there. It always made him think of Ben Obi-Wan Kenobi telling the stormtroopers in the first Star Wars movie, "These aren't the droids you're looking for," or the penguin in the movie Madagascar saying, "You didn't see anything."

Sam was sure that was what Leif had done with Valerie and the two children. He had hidden them in plain sight.

After contacting his men, Sam stopped in Ava's kitchen to get a cup of coffee, and glanced outside where he saw Emily standing all alone on the back patio. Taking his coffee with him, he stepped up beside her and together they watched the last of the autumn leaves twirling on the trees at the edge of the woods.

"Will things ever feel safe again to me, Sam?" Emily asked.

"When did things feel safe before?"

"I suppose when I was little, and it was just mom and me. But even then, I was afraid. However, it wasn't because I thought there were evil people in the world who did terrible things because they wanted to, or thought it was fun, or to prove themselves. I was afraid of spiders, or maybe a monster that lived in the closet."

Emily paused, thinking, "I suppose it's still the same. Evil masquerading as people who hide in closets or out in the open. There have always been people who have convinced others to follow them into doing horrible things."

"Yes," Sam responded, "And there have always been people who have stood for the power of good, and that light they wield will sooner or later destroy the darkness in whatever form it takes."

"If I hadn't come looking for my Aunt Jean, or decided to build an art retreat out on that hill, then those bodies might never have been discovered. Would that have been better, do you think?"

Sam turned to look at Emily and took both her hands in his. "Emily, sooner or later, doesn't matter. It happened. And because you came to town, there is more laughter and joy than there was before. That's what matters."

"Thank you, Sam," Emily said, smiling up at him. "And thank you for being here to help us."

At that moment, Sam's phone pinged. He looked down at the text on his phone and turned white.

"What is it?" Emily asked.

"They lost them again! They saw Joe and Edward come out of the field. When my men started moving towards them, they were startled by two deer. When they looked again, Joe and Edward were both gone."

"Oh, no," Emily whispered. "Now what?"

"I have no idea," Sam answered. "We'll have to start looking everywhere. How could they have disappeared?"

"Maybe Joe made your men think they saw two deer, and it was really Joe and Edward?"

"That is so possible it's terrifying. If Joe can do that, how are we ever going to win? He can be anywhere, be anything, make us see things that aren't there, and not see things that are."

Just as Emily reached out to pat Sam's arm, the back door opened and Hank yelled, "Hey, you two, we could use your help in here."

Rushing inside, Sam and Emily found the men huddled around the dining room table. Craig had a paper map of the area laid out on the table and had placed a marker on the lake.

"You think he is going to the lake?" Sam asked Craig.

"Well, it was a thought."

"Why? Why the lake?" Emily asked.

"Because it would make sense to Joe. He likes to manipulate emotions. The lake is where he had Harold take the first four women to be buried. It's where he used to take Edward and his mother for outings. They would go out on the lake together and fish. And it was where May and Edward hid the documents that

Edward eventually brought to us. It has a lot of emotional value to Edward, and in a strange way to Joe. He might think that it would be a nice completed circle to kill and bury Edward there."

"Okay," Hank said. "But why would he go someplace so obvious. Wouldn't he be more subtle?"

"Not if he wanted you to come after him," Craig answered. "But your point is well taken. If he is letting us know where he is taking Edward, he must be planning something else, somewhere else."

"Okay, we split up," Sam said. "Some of us stay here, and some of us go to the lake. The women and children will be safe here."

"No," Hank said.

"No what?" Sam demanded.

"No to all of that. No splitting up. No leaving the women and children here. That's just what he wants. We don't have to run around like that. You have men that can watch the lake, and search other places. And most of all, we don't leave the women and children by themselves!

"Right, Sarah?" Hank said, turning to look in the living room where Sarah and the women's council were sitting together in a circle.

Sarah stood up from where she was sitting on the floor and said, "Exactly right, Hank.

"We all stay here. Let's see what Joe does when no one comes after him. In fact, if it were my call I would say that you should send all your men home."

"What?" Sam yelled, and then seeing Mira's face he calmed down and asked more politely. "You don't really mean, send all the men home, do you?"

"Well, actually, I do. But that goes so much against your grain, why not just send all your men back to the barn, and ask them to wait for you there. Make sure you do this on a channel and in such a way that you know Joe will be listening."

Sam smiled at Sarah, seeing exactly what she was doing. Or at least he had a reasonably good idea of what she was doing. "Will do, my lady," he laughed and so did Sarah, as they mock bowed to each other.

"Wait," Emily said, "What about Edward?

"Don't worry, dear," Grace replied. "My Eric will find Edward. He'll be fine. Or at least, he will be fine in the long run."

The men all looked at each other and shook their heads, and the women turned back to their coffee and pastries that Mandy had brought with her. They looked like they were having a grand time together laughing and joking with each other.

Sarah took out her phone and snapped a picture of them all enjoying themselves, and then uploaded it to her Facebook page. Once that was done, all the women stood, put their coffee cups down, and joined the men around the dining room table.

"Okay, Sarah said, "Now that we have taken the attention away from Joe, we can get on with finding Edward."

# FIFTY TWO

Joe couldn't believe what he was looking at. He expected to see a plea for help to find Edward, Valerie, and the children on Sarah's Facebook page. Instead, Sarah had just posted a picture of a group of laughing women having coffee and pastries together, as if they didn't have a care in the world. That witch Sarah was at it again. Did she have them all fooled? Didn't they know that Edward was in danger, and for all they knew, so was Valerie and the children?

On the other hand, Joe knew perfectly well that Sarah knew what was going on, so she had to be teasing him. Taunting him. Telling him they didn't care.

Well, he would see about that! He looked over at Edward sitting painfully against the wall, looking drained and dejected. He would post a picture of that on Facebook if he could, but he restrained himself. That was an excellent way to get caught before he had done any real damage, and before he got himself out of town on the way to freedom.

He had felt Sam's men waiting for them as soon as they stepped out into the field. Instead of continuing, Joe had pulled Edward back down, and they returned to the bunker. Now that Sam's team thought he and Edward had left the bunker, he just had to wait until they went elsewhere to look for him before the two of them could move on. It wouldn't be long.

The scanner he used to listen to messages from Sam to his team squawked, so he turned the sound up so both he and Edward could hear. He was expecting worry, but instead, he heard Sam tell all his agents to go home. "You have got to be kidding," Joe yelled at both the phone and the scanner. In the corner of the bunker, Edward had no idea what was happening. However, when Edward heard Sam tell all the agents to go home, he had a moment of pure panic. They were abandoning him. It couldn't be happening.

Then he realized that was true. It couldn't be happening. They were playing some kind of game with Joe. Even if Joe didn't believe what they were posting or saying, they apparently didn't care. Sam and Sarah were trying to disrupt and distract Joe, and it was working.

They were making Joe doubt what he was seeing and hearing. They were doing to him the same things he did to others. It was new to Joe because no one had attempted this kind of mental game on him before.

Without moving a muscle for his father to see, Edward smiled to himself. Edward knew that it was his new friends in action. It was something he had never experienced before—a community working together for each other, and now for him.

As he watched his father bluster, rage, and not know what to do, Edward had an epiphany of sorts. Joe wasn't powerful at all. He was a corrupt little man who needed attention. Take the attention away, and Joe had nothing to work with. Nothing to manipulate, Nothing to fight again. No one to test his power over.

Yes, Edward thought, my friends have realized that they can turn the tables on Joe. So far it was working. He could play along with it too. Edward turned his face to the wall, closed his eyes, and relaxed into as close to sleep as he could get.

· · · ●· ●· ● · · ·

After clamoring out of the car and running into the woods beside the road, Valerie, Lex, and Hannah had hidden in a clump of trees. Actually, Hannah had them climb the trees. None of them thought Joe would come running into the woods after them, but it didn't hurt to take the extra precaution.

Valerie hadn't climbed a tree in years, but Hannah had found one where the first limb was fairly close to the ground, and she and Lex had boosted Valerie up onto it. After that, Valerie's childhood memories kicked in, and she quickly scrambled up the tree and found a reasonably comfortable place to sit. If Valerie hadn't been so terrified for Edward, she would have enjoyed the experience.

The first hour in the tree, Valerie remained worried for all of them, even though Hannah kept telling her that Leif was there with them, and he would let her know if they needed to move. Valerie finally realized that there was nothing she could do other than try to relax. Once she did, all the birds returned to their regular routine, and she had a delightful time watching their antics.

A few hours later, Leif told Hannah they could come down and start walking towards town. He said that he would lead the way because they would be walking the back way through the woods. Once they got to town, given that it was Halloween, there would be many people walking around, so it would be relatively easy to go unnoticed. They would be just two kids out Trick-Or-Treating with a parent. Totally normal.

The five-minute car ride was an hour's walk back to town. Leif hadn't been kidding about taking the back way. A few blocks from Doveland, he asked them to wait until they saw the

Trick-Or-Treaters come out. Once they did, he still had them walk through back alleys until they were back at Valerie's home.

And that is where they had stayed. Not in the regular part of the house, but in the new construction in the back, where Mandy's design studio was being built. They kept the lights out and whispered so no one would know they were there. Hannah and Lex began to think of it more as an adventure, and Valerie encouraged their mood.

She had snuck into the main part of her home and brought back blankets, pillows, and food from the refrigerator. They even had a bathroom. If they hadn't been hiding out, it would have been fun. Even though they were worried about Edward with Dr. Joe, they found a way to enjoy it. As Lex said, it was a funny kind of sleep-over.

Hannah thought it was brilliant of Leif to have them hide in plain sight. And because they were in the house peeking out the window late the next morning, they saw what Joe did next. It wasn't that unexpected, but no one would have guessed what he was planning if Lex and Hannah hadn't seen it for themselves.

# FIFTY THREE

*Well, I am not as unprepared as I thought,* Joe said to himself as he loaded the supplies into the boat. At this point, he wasn't trying to hide. Joe didn't mind being seen at the water's edge. In fact, it might help with the trap, so he allowed himself to make a little noise. He was still angry about being ignored, but it was a cold, controlled anger now. He was going to make them pay attention if it was the last thing he did.

That thought made Joe laugh out loud. There was no way this was going to be the last thing he did. He still had a few more things to do in town to pay them all back for taking his life away. Then he would leave.

Joe had heard that the best revenge was living a good life. Well, he was going to have both. The cold-hearted, destructive revenge and the good life which he was planning to deprive a few other people of first. Starting with Edward, of course.

The trick was going to be making sure it still looked as if he and Edward were heading out to the middle of the lake when they weren't.

Instead, Edward was still locked in the car, sleeping. After they had made it out of the bunker and into a vehicle Joe had kept in another garage a few blocks away from his house, Joe had injected Edward with enough drugs to keep him sedated while he made plans for the two of them.

Joe hefted the dummy that he had dressed in Edward's clothes into the boat and secured him with a rope tied around his waist onto the seat. Next, he tied the hands to the side and allowed the fake Edward to drape over and rest his head on the edge of the boat. The hat Joe had put on its head was glued on so it wouldn't fall off. It very effectively hid the dummy's face. No one would think it strange that Edward was sedated and couldn't sit up straight. They would investigate, and when they got close enough, kaboom.

It didn't matter who came looking. Joe was looking for a quantity of dead bodies, not quality. Once they had discovered this decoy, he would set another, using the real live Edward this time. Of course, that meant he was going to have to wake him up to make it work, but first, he had to set this trap.

Initially, Joe was going to get into the boat and raise a body dressed like himself to sit with the fake Edward, and then he was going to slip off into the water and swim back to shore. Then he decided that was too risky. He wasn't as strong a swimmer as he used to be, and besides, he wasn't sure how many of Sam's men were waiting on the shore for him to do something stupid. He suspected that although Sam had asked his men to pull back, they probably hadn't.

He couldn't keep himself invisible to them for long, and definitely not when he was wet. But he still had to have it look as if he was in the boat, so Joe did the same thing to the body that was dressed like him that he did to the dummy taking the place of Edward.

The rescue team was going to have fun piecing together the parts of the body he had stolen from the university research lab years before. Once again, it was excellent advance planning on his part. Joe had been keeping the body in the bunker's freezer waiting for a moment like this. Body parts, that they would assume were Joe's, would be scattered all over the lake. The rescue team would think he was dead.

However, the false identity wouldn't hold up for long. Tests would show that the body wasn't his, primarily because they would discover the frozen stiff parts. But that didn't matter. He just needed a few hours of stolen time. A time when they thought he was dead and then perhaps let their guard down long enough to be disoriented when he set the next trap.

He was hunting. *Yes,* Joe said to himself, *I am hunting.* Taking out the vermin. Joe pulled the cord of the onboard engine and pushed the boat out towards the middle of the lake. He had fished this lake enough to know that when the quarter gallon of gas he had put in to get the motor started was gone, and the engine quit, the boat would drift to the center of the lake and sit there.

As he pushed the boat into the water, he reached down and set the bomb. Once someone tried to board the boat, it would go off and take out anyone within the radius of the lake. *Poor fish,* Joe thought. *Oh well, sacrifices must be made.*

Once the boat was off, he made his way back to the car. He had parked it on an incline, so he didn't need to turn on the engine to drift back to the road. He expected Sam's team to think it might be a trap. So what? They would still investigate, and the bomb would still detonate.

Once the car reached the road, Joe headed back to town without looking around. Even if he were followed, it wouldn't matter. In fact, it might be a good thing. He had a plan on how to lose anyone following him, and when he disappeared again, it would add to his mystique.

Besides, how could he be in two places at once? If they began to wonder how he was doing things that seemed impossible, it made them more vulnerable and him more powerful.

He looked in his rear-view mirror and checked to see how Edward was doing. Joe smiled. His son looked pretty good. Edward was still lying on the back seat, entirely out of it. He even looked a bit peaceful. Soon Edward would be at peace for eternity. If there was such a thing.

Despite being furious with Edward for betraying him, Joe could see how Edward thought he was doing the right thing. If there were a God, which Joe fully expected that there wasn't, then Edward would be rewarded.

*On the other hand, will I?* Joe wondered. *In the beginning, I did all of what I did for the good of humanity. Now. Not so much.* Everything that Joe was doing now was strictly for his own pleasure. Rationally, that would mean he would not be at peace when he died. The thought flew through Joe's brain, taking up a second of time before he dismissed it.

*There is no God, and there is only now,* Joe thought to himself. And he deserved all the pleasure he could get right now, since there would be no later. After all, he had dedicated his life to serving his fellow man, and what did it get him? Hunted and hated. No, he was going to serve himself from now on.

Through the police scanner in his car, Joe heard about the boat drifting in the middle of the lake with what looked like Edward and Joe. Since there were only a few police officers in town, Joe knew it would be Sam's men who responded.

Joe smiled and laughed out loud. Yes, the pleasure had begun!

# FIFTY FOUR

At the Anders' home, the news about the boat in the lake with what looked like Joe and Edward onboard came as no surprise. Once the team that had been watching the lake reported on what they had seen, Sam alerted Doveland's Chief of Police, Daniel (Dan) Winters, and asked him to meet them at the house.

It was a small police force, and Dan had worked with Sam and the Stone Circle before, so he agreed to come in his private car, and not to tell anyone where he was going. He arrived in street clothes, wearing his baseball hat on backward, and his checkered shirt hanging out of his pants with a french tuck. Mandy, who noticed such things, wondered where Dan had learned such a thing, but it wasn't the time to ask.

After discussing the situation, and at Sam's direction, Dan sent out the notice about the boat over the police frequency to the two other men on the force and asked them to check out a report of a boat drifting in the lake. They weren't to do anything. Just look and report back. Dan and everyone present at Evan and Ava's knew Joe was listening, so Dan made sure to make the announcement very low key, almost lazy.

However, immediately after that, private messages were sent to the two men on the police force and to Sam's team. They were to do nothing about the boat on the lake. Sam was confident that neither Edward nor Joe were in the boat. And even if they were, it was obviously a trap. At the minimum, it was a trick to throw them off base, and at the worst, it was dangerous.

However, Dan wasn't so sure. Like most of the people in Doveland under fifty, Dan's doctor was Dr. Joe. Joe had delivered him and then taken care of him and his family his whole life. It was hard to wrap his thought around the fact that Joe was responsible for all the deaths on the hill. Let alone all the other deaths Sam assured him Joe carried out.

Still, it was obvious that Joe had Edward as a hostage, well as obvious as a father trying to hurt his son could possibly be. Dan was a family man. He couldn't imagine hurting his child. But he knew if even a small percentage of what they had discovered was true about Joe, then he wasn't really a family man at all.

Dan knew he couldn't let his emotions get in the way, but still, he worried. What if it really was them in the boat? What if Joe killed Edward while he did nothing? How would he be able to live with himself? Dan was trained to check things out, and that is what he wanted to do. Dan asked Sam for permission to go for a look. Dan said that he and his men would be careful.

However, Sam asked Dan to wait. Instead of sending someone to check out the boat, they would send a drone, while they quietly watched for what else Joe would do.

It was only because Sam had been right before about how to capture Grant and his second in command Lenny, that Dan agreed. If Grant had been trained by Joe, as Sam had told him he was, then it was all the more likely Joe would be even better at tricking them than Grant had been. The thought of that was terrifying, which is why he agreed to hold off from what his training wanted him to do.

It was only an hour later that Leif contacted Sam and everyone else still gathered at the house and told them what the children had seen. Ava and Evan had a moment of panic thinking that Joe might have seen the kids, but Hannah was positive that Joe hadn't known that they were watching.

It was the first break they had where they were ahead of Joe, instead of following him. And they were going to make full use of it. Hannah and Leif would be watching over Edward and report back what they saw to Sam. With that kind of Intel, they hoped to deliver Joe right into Sam's team's hands.

Leif also assured them that neither Edward nor Joe were in the boat, so no need for a drone. But a bomb was, so he asked them to keep the men away and not even try to disarm the bomb. The plan of making Joe think no one cared about him or his plan was in full motion. When the bomb didn't go off, and there was no activity at the lake, Joe would be confused.

Sam's team had strung up yellow, no-access ribbons across all the roads leading to the lake and were on the watch for anyone that might sneak through and be in harm's way.

Sam kept reminding his team that a fire burned because there was oxygen. Joe was like a fire. He needed attention in any form to thrive, maybe to survive. In effect, they were taking the oxygen out of the room by not giving in to any of Joe's threats, implied or direct. They wouldn't notice or care.

At least that was the message that they would send. Joe would feel ignored, while the exact opposite would be going on. Sam reminded his team again about not projecting their energy. There was no need to tell the Stone Circle and their friends. They already knew the why and the how.

# FIFTY FIVE

J oe couldn't believe the town. Where was everyone? Neither the Diner nor Your Second Home was open. He couldn't read the signs from where he was, but he assumed that they said they were closed due to a family emergency. Plus, the schools were closed, and all the children were home with their parents.

"Cowards," Joe wanted to yell at all of them. "Think I am going to hurt your precious little ones?" That thought made him pause. Was he? He had delivered most of them. He had been their doctor all their lives, how could he hurt them? Well, he thought, he had been planning to hurt Hannah and Lex. But he couldn't put the two things together.

It was the new people in town that needed to be stopped, and that included the children. In fact, it was probably more important to eliminate them because they most likely already had more gifts than their parents did. Not because of heredity, but because of expectation and opportunity.

These children lived in a culture of not accepting the normal as truth or limitation. Just as children easily learned two languages when living in a bi-lingual home, these children were learning the paranormal. Their imaginations and possibilities were encouraged. They heard the adults speaking about seeing spirits, talking to each other mentally, and being in two places at once.

For Joe, and others like him, it was unacceptable. If people could see beyond what they were told to believe, then how could they be controlled? Whenever Joe allowed himself to think about this, it terrified him. If more people became aware that they were being manipulated, the era of people like him could be over.

Joe thought about all the people who chose power and greed instead of morals or ethics. Who chose themselves over the masses. They did things that the world believed were evil.

But they got away with it because most people were distracted by all the stories that were thrown out into the world. That was the point. They were meant to distract people from noticing what was actually going on.

Or after all the stories were told, people were too discouraged or tired to do anything about it. Plus, while distracted, tired, or depressed, most people were easy to manipulate.

All his fellow conspirators, some of whom he had trained, would lose the edge they had over people if they woke up. If everyone knew how to see, listen, and be places that were currently hidden from them, the powers behind the scenes would be exposed. Like Oz behind the curtain.

It wouldn't be just Joe who would be exposed. All of them would be. And then instead of weeping over the tragedies in the world, people would rise up and stop them from happening. All because they would see what had been hidden, and they would know what to do about it.

Therefore, Joe reasoned, he had to do his part and stop the ones he could stop. Perhaps it would encourage others to do their part and increase the distractions, and if necessary, the deaths.

For Joe, it meant that Edward would have to be punished for his part in exposing his own father. First, by watching his friends die, and then by dying himself.

• • • ● • ● • ● • • •

The old gas station smelled musty. It had been closed up since
Tina sold it last spring. Tina did not know that it was Joe who had
purchased it. If she had, she would never have allowed it to happen.
Tina hated Joe. She knew that Frank could have chosen a different
life, and she had stopped loving him long before he went to jail.
But still. Joe had killed him. Just because he could.

Tina thought she had sold the gas station to a corporation
that would be renovating it. Since taking her two children to
Pittsburgh, Tina had not yet returned to see what was going on
in town. She wasn't even able to make it to Johnny's going away
party.

Doveland, and the gas station, were far from what was going
on in Tina's mind, so she hadn't given a thought to the fact that
nothing had been done. She had other things on her mind. Besides,
everyone knew corporations took a long time to accomplish
anything.

*Well, something is going to be done right now,* Joe thought.
*Maybe they will build a new one after the bomb blows this one away.*
Of course, they would also have to build a grocery store too. If he
timed it right, probably Harold's old house would go too. *Wow. He
would be responsible for redesigning a whole new town square.* The
thought made him momentarily giddy with happiness. Of course,
the town would need money to rebuild it. But that wouldn't be a
problem. Thinking ahead, he had already put money in a trust for
the village for the restoring work.

*It will be so confusing to them.* Joe chuckled to himself. How
would the people of the town reconcile that the same man who
blew up the town square, and killed their friends, also gave them

money to rebuild it? That confusion was precisely what he had promoted his whole life. It worked the same way as showing people a cute kitty video while describing a terrible event. People see the cute kitty, and don't notice, or at least barely remember, the horrific event. That's what Joe was counting on after all this was done. There was still a possibility he would come out a hero in the long run. If not that, at least he would be free.

He checked the remote control devices he had set up months before. Everything was in place. Landmines in the grounds of the square, and small bombs in the lamp posts in the parking lots. And finally, the big act. The bomb set under the gas tanks that had never been drained.

Everything was set. He only had to get Edward ready to be put on view. Joe set Edward in a chair in the window of the gas station's convenience store, bound and gagged. The blinds were still closed. Once he was out of the range of the bombs and on his way to the airport, where he had booked a private plane that would take him out of the country, he would remotely set the explosives and open the blinds.

Everyone would see Edward there, all alone. They would rush to help, and Edward would watch them die because the biggest explosive would be last, after the first responders rushed in to help. It was all Edward's fault, actually, because he had the audacity to betray his own father. Joe would teach Edward a lesson that more people needed to learn. Edward was his father's son, and because of that, Edward owed Joe allegiance.

As Joe checked the camera app on his phone to make sure he could see the entire square, he leaned over and kissed Edward on the cheek. There was no response from Edward, but Joe whispered "Goodbye" to him anyway, and slipped out the back door. For a brief moment, a feeling of sadness passed through him. Joe took it as a result of being under too much stress.

# FIFTY SIX

"Okay, he's gone. You can open your eyes," Hannah whispered.

Edward slowly opened his eyes, trying to bring himself out of both the drugged sleep his father had put him into, and the self-imposed shut down he had been doing for the last day.

Even with his eyes open, he still couldn't see Hannah. It's like last time, he thought. She's not really here. The world was spinning, and he couldn't see the room where he was sitting. All he knew was that it was dark and musty, and all he could feel was pure terror. He was all alone. He was abandoned. All his work was for nothing. He was going to die, and his father would win. His life was a complete and utter waste. He shut his eyes again. There was no point in trying. *I'm dead anyway,* he thought.

Watching Edward close his eyes again scared Hannah. She knew he must be giving up, and that he didn't really believe that she was there. She wasn't really. She was at home, sitting among all her friends, her mother hugging her, and Valerie and Lex staring at her wondering what she was doing.

Back at the house, Hannah motioned for Sarah to join her and then returned to Edward, saying, "No, Edward, I'm here! I know you haven't learned how to see me yet, but I'm here to help you, and I won't leave you until you are free. Can you get to the knife you put in your pants when you were back in the bunker?"

It took a few moments before Edward opened his eyes again and nodded. He was so drowsy he wasn't sure if he was dreaming or awake, but he did remember that he had a knife in his pocket. The one from the bunker. The one he had hidden there when he was just a boy. For a moment Edward wondered how he knew when he was ten years old that he would need that knife almost forty years later, but decided to explore that question later. Right now, he had to listen to Hannah. He had to be free and find Valerie.

Hannah waited until Edward had wiggled around enough to drag the knife out of his pocket. Then another few minutes went by as he struggled with cutting through the zip-tie. She wanted to say, "Hurry up," but knew that would make it even worse for him, so instead, she kept whispering, "Good, good, you can do it!" She knew he was too exhausted to lead him through the way he had gotten out of them before. This time he would have to cut his way through. Finally, he got the zip-tie cut that was binding his hands, but not without nicking himself a few times, even though he didn't feel it. Once his hands were free, he pulled the gag out of his mouth.

As he took deep, ragged breaths, Hannah said, "Good job, Edward. Now, you need to get yourself out of the ropes around your ankles. I can't help you myself since I'm at home. So you need to get out yourself before Joe looks on his phone and sees that you are free. Sam has shut down local cell phone coverage, but once Joe is further away, he will be able to see what you are doing."

"Wait, aren't you all trying to stop him?" Edward croaked, his throat parched from the lack of water and the gag in his mouth.

"Of course we are, Edward, but we need to get you out of here anyway just in case. We have already evacuated everyone in town. Sam's team is heading toward Joe now. We know where he is going.

We'll catch him. Leif and Eric are staying with Joe and guiding Sam's team to him, but they don't want to do anything until you are out of here."

Edward listened as he sawed away at the ropes, nodding in acknowledgment of what Hannah had told him. He was terrified. Not for himself, but for the team going after Joe. Did they know how dangerous Joe was, the extent of his powers of illusion and manipulation?

"Yes, we know, Edward," a new voice said to him.

"Sarah?" Edward asked.

"Yes, it's me, Edward. I am standing right in front of you, along with Hannah. You are not alone. Neither are the people going after your father."

"Valerie?" Edward pleaded.

"Is safe. Now you. We are all waiting for you. Come on. You can do it."

For the next few minutes, Hannah and Sarah prompted and supported Edward as he worked on the ropes. It was obvious that he was dehydrated, drugged, and barely functioning. But they kept telling him that he had the courage and strength that wouldn't fail him now.

Eventually, the ropes were cut, and he staggered out the back door of the gas station and slowly made his way through the back alleys, guided by Hannah and Sarah, to a few blocks away from the store where an ambulance was waiting for him.

Rounding the last corner, he saw Hannah and Sarah. They had insisted on being there for him once they understood how badly off he was. Hannah and Sarah had been driven there by one of Sam's men at breakneck speed.

He was keeping a close eye on the two of them and held them back as long as he could from going after Edward as he made his way towards them. He knew Sam would have his head if anything happened to them.

Once he let them go, Hannah ran towards Edward and grabbed his hand, while Sarah put her arm around his shoulder and led him up the last few steps.

"Okay, rest now. We can take care of everything else," Sarah said.

Their smiling faces were the last things Edward saw as the ambulance doors closed, and he drifted into sleep.

# FIFTY SEVEN

J oe kept looking at his phone, trying to get a signal. He was
definitely far enough out of town to raise the blinds and reveal
Edward. Joe was hoping to hear a few landmines and bombs go off
before he boarded the plane, and none of that was going to happen
until the blinds went up. He could imagine people rushing to help
and Edward screaming inwardly at what was happening. Perhaps
he could have the plane circle a few times before flying on so he
could see the big bomb blast take out the square and buildings.

Frustrated, Joe pulled off the road and searched his phone,
trying to understand why he wasn't getting a signal. No bars at
all. How could that be? Joe shook the phone in frustration. Was
it possible that Sam had shut down the signal?

"Not only possible, but yes, he did," a voice spoke to him out of
nowhere. He recognized it immediately.

"So it's true, you can remote view people, Sarah."

"Oh yes, it's true," she answered.

"Well, fat lot of good that does you. You can't physically stop
me," Joe said, trying to start his car. Nothing happened.

"You're right. I can't, but good hackers can stop your car, just as
you stopped Edward's."

Joe swore and stepped out of the car. He wished he had worn better walking shoes and a heavier coat. But Joe thought that he was just getting on a plane. All he had on him was his passport and money. The rest he could buy or it would already be at his home in Morocco. He looked around at his options and turned to walk into the woods.

He wondered where the phrase madder-than-a-wet-hen came into being, because that was precisely how he was feeling. Apparently, he was going to have to revamp his plan. Somehow, Sarah had broken through the barrier he had learned to build against people like her, and now he had that bitch in his head.

"I see that you are wondering how I got through to you. It was when you let yourself be angry and frustrated, Joe. And since you know how to raise that barrier, again before you do, I know something I think you will want to know."

Joe kept trudging through the woods, consciously calming himself down so that he could block Sarah. But his curiosity had been triggered. Even though he knew that Sarah had effectively found his weak spot, the desire to know, he couldn't seem to turn off that desire at the moment. His curiosity was working overtime.

"What could you possibly tell me, that I don't already know?" he asked.

"Well," Sarah said slowly. "How many children do you have?"

"Oh, for heaven's sake," Joe huffed. "You know I have one. Edward. The lying, thieving, traitor."

Sarah didn't answer, and Joe kept walking. He didn't know this stretch of the woods well, so he was being extra careful. He planned to get to where he could hide out from the men Sarah would send after him. But first, he had to get rid of her so she wouldn't know where he went.

Joe knew he would need to build a shield around himself so he couldn't be found, but he was tired from struggling through the trees. It felt as if the roots were reaching up to trip him, and branches were grabbing at him. The woods were not his favorite place. He couldn't manipulate trees. People were easy. Except for Sarah.

The thought that she was probably still there but not talking made him crazy. He was losing control. "Okay," Joe said, panting and stopping to lean against a tree. At least they were good for that. "Tell me what you want to say and get it over with."

"Are you sure, Joe?" Sarah asked.

"Yes, for God's sake. Why ask me how many children I have when you already know? I have one," Joe said, slowing his breathing down. He knew enough to know that stress was not good for him. His heart wasn't as strong as it used to be. As he leaned against the tree, trying to catch his breath, Joe realized that perhaps he should have taken into account that he was an elderly man.

If he would have stayed in Morocco and not come seeking revenge against Edward, he could be happily content in his home. Beautiful women. Delicious food. Constant attention from the people he had hired to take care of the house and garden.

And him, he thought. He could be taken care of right now instead of running through the woods. Perhaps he was an idiot after all. The thought of being an idiot after being so careful and in control all these years scared him. Maybe, along with a weak heart, he was also losing his mind. Could there be anything worse? he wondered and decided that for him there wasn't.

"Oh, but there is," Sarah said.

"You! How can you be reading my thoughts? Stop it."

"Well, as you mentioned to yourself, you are losing your mind. Perhaps it's true. Doesn't matter. Now you are an easy read. So, do you want to know what I have to tell you or not?"

Joe could feel his heart beating so hard it felt as if it was popping out of his chest, and instead of his breathing getting easier, it was getting harder to breathe."

"Are you doing this to me, Sarah?" Joe asked.

"No. And I'm sorry to see this happening to you. But no one is doing it to you, you are—or have—done this to yourself."

Joe nodded and slowly slid down the tree until he was sitting on the forest floor, knees drawn up to his chest. He continued to lean back against the tree, which for some reason no longer felt hard and mean, but soft and yielding. It is a nice place to sit, he thought.

"Tell me, Sarah, what you want me to know. How many children do I have?"

"Well, Edward, of course. And one more that we know about. And so do you. Know her, I mean."

Joe put his hand on his heart. "I have a daughter? Where is she? What kind of person is she?"

Sarah laughed, "Not like you, Joe. She is kind, generous, and a great mother."

"I have grandchildren?" Joe whispered. For a moment, he let himself drift into what it would have been like to be a grandfather. He had seen the look of grandparents as they gazed upon the grandchildren. How much fun they had with them. He had always harbored a secret wish to have a few moments like that for himself. But Edward had never married. That wish had died long ago. Or so he thought.

"Wait, you said I know her? Do I know the children too?"

"You do, Joe," Sarah said softly. "You know them well. In fact, you delivered them."

Joe grew afraid. All that he had planned had come to this, slumped against a tree, learning that he had missed out on something that could have been wonderful. He saw himself young and in love with May. They were happy together. Edward was a sweet boy, always trying to give him hugs until he grew old enough to know they would never be returned.

He had traded power for a life. At the time, it seemed a fair trade. More than a fair trade, worth it all. But now, knowing that it was all coming to an end, he questioned his decisions for the first time. Was it worth it?

"Was it, Joe?"

"Tell me then. I need to know. Who is she?"

It felt to Joe as if Sarah had grown even closer. He could almost feel her presence. She whispered, "Valerie."

Joe's eyes flew open. Harold's wife? Valerie was his daughter? How? Why? He could feel his heart pounding harder, and a great pain ripped through him, as he thought he heard Sarah say, "Choose better next time, Joe."

Moments later, Joe opened his eyes. The pain was gone, but he was still in the woods, sitting against the tree. Standing in front of him were Harold, Grant, Frank, and Lenny.

"I thought you were dead," Joe said.

"We are," they answered.

# FIFTY EIGHT

V alerie leaned against Craig, and he put his arm around her. They were back in the hospital again. This time, they were watching over Edward. When he woke up, they both wanted to be there for him.

The last time Craig and Valerie were together in the hospital, they had been watching over her husband, Harold. They were waiting for him to recover, not knowing that there was nothing wrong with him except what Joe had made him believe and that Harold would die from that belief.

Valerie still had a hard time accepting that it was a lie that had killed Harold. It seemed so ridiculous that Harold's death happened because Joe told him to die. But they had proof that Joe did that kind of thing, and did it well. He was a master of deception.

Valerie would never have believed that it was possible to kill someone by suggestion until Harold died. Like the women on the hill, there had been no apparent cause of death. Nor was there anything found that killed the four women whose bodies had been buried in the lake.

There was no reason other than a phone call to cause both Frank and Lenny to attack the guards at their prison, which resulted in their deaths. All these deaths because Joe was experimenting. It made Valerie wonder how many other people Joe had killed.

They would probably never know. Joe had died alone and afraid out in the woods. Well, not entirely alone. Sarah had stayed with him until Sam's men had come to take him away. Perhaps that was some comfort to him, if he had known. She wasn't sure if she cared.

What they had all wanted most was to prove that Joe had killed the women, and now they could. Edward had brought all that they needed to establish Joe's guilt. He had brought tapes his mother made of his father telling her what he was doing. He had brought documents that showed which experiment he used on which women. His mother had risked her life to get the tapes and documents, and Edward had sacrificed a normal life to hide from his father. And then, after all that, he was willing to die to save his new friends and his sister.

Valerie sucked in her breath at the thought. He was her brother. It was a hard fact to accept, but once Sam had shown her the result of the DNA tests, Valerie understood why she had felt so connected to Edward.

It wasn't that Edward was her half-brother that bothered her. In fact, once Valerie recognized that she had put the feelings she had for Craig onto Edward, she was delighted that she had found a family.

What was hard was the fact that she was Joe's daughter. All the talks she had had with Johnny about him not being his father's son now applied to her.

She was not her father. Nor was Edward. They were their own people, shaped by their own choices, and they had both chosen to be good people, with integrity and purpose.

She was proud to call Edward her brother. She hoped that once he heard the truth, he would be proud that she was his sister.

It took a bit of digging through the records that Edward brought with him to glean what had happened. Valerie's mother had been one of the first women who had come to the compound, about the same time as Emily's Aunt Jean. But she hadn't stayed. She had run away after Dr. Joe raped her. He hadn't called it rape. It was merely a condition of being at the commune. He gave them money for food. He was their guru, their leader. It was required.

But Valerie's mother had seen Joe for what he was and ran as fast and as far away as she could. Valerie was sure she didn't know she was pregnant when she ran away, which was a good thing. If Joe had known she was pregnant, he wouldn't have let her go, ever.

Obviously, he had never learned of her mother's pregnancy because he had never come searching for her to either take her child away or kill them both. Now Valerie understood why her mother had been so insistent that the man who married her, a childhood sweetheart, was her father. It was to keep them all safe.

But it made her sad. Apparently, her mother's husband knew she wasn't his daughter, but he always treated her as if she was, and she had not always reciprocated. Not because she didn't love him, but because she knew he was keeping a secret. If only they would have told her so she could have let herself love them as whole-heartedly while they were alive as she did now.

As Valerie's thoughts drifted into the past, Craig's arm tightened around her. He too was thinking of the past and how close he had been to losing her because of his stubbornness and unwillingness to wake up.

He vowed to do everything in his power to let nothing harm Valerie or her boys again. He would not allow evil, in whatever form it presented itself, to deceive him again. Craig knew that from now on he would recognize when a dangerous resemblance to truth was presented to him as Truth. He would learn more about how deception worked. He would not be blind to what was happening because he didn't want it to be true.

He wasn't worried. Craig knew he would recognize the signs of a master manipulator and deceiver when he came across one again. He could wish that he never would find another person like Joe, but it was unlikely. Craig knew he would need the skills he had learned again and again as long as there was evil in the world. *But I will never be oblivious to it again,* he vowed.

Craig thought about Joe, the master criminal who had hidden in the shadows his whole life and trained and directed Grant and Lenny to come after Craig and his friends. Joe could never hurt them again. He was dead. Edward would recover, and they would all be free to live normal lives.

"Right," Hannah said, coming into the room and hugging him. "Normal lives. As if."

"Okay Hannah," Craig answered, realizing that Hannah had read his mind, "I mean lives that allow us all to explore our gifts, practice them, and perhaps teach them to those that want to learn."

Hannah nodded. She hoped it would be that easy. But for now, they were okay, and that was good enough.

# FIFTY NINE

When Edward opened his eyes a few hours later, he was delighted to find Valerie waiting for him. He had been so worried about her. She assured him that she was fine, and so was he.

He had become dehydrated, and the drugs Joe had given him had made it worse. Another hour or so, it wouldn't have mattered about the bomb, he would have died sitting in the chair. "I am so grateful you are alive and well," she said holding his hand.

However, when Craig came back in the room carrying two coffees, Edward was confused. Especially when he saw Valerie's face when she looked at Craig. Edward had known that Craig loved Valerie. Everyone in town knew that. But Edward had thought that he and Valerie were becoming more to each other and that Valerie had chosen him.

"What did I miss?" Edward asked Valerie, looking at her with tears in his eyes.

"I'll leave," Craig said, setting the coffees down.

Valerie nodded at him and turned back to Edward.

"Edward, there is something I have to tell you," she began.

"It's okay," Edward said. "I know you loved him first."

Valerie took both his hands in hers and said, "Maybe, but I love you, too."

Edward turned his face away, and Valerie continued, "Listen, Edward, this may not be what you want to hear, but once you think about it, I think you will be as happy as I am to know ..."

"Know what?" Edward broke in.

As Valerie told Edward the story, and what she had learned, they both burst into tears when she ended with, "So you see, dear brother, I can and do, love you too."

When Craig returned later he found Valerie holding her brother's hand, and Edward sound asleep.

He sat down next to her once again, and she leaned against him while they waited for Edward to wake up again and begin his new life with his found family.

· · · ● · ● · ● · · ·

Because Edward needed time to recover, it was a week before Joe's funeral was held. Mandy and Valerie had helped Edward plan it. In fact, everyone in the Stone Circle had assisted Edward with the arrangements. It was a far cry from the simple and profound funeral they had held for Melvin earlier that year.

However, like Melvin's funeral, it seemed as if everyone in town attended. True to his nature, like Melvin, Joe had left instructions as to what kind of funeral he wanted. Joe had every detail down to perfection. Instructions were given on everything right down to the music played, songs sung, flowers on the grave and Bible passages read. He had left no detail untouched.

Unlike Melvin, who wanted a simple send-off, Joe wanted pomp and display. He didn't want any expense spared and had left cash with his attorney to make sure it was carried out to his specifications. Joe had planned what he wanted to have happen at his funeral believing that when he died, the town would want to honor him because he would still be a hero. Now he wasn't, or he shouldn't have been. Everyone knew what he had done. The evidence had been carefully laid out for everyone to see.

The remaining members of the families of the murdered girls had been given all the facts. The authorities said that the families deserved to know everything having waited for so long to find out what had happened to the women that had disappeared so long ago. Most of them had shaken their heads and said they didn't understand how he had killed them, but were grateful to find out who was responsible. All of them were glad Joe had died. Perhaps a trial would have been a good thing, but more than likely, Joe would have figured out how to wiggle out from under all the evidence.

For many longtime residents of Doveland, it was a different story. They had heard what was alleged that he had done, but found it impossible to believe that the doctor who had taken care of them their whole lives was a master criminal. They tucked away what they had heard and decided not to talk about it again, ever.

They were at the funeral to honor the Joe that they knew. The man who had given so much to the town for the past fifty years that there were babies named after him. Edward chose to let them continue to believe that his father was a good man, and gave him, and the town, the funeral that Joe had planned.

It was as Joe had predicted. Even with the evidence that he had prepared to blow up the town square, and anyone in it, most of the town couldn't accept it. It would mean they had lived their whole lives with an evil man and hadn't known it. Dr. Joe had done too much good for them to accept anything other than the doctor that they knew and loved. Not the man their police chief tried to tell them existed.

The people that knew and accepted the truth were at the funeral too. Sam thought that they were all there for two reasons.

The obvious one was to be part of the community. They loved the people of Doveland, and it served no one for them to divide the community between those who supported Joe and those that didn't. It would have been what Joe would have wanted—separation and disagreement. They were never going to give him that satisfaction, even if he couldn't see it.

The other reason, which no one wanted to say out loud, was to prove Joe was really dead. They were grateful that he had chosen an open casket. It gave them all a chance to look one more time, just to be sure.

As Mandy and Mira stood hand in hand looking down at the man who had caused so much death, Mandy whispered, "He really is dead, isn't he?"

Mira nodded and added, "May we never meet another like him."

Leif and Eric stood in the back corner of the church watching the funeral. "What about the others that Joe trained? Will we ever meet them?" Eric asked.

Leif shook his head. "They're out there, but let's hope they don't give this little town any attention at all."

Behind the casket, the town's choir sang, "Turn, Turn Turn." It was not the song Joe chose. But no one knew that except Edward and Valerie. They wanted this one, to remind everyone that times change. Joe's time was over. Now it was their season to be a family and community.

They buried Joe in Doveland's cemetery, next to his wife, May, as he had requested. They never did take the time to dig May up. There was no need to disturb her remains. They knew it was Joe that had killed her, and that was enough to know.

Edward thought that it was going to be hard visiting his mother's grave with his father's right beside her. But, he knew that his mother would have wanted it that way too. He hoped that if his parent's lives met up again, Joe would choose differently.

For now, Edward knew what he was going to do. Live free from his father's influence for the first time in his life. He had a family, Valerie and her children. He had friends. Life was good, and he was going to do everything he could to keep it that way.

# SIXTY

I t was a Thanksgiving none of them would forget. It was full of delicious food of all kinds, including a lovely vegan and vegetarian version for Mandy, Emily, and Sarah. They were sitting around the fire in Evan and Ava's living room remembering the past year, being grateful for what they had learned, and what had been discovered, and what had been completed.

It had been a hard year in so many ways. They had said goodbye to a man that they all loved. Melvin would be forever missed. Hank continued to discover little notes from Melvin hidden away for him to find. Melvin knew that Hank would renovate the house and uncover the notes as he went along. Hank thought that for the rest of his life, he would never get lost again. Melvin had found him and given him a father. Actually, Melvin had given many people a father and a grandfather. Hannah turned to Hank and smiled. "Yes," she said, "I miss him too."

As a group, they had kept Joe, the town's hidden monster, from killing any more people, and Valerie had found her brother, and her sons had an uncle they could look up to.

Johnny looked across the room at his mom holding Craig's hand and at Edward, who sat at her side and decided once and for all that he was not his father's son.

Johnny wasn't particularly religious, but he liked thinking that he was Love's son. He had made a choice to live life as a good man, just as all the men sitting in the living room together were choosing. Seeing Johnny's face, Pete leaned over and hugged him. "Missed you when you were away, buddy. Come work at the Diner over Christmas break? Maybe help me set up the pizza oven?"

Johnny laughed, "Sure, Pete. So Barbara said you could put one in?" They both laughed, and Barbara smiled at them both, thinking about how grateful she was for her new life in Doveland.

Mandy was thinking the same thing that Johnny had been thinking. She hadn't yet discovered her birth parents, but at the moment, it didn't mean anything anymore. The people sitting in Ava's living room were her family. Valerie had made a place for her in her home, and Tom had opened his heart to her. Life was good. She chose who she became in the world, not her family heredity.

Sarah and Grace sat with their husbands on the couch. If you couldn't see Eric and Leif, the space between Sarah and Grace seemed odd. Edward still couldn't, but he accepted that they were there and that someday he would see them, too.

"I was thinking," Leif said, and all those that could hear him stopped talking and looked his way. "Perhaps Eric and I should begin to tell you about the other dimension that we live in."

Hannah jumped off her chair and yelled, "Hooray!"

Ava gave Hannah the mom look, and Hannah sat back down while saying, "Sorry, but still, hooray?"

Leif turned to Sarah, who smiled back at him and nodded. "Hooray it is then," Leif said, thinking that he might be the only person in the room who knew what would be required of each of them as a result. And then both Sarah and Hannah winked at him, and he decided not to worry about it, but enjoy the adventure.

# EPILOGUE

Suzanne Laudry was so still both men wondered if she had drifted off somewhere. But her eyes gave her away as she stared at the two of them as if she could see through to their souls.

They waited, wondering what the verdict would be.

"It can't happen now, Leif," she finally said.

Neither Leif nor Eric moved. They kept on waiting. They knew she had more to say, and it was not wise to interrupt her while she was thinking. The answer to the question was too important to them.

The three of them were standing or drifting in the middle of nowhere. At least that's what it always felt like to Leif. The first time he had traveled to the Forest Circle's dimension, he had no recollection of how he got there. In fact, it was many trips before he began to recognize that he passed through what felt like a tunnel before it opened up to what Sarah called elsewhere.

For Sarah, that elsewhere happened even when she was in the earth dimension. She said it always had. But she had never left earth or physically traveled to another dimension. She experienced it as if it was a waking dream.

For Leif and Eric, it was different. They had left their earth dimension's bodies and now traveled between earth and their new realm almost as easily as walking through a door. Or taking a trip to the store. But it was Suzanne and her friends who had brought them there first, and then taught them how to travel on their own, without telling them how it worked. It was like driving a car. You drove it, but most people would not know how to build one by themselves.

Now, Leif wanted to teach others how to travel between dimensions or realms, as Hannah called it, without leaving their bodies. Or perhaps they would leave their bodies behind as they traveled. He wasn't sure which way it would happen, or how it would happen, or even if it could.

But since Suzanne hadn't said no to his plan, just that it couldn't happen now, Leif suspected that there was a way after all.

"May I ask why not now?" Leif asked.

"You are missing someone who needs to be there before we can even consider it. Once that's in place, we can speak of it again. But there is no guarantee that it will be allowed, or that anyone will be able to navigate the passage between our two realms."

"I understand," Leif said. And he did. "Should we be looking for this person?"

"No, he'll find you. However, it will be up to you to recognize him, and then help him find what is needed. Remember, even then, it may not be allowed. We'll have to let the event play out first. In the meantime, you can tell a few stories about our dimension to the trusted few. Perhaps in that way, we'll discover which ones would be ready—if it comes to pass."

Suzanne was gone even before she finished speaking, her words hanging in the air as an unattached sound wave.

"I don't think I'm ever going to get used to the strangeness of this no-place called a passageway," Eric said. "Even without a body, it makes me feel dizzy watching what happens in here."

"And you're used to it, Eric. I think that is one of the things that bothers Suzanne the most. How will our friends be able to deal with the non-locality of it while keeping their human bodies?"

"I guess it's not something we have to worry about right now," Eric responded. "First, we have to wait for someone to find us, recognize it's the right person, and then help him find something we don't know anything about."

Leif laughed, the sound of which moved out of his mouth and hung sparkling in the air before dissolving into nothingness. "That sounds about right. We watch for someone that seems normal, but isn't."

This time, it was Eric's turn to laugh. "You mean like all of the Doveland Karass? Heck, he'll fit right in."

Suzanne watched the two of them drift through the open door to the Forest Circle's realm. She hadn't gone anywhere. Instead, she had turned off the projection of her body and waited in the emptiness of the passageway. She waited until she was sure that no one else had entered the no-place passage before shutting the door to the earth realm, and then turning to close the door on her side once she exited. It was just one of the many things that needed to be discussed. How to keep the passage safe.

She and her friends had time to figure it out, though. And the Stone Circle would be busy enough with what was coming to be doing too much questioning about visiting other realms. That would come later. By then, she thought the decision would be made for them.

All characters in this book are fictional. Some are composites of people I have known. Most are entirely made up. As this series goes on, the characters and situations come more and more from my imagination.

Some places are real, others, like Doveland, I imagined. However, I grew up in State College, PA, where my father was a professor and dean at Penn State. I believe he would be delighted that Johnny chose Penn State for his college education.

In this book, I explore the idea of a family tree, of heredity, and choices, all summed up for me in the word, Stemma.

I think we all ask ourselves if we are our parent's children. Sometimes that feels like a good thing. There may be gifts we received from them that we want to acknowledge. Other times, we know we don't want to carry forward ideas that are not good or be responsible for what came before us. I had wonderful parents. But many people don't.

Either way, I believe it is our choice of what we do with what we have found within this lifetime that determines the life that we lead and the impact we have on others.

Perhaps we are here in this lifetime so that we will continue to learn how to choose to live for the good of all.

In this book, as I close with Sarah telling Joe to choose better next time, I am expressing my belief that he could. We all can. And as always, it is much easier within a community.

Our first choice might be to decide what we want to carry forward. Our second choice revolves around the community of people we want to express it within.

We choose that community, and they choose us. Our community may not be local, but given our ability in the world today to be everywhere at the same time online, it is always available.

Every day I hope to choose better than I did the day before, and I am always grateful for my community, my Karass, for walking the path with me.

And I am always grateful for you, dear reader, for traveling with me through my books.

As you read this series, let me know what you think! Find all my books, any of your favorite places to buy books.

There are nine books in these Stories From Doveland series. After that, I wrote two fantasy series that include some of the characters from these books.

If you would like to read a short prequel to these series, I'll send it to you for free.

Get this free short story here: becalewis.com/fantasy.

# ALSO BY BECA

**The Rivers of Time Series: Women's Lit, Friendship, Small Town, Mystery, Magical Realism, Small Town Fiction**
*The Returning, The Awakening, The Rising*

***Follow Me Here:*** **Women's Lit, Friendship, Small Town, Mystery, Magical Realism, Small Town Fiction**

**The Ruby Sisters Series: Women's Lit, Friendship, Mystery, Small Town Fiction**
*A Last Gift, After All This Time, And Then She Remembered, As If It Was Real, Almost Innocent*

**Stories From Doveland: Women's Lit, Friendship, Small Town, Mystery, Magical Realism, Small Town Fiction**
*Karass, Pragma, Jatismar, Exousia, Stemma, Paragnosis,☐ In-Between, Missing, Out Of Nowhere*

**The Return To Erda Series: Fantasy**
*Shatterskin, Deadsweep, Abbadon, The Experiment*

## The Chronicles of Thamon: Fantasy
*Banished, Betrayed, Discovered, Wren's Story*

## The Shift Series: Spiritual Self-Help
*Living in Grace: The Shift to Spiritual Perception*
*The Daily Shift: Daily Lessons From Love To Money*
*The 4 Essential Questions: Choosing Spiritually Healthy Habits*
*The 28 Day Shift To Wealth: A Daily Prosperity Plan*
*The Intent Course: Say Yes To What Moves You*
*Imagination Mastery: A Workbook For Shifting Your Reality*
*Right Thinking: A Thoughtful System for Healing*
*Perception Mastery: Seven Steps To Lasting Change*
*Blooming Your Life: How To Experience Consistent Happiness*

## Perception Parables: Very short stories
*Love's Silent Sweet Secret: A Fable About Love*
*Golden Chains And Silver Cords: A Fable About Letting Go*

## Advice / Journals
*A Woman's ABC's of Life: Lessons in Love, Life, and Career from*
*Those Who Learned The Hard Way*□
*The Daily Nudge(s): So When Did You First Notice*

# OTHER PLACES TO FIND BECA

- Facebook: facebook.com/becalewiscreative

- Instagram: instagram.com/becalewis

- LinkedIn: linkedin.com/in/becalewis

- Youtube: www.youtube.com/c/becalewis

- Buy Books Direct: https://becalewis.org/

# About Beca

Beca writes books she hopes will change people's perceptions of themselves and the world, and open possibilities to things and ideas that are waiting to be seen and experienced.

At sixteen, Beca founded her own dance studio. Later, she received a Master's Degree in Dance in Choreography from UCLA and founded the Harbinger Dance Theatre, a multimedia dance company, while continuing to run her dance school.

After graduating—to better support her three children—Beca switched to the sales field, where she worked as an employee and independent contractor in many industries, excelling in each while perfecting and teaching her Shift System and writing books.

She joined the financial industry in 1983 and became an Associate Vice President of Investments at a major stock brokerage firm. She was a licensed Certified Financial Planner for over twenty years.

This diversity, along with a variety of life challenges, helped fuel the desire to share what she's learned by writing and speaking, hoping it will make a difference in other people's lives.

Beca grew up in State College, PA, with the dream of becoming a dancer and then a writer. She carried that dream forward as she fulfilled a childhood wish by moving to Southern California in 1968. Beca told her family she would never move back to the cold.

After living there for thirty-one years, she met her husband, Delbert Lee Piper, Sr., at a retreat in Virginia, and everything changed. They decided to find a place they could call their own, which sent them off traveling around the United States. They lived and worked in a few different places before returning to live in the cold once again near Del's family in a small town in Northeast Ohio, not too far from State College.

When not working and teaching together, they love to visit and play with their combined family of eight children and five grandchildren, walk, read, study, do yoga or taiji, feed birds, and work in their garden.